AND THE DEVIL MAKES FIVE

DUSTY RICHARDS

THE O'MALLEYS OF TEXAS

AND THE DEVIL MAKES FIVE

PINNACLE BOOKS
Kensington Publishing Corp.
www.kensingtonbooks.com

PINNACLE BOOKS are published by

Kensington Publishing Corp.
119 West 40th Street
New York, NY 10018

PUBLISHER'S NOTE
Following the passing of Dusty Richards, the Richards family is working closely with a selected author to complete a number of unfinished manuscripts to create additional Western adventures—all inspired by Dusty Richards' unique and entertaining brand of storytelling.

All Kensington titles, imprints, and distributed lines are available at special quantity discounts for bulk purchases for sales promotion, premiums, fund-raising, educational, or institutional use.

Special book excerpts or customized printings can also be created to fit specific needs. For details, write or phone the office of the Kensington Sales Manager: Attn.: Sales Department. Kensington Publishing Corp., 119 West 40th Street, New York, NY 10018. Phone: 1-800-221-2647.

PINNACLE BOOKS and the Pinnacle logo are Reg. U.S. Pat. & TM Off.

First Printing: February 2022
ISBN-13: 978-0-7860-4565-5
ISBN-13: 978-0-7860-4566-2 (eBook)

10 9 8 7 6 5 4 3 2 1

Printed in the United States of America

Prologue

The cool night air chilled the perspiration on the man's trembling body. There was a great deal of sweat as he sat with his gloved hand tightly on the throttle of the steam locomotive. He did not need to hold the lever in place. He had stopped the engine, as planned, but he did not want to let go. He feared, if he did, that his quaking body would shake itself apart.

"Lord, God, what am I doing?" he muttered as he waited.

Fear, guilt, despair, and other emotions ran through his once-powerful body. Yet those feelings, while powerful, were all crushed down by hunger. His flesh sagged where it was once full and robust. His rheumatism was worse to the point that his thirty-three-year-old knees and elbows were in constant pain. Discomfort was expected by a trainman. He was sitting in a cramped space for endless hours, on a rattling seat and floor, working with often stubborn equipment that froze in the cold or expanded in the heat.

The ache in his belly had been a constant companion for months, the worse since any food that came into the man's tiny apartment did not go to him but to his wife and their young child.

A six-year-old so weak that if he did not soon get regular plates of bread and glasses of milk, the little boy would die. A downstairs neighbor had already lost their daughter.

"I don't have a choice," he said quietly, as if in apology to that same God.

The *Storsvagåret*, the Year of Great Weakness, was like nothing the Swedish nation had experienced. The famine struck the northern provinces hard during a mercilessly, endlessly cold winter and spring. It wasn't just that harvests were poor. They did not happen. Emergency funds were allocated by the government, food was purchased from other lands, but in the north—

It is too late, thought Torn Wallström. The food went to those who could pay, and the train engineer was not among those. The merchants, the land owners, the politicians— they ate first. Wallström and his family were still starving.

That was why the twelve-year veteran of the Nora-Ervalla-Örebro railway had taken the gold from the Spaniards and their diminutive leader. He had confirmed the cargo he was carrying, agreed to stop the steam locomotive outside of Närke, and permit them to board.

And that was where he sat, stiff and tense inside the small crew compartment of the locomotive. The metal behemoth around him hissed, the coal firebox howling behind its closed door, the pistons still but the blast pipe still hissing steam from the chimney. This run had been particularly hard because he had convinced his long-time fireman Augustus to stay home with his ailing mother. Torn had fed the fire hole himself.

The engineer started as two horsemen rode up from the front of the locomotive to the ladder. They stopped outside the open door. One of the two men held a shotgun. The other, a diminutive, well-dressed man, held a purse.

"It is aboard?" the small man asked in clumsy, Spanish-accented Swedish.

Torn nodded. "In the caboose," he said in a soft, reluctant voice. "A black chest."

"Guards?"

"One, plus the conductor," Torn informed him. "The—the conductor will be making his way forward by now. Through the six cars, first, and then outside. He carries a pistol for derelicts but he won't—"

"I see him," said the man with the shotgun, galloping toward the rear of the train. There were shouts for the conductor to stop, and then a resounding shot that echoed through the cabin.

Torn cringed. It was not the conductor's small-caliber handgun.

Sweet Jesus. Hampus—why didn't you listen?

The diminutive man threw the purse into the open door. It landed with a heavy clank on the iron floor. It bulged with silver *riksdaler*.

"For your services, as agreed," said the rider.

Torn did not thank him. He sobbed as the man moved on, followed by two armed men in a wagon. The driver halted briefly.

"Take your money and get out!" he yelled in perfect Swedish as the man beside him produced a bottle. The bottle had a cloth stuffed in the top. "And remember the name you will tell them you overheard."

"Zuloaga," the man said. "Zuloaga."

"That is correct," the other man replied. "Remembering this name will *keep* you alive."

The man below lit the cloth ablaze. Torn watched the process, frozen and confused.

"Get out!" the man repeated. "An attack. This bottle. That is the reason you stopped for us!"

The bottle flew through air, a red comet against the night sky. It smashed on the floor, between Torn and the purse, and the kerosene inside poured out, instantly ablaze.

The wagon moved on, and Torn forced his stiff, pained legs to move. He jumped over the fire, which spread to the coal, and stopped only long enough to scoop up the purse. He swung round so he could descend the ladder but flames licked at him and he fell the four rungs onto his back. The wind was knocked from his body, the small of his back hit gravel, and the reverberations of both left him too weak to stand. He rolled, rolled hard, as black smoke from the igniting coal and burning liquid poured toward him.

The gravel beside the track ended and there was dry grass beyond, on a small incline. Torn rolled down and took a moment for life to return to his legs. Lying on his belly, he saw the conductor, dear Hampus, lying on his back. He had walked through the train to the engine, and lay dead on his back, his arms splayed across the small stones.

"Oh, God," Torn moaned.

The diminutive fellow who had first come to him at the station—the man had said nothing about murder. And he realized, then, that the other man who had spoken was Swedish. Another hungry man with a family?

"Oh, God," the man uttered again, weeping into the dry, dead earth.

At least Hampus would no longer have to suffer hunger. He had no family, but he had a belly and that belly had shrunk. So many times over the last four months, he had come forward at train stops to remind Torn to stop farther along at this very river where he paid a fisherman for a portion of his catch. He would cook it on the stove in the caboose, saving a little for Torn. Hampus never had to offer him money. Scraps of food were currency, now.

The heat from the locomotive crawled above him, the metal whining and sharpening the heat. It brought a choking cloud from the burning coal, along with loud pops and snaps from the wood in the seat, the window frame, and other non-iron materials in the cab. Like some obscene, sideward crawling lizard, the engineer moved to the side as he waited for the surviving conductor, Åke, to evacuate passengers. The veteran would have been somewhere in the train, resting between stations. Unlike Hampus, in the caboose, his role during an unauthorized stop would have been to move from car to car instructing the passengers to remain where they were.

There was more gunfire, one shot from inside the caboose then a blast of yellow-white on the outside. There were no further sounds from within. The men from the wagon boarded the caboose.

Passengers had looked to the windows at the first shot, but now he could hear them screaming, saw the faces vanish from the windows. He saw the men very slowly, carefully move the large box from train to the wagon. Torn had no idea what was inside. It could not be gold. They would be moving faster than this. They acted as though they were carrying a newborn babe.

"Kaarina, what have I done?" he said to his beloved

wife. *You have saved her life, and the life of your child,* he told himself.

Choking smoke began to settle around him and, coughing, he managed to get to his knees and crawled toward the level ground below. There was a river beyond. Following it, he knew he would reach the city.

Behind him, he heard the clatter of wheels and the thumping of hooves as the horsemen and the wagon departed. He heard people begin to run from the train, led by the other conductor who had remained inside. There were shouts as passengers saw the burning locomotive, the dead conductor. The commanding voice of the conductor as he attempted to organize the exodus was lost in the panic of those on the ground and those inside the cars that were swiftly filling with smoke.

Torn could not watch. He did not want to see any more of what he had caused. It was not supposed to be like this. They were to stop him at gunpoint, take the chest, and leave.

"Oh, God," he said again, this time adding, "Please forgive me my ignorance."

Reaching the bank on bleeding knees and elbows, Torn shoved his face into the waters and washed away the grime of travel.

But he knew he would never be clean again. And there was one thing more. When he pulled his face from the waters, he saw the fisherman running over with his catch. The catch he was going to seek to sell to Hampus.

Torn began to laugh, and he knew it would be a long, long time before he was able to stop.

* * *

Four weeks.

That was how long the *Juaristas* had given their agent to carry out the plan. That was how long they had before decisions about railroads moving west in the United States were made. Free of war, industrialists and banks were busy establishing routes to the Pacific. Stability in Mexico would decide whether some of those tracks and terminals would be situated near or perhaps even over the border.

The future economy of the Mexican nation depended upon trade with its growing northern neighbor.

Gabriel Martinez enjoyed working under pressure. It had been a leisurely sail to Europe from the Gulf of Mexico, during which he took stock of the waters, the route, the stillness of the sea. His military advisor had said those things were crucial. All of those things fell within the boundaries that had been described to him. Striking up relationships with the captain and crew, he had learned more about the Atlantic route.

Making that return crossing, his passage would be in the hands of the efficient and well-prepared men he had already met in Mexico City. For now, though, it would be a somewhat busier return as he worked out details for the final phase of the plan. By the time he was on firm ground in America, there would be no leisure, not time to waste.

A land crossing to the Pacific. A quick sail up the California coast to determine speed, winds, and the reliability of a much smaller ship than he would use to cross the ocean.

And then, the final journey, a voyage to destiny. History being written by a man whose stature people had long mocked.

Dusty Richards

Hopefully, the *Juaristas* would have made the arrangements with the shippers in San Francisco. If not, the cargo would have to be revealed. That would mean a much more dangerous journey across land. He hoped it would not come to that.

The small man sat in the rocking buckboard, confident that he would be able to deal with any eventuality. Like today. He was sorry for the loss of life but he recognized that great goals make sacrifice necessary.

To achieve this one, he would let nothing stand in his way. There was only one thing he had been warned about before leaving Sweden.

"The smell," he was instructed by the old man who first told him about the cargo. "When it is sweet—and you only have two months before that begins—be nowhere nearby."

It would be close.

But the goal was worth the risk.

Chapter 1

"I now pronounce you—"

"*Man and wife*! Yay-*hoo*!"

"B.W." Beauregard Lafayette shouted the words and whooped, jumping from his seat and waving his weather-worn hat over his head. Lolling nearby, the collies Blood and Mud came alert and barked at him, though it was too hot for them to move any closer. They stood as if waiting for something to happen. But no one moved or spoke. Brother Whip just stared ahead, searching for a sign of support, his cry quickly, mercifully, lost in the blue skies and yellow-white sun overhead and the expanse of plain that surrounded them in all directions.

The officiant, Reverend Merritt Michaels, looked with open shock past the couple standing before him. The couple remained stationary under the lace canopy protecting them from the sun. When the reverend—the bride's brother—failed to immediately continue, the young woman turned. A sharpshooter, if she had her rifle, the bride looked as if she would have used it.

At the same time, by habit, the hand of the groom drifted

to the spot on his thigh where he usually wore his Bowie knife. It was not there this afternoon because of the occasion—though there had been a discussion with his fiancée about not having wanted to leave it behind.

"It's as much a part of me as my lips," he had said.

"I will not be kissing your knife," she reminded him.

"But I always have it," he remarked to no avail.

Now, on the verge of being Clarity O'Malley, Clarity Michaels turned blazing eyes from B.W. to the groom.

"You were right about the knife," she told Slash O'Malley.

"I coulda thrown it and I wouldn't never have had to leave your side," he assured her, cooing.

Clarity's harsh expression cracked, and she smiled sweetly. They both turned back to the pastor.

The man who had leapt to his feet remained dumbly, firmly planted on them. He was still stunned to be the only one who had risen from his seat.

"Why'd y'all stop?" the stagecoach driver stubbornly inquired of the preacher.

The round-faced clergyman had no answer beyond what was self-evident. Neither did anyone in the small group of people seated on the wooden chairs that had been carried from the Whip Station, along with a pair of stools and an empty water barrel.

Without turning from his front-row seat, the head of the family, Joe O'Malley spoke quietly from under his broom moustache.

"B.W.—*sit* yourself down."

The collies promptly obeyed. B.W. defiantly did not. He stood there still with a look that was half-surprise, half-humiliation. Joe continued to look toward the canopy though his salt-and-pepper brows now dipped disapprovingly.

The rugged seventy-year-old was seated directly in front of B.W. He was glad it was noon, so he couldn't see the man's shadow clearly. Seeing his throat, he might be tempted to turn and choke the real one.

To Joe's left was his granddaughter Gert, twin sister of the groom. She was hiding a smile with an Apache fan made of snake bones and eagle feathers. To Joe's right were his frowning son Jackson and Jackson's frozen-faced wife Sarah, parents of the groom.

To the left of B.W. was Dick Ocean. The stagecoach shotgun rider just shook his head very slowly. They were surrounded by the Isaiah Sunday family from the Vallicita station and the Mission Indians Sisquoc and Malibu out of Fort Yuma, in the southeastern-most corner of the State of California. The Indians were wearing their uniforms, the only somewhat formal attire they owned.

Inside the station were the two passengers who had come in on the Butterfield Line stagecoach, Sebastián Sanchez and Rafael Gonzalez. Sarah and Gert had fed the two men and then asked if they wouldn't mind helping themselves to anything else they might want. The men were only headed to Vallicita, the next stop on the way back to St. Louis, Missouri, and had obligingly said they understood completely.

"Please enjoy your ceremony," Gonzalez had told her.

Sarah had thanked him in her soft German accent. "This is the only time the driver and his Shotgun can be here," she apologetically explained to the young men. "They didn't want to miss it."

"The bride is lovely, they are not to be blamed," said the courtly Sanchez.

Now, Sarah wished they had done the ceremony an hour earlier, while the stage was still up north a way and headed toward them from Oak Grove.

Despite the admonition from Joe, and in spite of tense moments that seemed to pass like B.W. was a mouse snared in tumbleweed, the man was still standing. Dick finally tugged at the hem of the whip driver's Sunday tweed jacket. Reluctantly, the burly driver lowered himself into his seat on stocky, bowed legs. His personal Bible, from which he was never separated, was held tightly in his left hand. His fingertips gleamed white, tightly pressed against the black leather covers.

The man landed heavily, the chair squeaking with his weight. In the nearby stable, a horse answered the sound with a whinny.

"I meant nothing—" B.W. began quietly as he settled in.

"Quiet," Joe said through his teeth, making two taut syllables of the word,

"Sure, Joe," B.W. said. "Sure." The driver turned his crinkled eyes toward the backs of the soon-to-be-newlyweds. Raising his voice, he said, "Y'know, where I come from, right before the ring goes on, the cheer goes out!"

"You're still talking," Joe said thickly.

B.W. looked absently at his right hand. He held it up, showed his soft fawn-colored gambler's hat. "Hey," he grumbled. "At least I took my hat off."

Octogenarian Willa Sunday, whose son ran the Vallicita station, leaned forward and whispered.

"I suspect that lest you want your head off, you still that tongue *at once*!" warned the former slave.

A hot wind blew a warm, enervating heat over the group. B.W.'s big shoulders finally rounded and gave up the fight. Reverend Michaels, dressed in black and standing just outside the canopy, took advantage of the break to dab his perspiring head with a handkerchief. He also looked to Joe for guidance. The patriarch nodded his uncustomarily clean-shaven chin.

"Continue, friend Merritt," the elder O'Malley said.

"Very well," Michaels spoke softly. He regarded the couple and found his previous smile. "I now pronounce you man and wife. Brother Jefferson Slash O'Malley, you may kiss the bride."

Everyone leapt to their feet and applauded—except for B.W. who, showing a cautious, perplexed expression, took a moment before rising slowly.

"Would someone tell me just what in the name of the holy prophet Moses I did *wrong*?" he demanded of everyone around him.

No one answered. They were all filing from the rickety chairs and improvised seats to wait their turn to hug the newlyweds, who were in the process of being blessed by Clarity's older brother. Jackson and Sarah tearfully signed the wedding certificate that Merritt had written out. The document sat on a crate, held there by the inkwell.

Gert was allowed to greet the couple first so she could get back inside to their guests. She was followed by Sarah, who trailed petals from the homegrown bouquet her daughter had given her to preserve. Jackson went third so that he could attend to the stagecoach horses and quickly get B.W. and Ocean back on the road. The thirty-seven-year-old required more time to do his work than he would have liked, having been seriously injured in a horse fall years before. His pronounced limp notwithstanding, Jackson always got the job done right, and on time.

As Isaiah helped his mother to her feet, his wife Bonita and son Joshua went to the bride and groom. Slash was distracted, admiring the ring on his finger. It had been the one Joe had worn when he married Dolley. It had never left the older O'Malley's finger until this morning.

"I am so happy for you both," Bonita told them.

"Thank you," Clarity said, pressing her cheek to that of the Colored woman. "And thank you for being here."

"I only wish we could stay for some of your mama's pie!" she said. "But we got a place to run."

"We'll bring one when we get back," the native Kentuckian assured her.

Isaiah stepped over. He bowed his head to the bride and folded the groom's hand in his own strong, five fingers. "May you be as happy as I am," the big man said.

"That's the kindest wish, friend," Slash said, genuinely moved. "I'm grateful you were able to get here."

"We knew there wouldn't be any stagecoach while we was gone." Isaiah grinned. "And we'll still beat him back."

The Sundays' boy Joshua stood between his parents. His mother bent and whispered in his ear.

The boy looked up. "Best of happiness, sir and ma'am!" he said through a big, missing front tooth and offering his small, spindly hand next.

"I thank you kindly, young Master Sunday," Slash said. "Me being married—that doesn't mean we can't still go hunting together. And you have to learn to throw a knife."

"My daddy says when I'm older," the eight-year-old replied.

Slash leaned down and whispered conspiratorially. "I learnt when I was young'n you," he said.

Joshua turned wide eyes to his mother. "Hear that, ma? Slash was—"

"On the trail from Texas and didn't have time to set traps, like you do," she said.

"We came all the way from 'Bama—"

"That was different," Bonita said and hushed him.

"How?" the boy grumped.

"We'll talk about it later," she said.

The boy knew, but did not understand, that his mother and son had been brought west by their former master, Brent Diamond. Isaiah and Willa had tracked them to California when the South fell. When Isaiah discovered his wife and child working at the Vallicita station for their onetime owner, Isaiah gave Diamond the option of vacating, at once, or staying—underground.

Complicit in a failed plot to establish a secessionist empire in the West, Diamond chose flight to parts unknown.

As the Sunday family boarded their wagon, Clarity tugged her husband over to see the Mission Indians. They had to return to Fort Yuma but stood patiently waiting to present their gifts.

"We brought books for your firstborn," said Malibu, pointing to the bundle he left on the seat. "It was those we used at the mission to learn English."

Clarity and Slash were deeply touched. The bride hugged both men lightly. The two seemed surprised by what would have been frowned on anywhere else. They stood stiffly, unsure how to respond. The groom shook their hands. That they understood.

Off in the distance, Joe stood at his usual spot near the trough at the porch. His shotgun rested against it, where it always was during the daytime. The thumb of his left hand was absently fingering the spot where his ring had been. It felt naked but it felt right.

He was taking in the last of the event—and calming from B.W.'s outburst. He scowled at Clarity's familiarity with the Redskins. "I got another Gert on my hands," he said to himself.

When the Indians went to the stable, the newlyweds went to "papa" Joe.

"Surprised you didn't use this on B.W." Slash grinned, nodding toward the gun before hugging his grandfather.

"He's a dunderhead sometimes, but who isn't?"

Clarity stepped up and embraced Joe. He was pointedly silent. That was so he wouldn't mention the breech in custom. She knew from just two weeks of living here that Joe was intemperate of Whites being close to Indians, especially women. It was a convention the man's granddaughter flaunted at every opportunity.

"You got yourself a lovely woman and a sharpshooter," the older man said to Slash after stepping back from his granddaughter-in-law. "Now you'll learn if she can sew, plant, and cook."

"I do not recall those words in the vows, but I am an admirable learner," she assured the O'Malley men.

Clarity's clear eyes drifted to B.W. and Dick Ocean who came up behind Joe—though not too closely. The men had waited to talk to the couple when Joe could also hear.

"I'm real, real sorry, Miss Clarity," the Louisiana-born

driver said, the Bible under his arm as he turned his hat round in his hands. "I hope you forgive me."

"Your enthusiasm cannot be faulted," she answered with a quick and easy smile. "The thought was pure even if the action was—"

"Disruptive," Slash interrupted scoldingly.

"That's a very good word for the Whip," laughed Ocean. "Disruptive."

B.W. scowled at the shotgun rider. "I don't have to hear that from you, and won't—lest you want your other leg shot."

A Massachusetts man of Caribe descent, Ocean was still hobbling from a bullet he had taken two weeks before at Civil Gulch, between Vallicita and Whip Station. Gert's quick attention and native ointments had helped it to heal quickly. He was able to rejoin B.W. for the delayed trip to San Francisco and, now, for the return to St. Louis.

The ceremony had broken up quickly. There was no celebration for the guests. The family would have one after the coach departed and before the newlyweds rode off to San Diego. The Sunday family had already passed through the big, stone entranceway and B.W. and Ocean left to check on the condition of the stagecoach before heading to the stable.

Though the team was changed here in just ten or fifteen minutes, B.W. was fond of telling impatient passengers, "Fresh horses won't help if the thoroughbrace tears and y'all drop through the bottom of the coach."

The driver made sure the luggage and mail bags were secure. There wasn't much of the former on this trip, but mail was crammed into both the back box and the free seats inside. San Francisco and Los Angeles were seeing an influx of new settlers every month. They were anxious to let folks back east know they were still alive.

The couple took a moment to themselves. They still had to see Clarity's brother, who had remained by the canopy, lost in pleasant, emotional memories of all that he and his sister had been through as orphans—up through the dire events that had brought them here.

But this isn't the time for reflection such as that, he reminded himself as the newlyweds approached. *This is the time to look ahead to a new life.*

Even so, though he thought it, though he hoped it, Merritt Michaels added a silent prayer for his dream to be so. The people they had crossed back in Murray, Kentucky, were powerful . . . and as wicked as any among God's too-many sinners.

Taking a little time to watch the water bugs as they skidded along the top of the trough, Joe headed inside, as he always did, to size up the passengers. He did it not to pry, not to judge, but to be knowledgeable about the land in which he and his family lived.

Since the end of the War, and in the two years the O'Malley family had been running this station, Joe had watched the West swell with all kinds of people. There was a time, in memory still green, when the entire land west of the Rockies seemed like it was home to just himself and a few other souls. That was when he worked as a scout and buffalo hunter for John Butterfield and his western operations. Then, well before the War, he saw mostly Indians, a few hardy prospectors, and surveyors looking to put in more stage lines, mail routes, or even establish rail lines to the Pacific.

Joe had not yet seen a train but he had seen pictures in

books and newspapers and he had heard stories from travelers. He did not believe he would like them or their tracks, which were spiked hard into the ground. It wasn't like a homestead, which was constantly in use. These rails just lay there empty, most of the time, like scars across the land. And when they were in use, the wheels apparently made a lot of noise and the locomotives spit choking smoke and black grit.

And for what? he wondered. To quickly turn the West into the crowded East. It made no sense to him.

The West already had new merchants and pastors, schoolteachers and reporters, card sharps and loose women—every kind of human being God had fashioned. They were all coming this way to find fresh opportunities.

That in itself was fair. People had first come to the shores of America seeking freedom and a new beginning. But boats took weeks to arrive, not days. He wondered how much the land could sustain.

Joe also wondered what his late wife Dolley would have thought of it all. She had never spoken about much other than the raising of Jackson and the challenges of tending to their little log cabin when Joe was away. Sometimes she talked about foods they'd had to try, like muskrat and buzzard, when cold weather killed their garden and made anything else scarce.

But she did it uncomplaining. She probably would feel the same about trains. She liked people, so whatever damage was done there would be compensation by the benefit of fellowship and new ideas.

Joe missed her steadying good sense. Her death was one of the reasons Joe had decided to set this place up with his son, his daughter-in-law, and their kids. He had a chance to work with ranching O'Malleys in Texas. But here, with the faintest salt water breeze in the air when the wind blew right—here was where he belonged.

Want to make sure the West settles right, he thought as he entered the station. *With decent values and law.*

That thought made him wonder about the two men who sat before him, comfortable and at their leisure—as if he was the stranger here, not them.

Chapter 2

Joe stood a moment, letting his eyes adjust to the pine-wood darkness. He smelled the remains of the meal that had been served, notably the chicory coffee that was presently being drunk with molasses for a sweetener.

Not all of those folks coming west did so from the east. A great many also came north from Mexico, like the two gentlemen who were sitting at the Whip Station table, smoking cigars and drinking their own tequila. The two men were well-dressed, around thirty years old. They had an attitude of affluence about them. One wore a pocket watch with a gold chain, the other a large, sterling silver and onyx sealing-wax seal ring. Joe didn't know the seal, but he knew the black stone. It was a treasured rock that local Indian tribes used for necklaces.

The cigars didn't smell cheap and rank either, the way the O'Malley root cellar or outhouse did. The smokes smelled nutty, like when Joe and young Jackson used to toss acorns into campfires.

Except for thin moustaches, the dark-eyed men were clean-shaven. Their hair was black and neatly brushed from their foreheads. They had obviously freshened up after they arrived at the wash basin in an adjoining room. The journey from San Francisco was not friendly to anyone's grooming.

If the men were Mexican nobility, they might well be looking for a place to settle in the United States. Their kind was not wanted in the *Juarista*-run state to the south.

Neither Joe nor Sarah engaged the passengers unless their guests spoke first. Most times, people on an hour-long layover during the arduous trip wanted to enjoy the fact that they had legroom and weren't bouncing. Most of what they had to say included an "ooooh" or some such.

There, too, these men were different. They had been in a mostly empty carriage, it was true, but they were relaxed, conversing softly in their native tongue.

"*Señor* O'Malley," said the one who was facing the front door.

Joe looked over at the man. Sanchez, he recalled the name. The Mexican wore a pleasant smile behind a cloud of smoke. He also wore two jeweled rings and a silver chain around his neck, both of which announced his social standing.

"Yes, sir," Joe replied affably.

"My congratulations on your son's marriage."

"Thank you very much, and call me Joe," he answered. He continued toward the window sill where Sarah had set a freshly baked cherry pie. That was not for the passengers but for the little wedding party to follow the departure of the stagecoach. The women were outside, washing the meal plates by the well. The dogs had roused from their torpor and were snapping up scraps. What they didn't eat, smaller varmints would.

Gonzalez was sitting opposite Sanchez, his back to Joe.

He wore a leather satchel, bulging slightly, over his right shoulder. He turned round to look at his host.

Unlike the first man, this one had a sly look and a long ash on his cigar. He also had a scar that ran from his left ear to his chin. It was old, with spidery stretch marks where the skin had grown over. It looked too fine, too regular to have come from anything but a knife.

"The Brother Whip—he speaks very highly of your family," Gonzalez said.

Joe stopped. He didn't know why, but the remark didn't sit right. Perhaps it was innocent. But it almost sounded like it was somehow a threat.

"Why were you and the driver discussing my family?" Joe asked. His own voice, now, had a trace of menace.

"The proprietor at the Oak Grove—it was he who mentioned you," the man said.

"That doesn't tell me why," Joe responded bluntly.

"Let me think," Gonzalez said, pressing his lips together in thought. "What were we talking about?"

Joe waited. He knew the folks at Oak Grove, but not well. Their relationship was not the same as it was with Isaiah and his family, who they took to like sun to summer. Station owners from up and down the line met twice a year with representatives of the Butterfield Overland Mail Company at a hotel in Los Angeles. It was not a time for socializing but for business. At least, that's how Joe took it. He was there representing the future of his children and grandchildren—and perhaps, one day, great-great-grandchildren, the Lord willing. After those meetings, he was itchy to get out of his best clothes. He was happy to talk to the St. Louis boys about profits, but not about dinner menus. When the work was done, he did not delay but set out for home. Even if it was after sunset, he would get some distance away from the dirty city, then sleep in the plains or by a clean, flowing river. Los Angeles and even San Diego made him feel like the clothes he wore when he went to them: they were too tight.

Gonzalez was still thinking, and Joe was still waiting. Noticing his ash, the Mexican dropped it into a copper ashtray.

"I remember," he said, then pointed the cigar at Joe. "We were discussing travel from Mazatlán to San Francisco, *Señor* O'Malley. Sanchez and I—we were trying to determine whether it was best to go by sea or by land."

"I suppose," Joe said, "that depends on whether you want to be tossed around or thumped around."

The men laughed a little too loud at Joe's dry observation. He was getting restless. With Indians, with bandits, with wolves, you knew where you stood almost immediately. There was a rogue coyote once who kept Joe guessing as he and the scraggly beast both made their way to the same watering hole. In fairness, the coyote had found it and Joe found the coyote. When they got there, on opposite sides, they eyeballed each other constantly as they drank and then walked away. They were two fellas just too tired to fight.

These men were not plain-speaking. They had the style of riverboat gamblers who were looking to lasso you into a game.

"That still doesn't explain where me and my family fit in," Joe said impatiently. "But if it's just the same to you gentlemen, I'm going to pump more water, then go to the stable—"

"A moment," Gonzalez implored.

Joe waited.

"The people to north, at the station, informed us that you were once a frontiersman, that you knew all the trails through the mountains, all the rivers and lakes," Gonzalez said. "And—ah, that was it, the mention of your family. The station mistress mentioned that it had to be hard on a family to have a man whose work keeps him from home."

"That's right," Sanchez said to his companion. "Then we told her that we had the same problem and—well, so on and so on."

Joe smiled crookedly. Maybe he was wrong. Maybe these men were nothing more than nanny goats who liked to "baaaaa" while they chewed on the grass.

"Well, sirs, you hit the bull's-eye," Joe said. "That's exactly why I'm here, with new roots."

He turned to go and the men went back to their cigars and conversing in Mexican. The whole conversation had amounted to a "blessed knotty nothing," as his own mother Bess used to describe little Joe's own stories.

Joe hung his good jacket on a rack beside the back door. Then he went around the outside eating table to the well where Sarah and Gert had just about gone through a bucket of water. He toed Blood out of the way then let the bucket fall with a *sploosh*. The man perched on the well as he cranked it up. He kept his mouth closed since flies and other insects liked the water and mossy walls here, and paid little attention where they flew.

Joe hauled the bucket over the stone wall, placed it on the ground, and stepped from the well.

"Did you have a nice conversation?" his daughter asked.

"I truly do not know," Joe said. "What d'you think of those men inside?"

"Very pleasant," Sarah said. She used a tin cup to scoop

out water to wash the utensils. "I was just telling Gert, I can't remember passengers going in either direction who seemed so completely relaxed."

"Maybe they were happy to get away from the turmoil in Mexico," Gert suggested.

Sarah made a sound of agreement.

"They was asking me about my family," Joe said.

"You sound surprised," Gert said.

"I was."

"Why?"

"I guess I'm used to people mostly minding their own business," he answered.

"A natural curiosity, perhaps," Sarah said. "They seem to be men of means and intelligence."

"The more people who come west—or north—the more people will be curious about local customs," Gert added. "Aren't you, when you go to see who has come in on the stage?"

"That's different," he said. "I like to know who is in my home. I'm not sure I'll ever be comfortable with folks being just naturally nosy."

"Being interested isn't the same as being a gossip, grandpa," Gert said.

"It is to me," Joe said. He locked the handle in place by driving his palm against a wooden peg.

"Didn't you talk to Clarity when you rode out to Civil Gulch?" Gert asked.

"That was different," Joe protested. "And impertinent."

"It was neither," the young woman politely disagreed.

Gert was referring to a trip they took two weeks earlier to try and locate Rebel raiders. That was shortly after Joe had learned she was a sharpshooter and took her with him on his nighttime hunting party.

"Miss Clarity was interesting," Joe said. "Now she's family."

Sarah looked up at her father and frowned. "That made no sense, pop."

He shrugged. "I was trying to say, if she didn't have that skill for shooting, we wouldn't've had anything to say and maybe she wouldn't now be your daughter-in-law."

"So the marriage is all your doing because she impressed you as a marksman." Gert grinned.

"In a manner of looking at it, yes," Joe agreed amiably.

Gert made a face as her grandfather walked over to the stable. He had said all he cared to say to the women and still was not convinced the two Mexican gentlemen were as innocent as the ladies seemed to think.

Since he did not have to lock eyes with the two men again, Joe tried to put the matter from his mind as he went to see how Jackson, B.W., and Ocean were getting on. On the way to the stable he passed Clarity and Slash who had just finished putting bags into their cart. The wagon had been a gift from the O'Malley family, delivered to the Sunday family waystation from Fort Yuma and brought over this morning.

The newlyweds didn't have much, but they were taking some clothes and guns with them. They would be away in San Diego for two weeks or so, some of which time they would spend camping and living off the land. They planned to buy some tent material in the city.

During that time Joe planned to do nothing but work on a cabin for the couple on the far side of the stable. Most times, they would be upwind from the smell of horses. Isaiah Sunday had promised he would be back to help as much as possible.

Joe saw the couple, who were with Clarity's brother. A

final kiss on the cheek for his sister, a handshake for Slash, and then Reverend Michaels left to help the O'Malley women. His back to the newlyweds, the pastor brushed tears from both eyes. Joe noticed, thought the pastor didn't see him. Merritt hadn't been the soft, Gospel-spouting man the frontiersman had first imagined. In fact, as soon as the wedding meal was done, the pastor would return to his horse and his new traveling ministry.

Joe was actually proud of the man, the quickest about-face he had ever made in his opinion of someone. Within a day of deciding to remain in the area, Merritt Michaels had used what savings he had to buy a horse and spent over a week visiting the homesteaders in the region, getting himself known and seeing about establishing a church hereabout. He had gone out with just a crude map and a general sense of who lived where. When Merritt reached the coast, he was given letters of introduction to clergy in the missions and churches. These were written by the O'Malleys' newfound friend, Cavalry Major Alexander Howard of the San Diego Barracks.

In just that eleven-day sojourn, the change in the pastor had been remarkable. When he arrived, he had been a pale, shy flower hoping to join a congregation in San Francisco. Now he had a sun-burned face and a new enthusiasm for what Southern California had to offer. The West did that to people. Either it broke them with its deviltry or lifted them on angels' wings.

Joe circled wide around the couple. He did not want to intrude. He remembered how he felt when he married his dear Dolley.

Like God Himself had forgiven me every stupid thing I ever did and said, "Here. Here is someone you never want to disappoint or hurt or even be away from."

Joe walked on toward the stable, but his mind was not on where he was. It was on where he had been. The death of his wife was like nothing Joe had ever experienced. Joe wasn't at home when his own parents died. He did not learn of it until weeks later, by post. His mother had died first, then his father, both at the age of fifty-nine. Not a bad age for folks who had crossed the ocean from Ireland where they had endured so much hardship—only to find more when they arrived on these shores in 1797. Seamus O'Malley had shod horses in the Old Country and did so again in New York, where he literally had to fight off men who wanted his job. As a boy, Joe never understood how a man could come home burned from a forge, bloodied from a fight, and still consider it a good day.

But Joe was with his darling wife as the cancer ate her, thinned her, paled her, weakened her, did every wicked thing it could to ravage her fading life without mercy or respite. There were times when she was in such pain that she begged God to take her, that Joe wanted to help her along. One time he went so far as to put his gun to her temple as she stared blankly at the dark roof, her mouth frozen wide.

But he couldn't shoot her. Not that fine hair and the skin he had cradled and kissed and loved. Not for love of her nor hate of the disease could he take her life. Only God had that right.

Joe did not know any of the scripture and proverbs that B.W. was always quoting. Until Dolley died, the frontiersman was not even sure he believed in God. No one with any sense would make the world so beautiful, then fill it with some of the first Injuns he had met out here, savages that tortured a man for days. Or bears that would claw out a man's lungs or storms that would sweep in and tear a baby from its mother's bosom or fires that would consume the warrens and nests of His helpless, lesser creatures. A generous, loving God would provide enough water so that settler would not have to murder settler to feed his sheep or cattle.

No. Joe believed in God for one reason. If there was a God, then there was a Heaven. And if there was a Heaven, then Joe would see his Dolley again.

Joe had intended to ask B.W. if he had heard or seen anything strange about the men he was transporting to Vallicita.

He didn't get the chance.

Chapter 3

For the first time in his long life at sea, Captain Alan Swift was troubled. And a man who had ridden out typhoons and survived shipwrecks, who had kept a crew alive in a longboat for thirty-three days in the cold North Atlantic—such a man was not easily troubled.

Dressed in a bell-crown hat and a long, blue frock that protected him from the wind but did not bake him under the sun, Swift stood on the gently swaying deck of his schooner, *The Dundee*. He was concerned about something other than the seaman's usual worries. Here along the California coast that meant the elements—which could change in a moment as the winds or contour of the land did—or what the Spanish called picaroons, high seas marauders.

Swift's ship itself was also not the problem. It was the best he'd ever sailed, let alone commanded.

"Lord no, I fear nothing that God or I can control," he said softly, as though assuring the vessel that his grave expression, wrinkled as whale hide, had nothing to do with her. "But you should be worried too," he confided to the graceful, young lady.

The seventy-foot, seven-inch coasting schooner was launched in San Francisco on August 23, 1866. *The Dundee* was sleek and modern. The wood from northern California was strong, healthy, and the oakum—the tarred hemp cordage caulking—sat tight and sure beneath the pitch that covered it.

"Hell, everything on this continent, on this coast, seems fresh and fit," he said with an affectionate glance at the rocky shore, which passed near enough that he could hear the undersea caves echoing back.

What troubled Captain Swift were his bosses. More specifically, his instructions for this voyage.

The vessel was launched just four months previously at the Ritchie Brothers Shipyard. The Ritchies had given Swift the entire story in their first letter to him.

The three men were three Scottish immigrants who had given up their seafaring trade at home, come seeking gold in 1855, and instead found poverty—and found it quickly. The greed-driven prices for tools, food, clothes, all goods went up as the need for them rose and the population swelled.

It was the brothers' good luck that Mexico was in turmoil. The tyrant Antonio López de Santa Anna had just been deposed, and *La Reforma* was underway. The salvation for the Ritchies came when Benito Juárez and the revolutionaries got rid of the *fueros*—the historic privileges held by both the clergy and the military.

Funded by the church, these displaced military officers and their friends among the nobility came north looking for weapons and ships. Agents found the Scottish brothers who had been hired by a shipbuilding company to find rich timberland. They knew wood, knew what to look for.

But then another Mexican agent came to them. One

who did not represent the landed interests. One who represented the new government. He said that the *Juaristas* wanted to *be* a new concern. Should the rebel government be driven out, should the French return, they would need a government-in-exile. They would need income and warships.

Money was provided, a swath of coastline was purchased, and the brothers were back in business. They were not working for the wealthy but for the men who opposed them.

There was nothing illegal in what the immigrant brothers did, accepting foreign funds to buy forests and set up a shipyard. In fact, the federal government encouraged such arrangements. It gave the United States influence abroad.

"Rebel foreigners funding Scottish immigrants to give power to the American government," Swift thought. It was an insane world.

Captain Swift had been one of the first employees of the new venture. He had been the one who put the Ritchies' new vessels through sea trials in Europe. And right now that was where he wished he was. Safe, at home, in his native Edinburgh.

"It's not the ship or the land, for I love you both," he said.

He missed people he knew and whose habits and desires and heritage he understood. He did not understand Mexicans or Canadians. The French hated anyone from across the English Channel so he avoided them. He wished they would do the same. There were people of African heritage who were a complete mystery to him. So were the Chinese, Japanese, Koreans. Until coming to America, he had never set eyes on an Asian.

Whatever strengths or flaws these people brought with

them were expanded because the virgin wilderness here was so vast and so ripe for exploitation.

But worst of all was Swift's current passenger, Gabriel Martinez. This man was the cause of the captain's current agitation.

There was something unclean about the fellow. He had come up from Mexico, and Mexico was still at war. They had just finished ousting the French. The liberal reformer Benito Juárez was in power. Martinez was too well-dressed to be one of his *Juaristas*. That would make him a noble. That in itself did not make Martinez bad. It was the natural arrogance and secretiveness that came with it.

The eyes of the taciturn, humorless man were dark and dead, like coal. There was a permanently critical set to his mouth, and his cheeks had a smooth, pale look of alabaster. He had a cultured accent and manner but they did not seem inbred, like the nobility Swift had known abroad.

In a word, there was something *off* about him.

The captain found himself looking away when he had to speak with the man, as if he were looking at something supernatural and unhealthy. As he did just a minute before. The schooner had just left San Diego port and was on its way to Los Angeles, Santa Barbara, Monterey, and then San Francisco.

"Mr. Martinez, are you very certain of your cargo?" Swift had asked.

They were heading into seasonally unsettled waters, and that had the captain watchful . . . careful.

Standing beside the captain on the forecastle deck, the diminutive man had his tiny hands clasped in the small of his back. The seas along the Southern California coast were getting choppy as they sailed north. The early after-noon skies, which had been clear less than an hour earlier, were starting to fill with dark-bottomed clouds. The winds from the west were nudging them toward the shore and the waves were starting to chop.

"I am most sure of my cargo," Martinez said confidently. He tapped the brown top hat he wore. "I wore this on the Atlantic, you see. It never left my head, and the cargo arrived safely. When this blows off, then, perhaps, I will reconsider my position."

"When your top hat blows off—" the gray-bearded captain began. The fifty-seven-year-old veteran fell silent when he realized that the passenger was having fun with him. "You mock me, sir, and the safety of this ship."

Gabriel Martinez smiled thinly, the line of his pale lips barely moving his frozen face. "Why so concerned, captain?"

"Because I don't know what you have down there." Swift wagged a stubby index finger in the direction of the hold.

"Since you *don't* know the cargo, your fears are—"

"A captain's natural caution for ship, crew, *and* passengers," Swift replied. "I have endured your silence since Mazatlán because those were my instructions. But I have never in my years at sea known of a captain who cannot be told what cargo he carries!"

"How would it matter if you knew?" Martinez asked pleasantly. "Suppose I tell you we are carrying a rare wine."

"Then I would advise you to turn back until the seas calm," Swift replied. "It may be smashed within that crate."

"'Caution is a seaman's most trusted companion,'" Martinez said. He was quoting a sign in the Ritchies' San Francisco office.

"That's right," Swift said. "We are nearer to safe haven back in San Diego than we are to the north."

The five-foot two-inch Martinez tugged on the sleeves of his dress coat before moving closer to the foot-taller sailor. The smaller man's smile remained fixed. His eyes were still lifeless.

"Your employers have ceded authority over your ship to me," Martinez said. "I have that guarantee, in writing, in my cabin should you wish to see it."

"I've read it."

"Fine. Then, captain, *I* will let you know if we are to turn around or lower the anchor or the sails. If, by some agency, we go down—*you* may give the order to abandon ship."

Martinez turned away before the captain could respond. Swift did not watch the man go but turned away. He remained on the forecastle, looking out at the Pacific Ocean. It looked increasingly as though the weather would not cooperate with a northern passage. The captain's concerns deepened. Either they were smuggling riches from Mexico—in which case a wreck would be salvaged and its captain incriminated—or something deadlier.

Swift lingered another minute. He had it in mind to turn back to San Diego anyway. He could convince his good friend Harbormaster Rog York to write a report that said the ship was in danger from the storm and the bay offered refuge.

"The favor would cost me a dinner at the Mariner's Cove but it would be worth it," he said.

But Swift's pride would suffer if he asked for help to do something he should have the backbone to do. Orders be thoroughly damned. Alan Swift *should* put the safety of his crew before whatever—or whoever—he was transporting.

"And, damn the Ritchies and Martinez," he decided. "That's what will be done."

Without showing the urgency he felt, the captain went below. He entered his cabin aft and went to his long drawer of carefully rolled charts. As he stood there, he felt the gentle nudge of the waves against the hull. It was more pronounced than just a few minutes before. He removed a chart and unrolled it onto a table. He wanted to note every cove, every inlet where he might put the vessel in the case of a serious blow.

"There are several spots," he muttered as the light coming through the big aft windows shifted from west to east in slow, steady panels. If the light began to move and jerk more swiftly, it would mean the undercurrents were getting stronger. As long as that didn't happen—

"As long as his bloody hat remains on his bloody head," Swift remarked with disgust. "A martinet *and* a dandy."

What frustrated the captain was that apart from his regular cargo, even his longtime employers, men he trusted, did not trust *him* to know what Martinez had brought aboard. The contents of a sea chest had been loaded in secret, the large locker carried onboard by four men while Martinez watched them carefully. Once the chest was aboard, Martinez had two crewmen secure it to a pillar in the hold with rope and closed it with a padlock.

"Like Ulysses before the Sirens," he thought.

Swift had offered him the use of chains, but Martinez had declined. He did not say why.

Then the Mexican gathered empty canvas storage bags, which were used to store additional foods taken in at various stops. He carefully padded the area between the crate and the pillar. Swift had only been informed, by youngest Ritchie brother Branan, that there was just one caution he could provide before Swift sailed south to Mazatlán—with

Martinez, who had come north on a different vessel, another Ritchie schooner *The Wallace*.

"The hold must not flood," Branan had said.

"Why?" Swift had asked.

"I do not know," Branan had admitted.

"You don't know what we'll be carrying?"

"I do not wish to know," Branan Ritchie had told him.

Swift had looked at the man with disappointment bordering on disgust. "Mr. Ritchie, you have given this man command of my ship," Swift had said.

"It is our ship to put in command who we choose," Branan had said. He had immediately softened. "I'm sorry, captain. I—*we*—mean no disloyalty to you, none whatsoever. You must accept my word on that. This man, your passenger, is an accomplished fellow. He speaks many languages. More importantly, he has many powerful friends. And we are—let us just say 'indebted' to Mexican concerns that have sponsored him."

Swift understood, then. Either he helped this *Juarista* or the funds for the shipbuilding operation would be withdrawn. It was a dangerous, foolish capitulation, he thought. But he had told Branan, for the sake of their long relationship, that he understood.

And Swift did understand. He simply did not like one, single stroke of the pen that had put him in this humiliating position. He thought of resigning, then and there, but his own sense of loyalty, damn it all, was intact.

But as Swift left the brother's office, his employer had looked uncommonly—*shamed* was the word that had come into Swift's mind at the time. Not because of any potential danger, the captain suspected. Seafarers faced danger every day they are under sail. No, it was because Branan apparently could not confide everything to Swift. That went against every code of the sea that either man held dear.

"A new world . . . a new code," Swift had thought as they set sail to the south.

From the start, when Martinez had boarded, the relationship had been tense.

The passenger did not speak much, and what he said was invariably condescending. He did not walk like a sailor, which was the first mark against him. How could Tomas Martinez know what was good for a ship if he had not spent much—*any*?—time at sea? What's more, how could he know what to do if there were some kind of danger? He would be ignorant of how much time might be required to turn about or evacuate the crew or—

"A captain, even if that's not his title, should know *everything* about his ship," Swift said angrily, slapping a beefy hand on the chart.

There were no convenient covers from a storm. Not in the next ten or so nautical miles. Thus educated, the captain decided he would educate himself about the cargo. At once.

Martinez had the only key to the padlock but Alan Swift had something nearly as good. A crowbar. This particular tool had been hand-forged at the Helmet Iron Foundry in Gorbals, Glasgow. It was one of the many reliable tools he had brought with him to America, tools that ranged from his own bung hole augur drill to his sextant. They were old and trusted friends. He knew their feel, their strengths.

The captain kept the crowbar in a ditty bag hanging from a peg in his closet. The cloth helped prevent rust by keeping the crowbar dry. When he opened his windows slightly, sea mist inevitably came in with the clean sea air. Stored here, the crowbar was also handy in the remote possibility they were attacked by pirates. Boarders would think to take the captain's pistols, which he kept in a case on the chart drawer. They might not concern themselves with a canvas sack.

He looked over at the closet. His iron friend beckoned.

"Aye," he said, smiling as he walked over on the rocking floor. He undid the ropes of the bag and removed the iron. It sat just right in his big, calloused hand. He felt like a man two-times-bigger just wielding it. Hefting it menacingly as he walked to the door with long, steady strides, the captain hurried up the ladder outside his cabin and crossed the deck—*his* deck—to the forward hatch. Swift looked around while he pulled it open. The captain noticed Martinez standing aft, now on the quarter deck, above the captain's own cabin. The man was gazing out at the sea. Swift couldn't imagine what such a narrow mind might be thinking, faced with such majesty. He also didn't know if the man had seen him leave, nor did he care. He also saw no reason asking for the key and being turned down. He was the commander here and, as such, he did not issue requests.

"I give orders," he said with quiet ferocity as he opened the hatch.

The captain shut the hatch behind him and descended a longer ladder to the hold. It was dark but he knew every foot of the ship by touch, by step. He struck a paraffin-tipped match in the holder next to the lantern and hung it on a central hook. The light swayed as though it were a Daisy Fairy flitting across flowers in the field. The rocking was more pronounced down here, suggesting that the seas were indeed getting rougher and that severe weather was on the way.

"A bloody crow's curse on all of you," he said, thinking of Martinez and Branan Ritchie both.

Amongst the crates and barrels bound for different ports was the strong, central wooden pillar with Martinez's chest lashed to it by spare halyards.

"What was wrong with chains?" the captain wondered aloud. It couldn't be the noise, since the tight ropes creaked nearly as loud.

Swift walked around the pillar. He was glad he would not have to undo the rigging to reach the padlock and raise the lid a little. There was room under the diagonal top rope to open the lid.

Kneeling in front of the chest, Swift examined the lock. It was iron and it was new. It might not break. He ran his hand across the lid. He knocked on it. The lid had a metal frame but was wood, mostly. There was room enough at the top for him to fit the edge of the crowbar, pry it up, and see inside. He didn't care whether he cracked the case or not. Branan could buy Martinez a new one—

"If we reach San Francisco," he thought.

Concern once again steeled his resolve. The captain hated that he felt like a buccaneer on his own vessel. He was being insubordinate, not in a nautical sense but in a personal one. That fact did not fill him with pride. The Ritchies might well dismiss him, though he had no doubt they would quickly reconsider. The corsairs in this region vastly outnumbered the honest men. The Ritchies would immediately find their cargo arriving short, if at all.

Swift snorted. Some of those men that Swift had encountered here, along the Barbary Coast, would have bumped Martinez from the quarterdeck into the sea and left him to drown. They would have opened the chest.

Finding a gold bar or a precious stone of some kind, they were as likely to sell it as to deliver it.

His heart thumping with anticipation and concern—he did not know what he might be releasing—Swift put the hooked end of the crowbar under the metal frame that ran around the lid.

Bracing the crowbar on the top, front side of the chest, Captain Swift rose on his knees and put his full body weight down on the crowbar. The ropes groaned, the padlock rose, and the chest itself squeaked from the pressure. Swift grunted, rose from his knees, and put even more of his weight on the crowbar. The wood complained loudly now—

"What are you doing?"

The voice from behind sounded crisp and annoyed. Swift relaxed his efforts and, unapologetic, looked over his shoulder. Martinez was standing there, his hands behind his back, glaring down. His shadow swayed in the lantern light as if it was another person.

"As you see, Mr. Martinez. I'm opening your chest."

"Step away. At *once!*"

Swift steeled his shoulders. "I will not," he replied. "Either you tell me what we are carrying or you will go back on deck and allow me to finish."

"I will do neither," Martinez responded. "Your superiors—"

"Are not here, nor are they the captain of *The Dundee*. I am. I will answer to them for my actions."

Martinez's mouth formed a disapproving line. "Get *away* from the chest, captain."

Swift scowled back at the man and returned to his work.

Martinez watched for a moment. Swift rose up, pressed down, and the crowbar once again worked against the chest.

The groaning of the iron against the softer metal rim grew more insistent.

With one quick move, Martinez's right hand came around his side. Held tightly in it was a belaying pin. He swung it. The hard wood struck Swift on the right temple. The wooden knob sent the captain to his left side. The crowbar fell from Swift's grip, dropping to the hull with a dull clatter.

The captain tried dazedly to get up. He failed, crumpling on the cool hull. He moaned, but only for an instant.

Martinez squatted. The man was still breathing. The Mexican drew a handkerchief from his shirt pocket and wiped the blood from the pin. Then he pressed the cloth against the captain's wound. The injured man groaned. Martinez left the handkerchief and picked up the crowbar.

"Be grateful I did not use something like this," he said and dropped it.

Martinez would replace the pin when he returned to the deck. For now, he leaned his face toward the older man.

"I know you are conscious, so listen well," said the Mexican. "I will summon the surgeon at once. When he arrives, you will inform him that you struck your head on the pillar while checking the cargo." The shorter man rose and tugged the ends of his jacket. He looked at the red stain that was running behind the sailor's ear and down his blue collar. "It is fortunate I followed you down. Otherwise, you might have bled to death before being discovered."

Swift wanted to say something, but he was unable to muster the strength to form words—and Martinez had already left. The captain's head pounded like a loose jib and, over the throbbing, Swift heard footfalls approaching rapidly down the ladder. The ship's surgeon, Russell Puckett, bent over him.

"Captain, can you hear me?"

Swift nodded once, weakly, a lightning strike of pain firing along his neck as he did. He heard Puckett rummaging through his medical kit, felt cool water on his injury. Then he felt a cloth. The pressure, though light, caused him to wince.

"Sorry, captain," the physician said. "I have to clean the wound."

Swift did not move. All he wanted to do was lie there.

And think about how he would not only best Martinez but make him pay for this reckless, craven act.

Chapter 4

"*Señor* Joe!"

Nearly at the stable door, Joe turned, squinting into the wall of sunlight. He saw both of the stagecoach passengers walking toward him, silhouetted in the sun. He could tell Sanchez by his leather satchel.

Curiosity my hind leg, Joe thought triumphantly. The men *had* been after something. Now he would learn what.

At least the Mexicans apparently knew something about horses. They were smart enough to have left their cigars inside, far from the dry hay.

"Yes, sir?" Joe asked without moving.

"May we speak with you?" the speaker replied.

Jackson and B.W. started moving the new team out. Joe stepped forward, out of the way. B.W. motioned for Jackson to stop. He leaned close to Joe and whispered.

"I wondered when they'd get around to this," the driver said.

"What're you talking about?" Joe asked.

"Ever since they got on in Frisco, at every stop, they asked if I knew any guides," the driver told him.

"To where and why?" Joe asked.

"Dunno," B.W. shrugged. "I said I knew a plainsman who was better than any guide and mentioned your name. They asked a few questions. I answered."

"You didn't think to mention this to me?" Joe asked.

"You had nuptials on yer mind," B.W. said. "I figgered if they had something to say, they'd say it." The Whip and Jackson started the horses again. B.W. looked over at the Mexicans and boomed, "You haven't got too long, gents!"

"This will not take long," Sanchez assured him.

Joe walked toward them, away from the horses. Too many people crowding around might make them skittish. He motioned the Mexicans to one side with an arm then faced them.

"What can I do for you?" Joe asked. "As long as it don't involve my family—"

"It does not," Sanchez said. "Not directly."

"What does 'not directly' mean?"

"*Señor* Joe—" Sanchez began.

"Just 'Joe,'" the older man reminded him.

"Joe," Sanchez corrected himself and dipped his head to one side in acquiescence. "We have a proposition for you."

"You want to go somewhere the stage doesn't go," he guessed.

"Ah, the Whip has spoken to you—just now?" Gonzalez said.

"That's right."

"Well, what you say is true—in a manner of speaking," Sanchez replied frankly. The man absently touched his scar.

Joe had known people who did such before. It usually meant they were lying, about to lie, or considering what lie to tell.

"Joe, when we reach Vallicita, we will not be returning to Mexico," Gonzalez said. "We have another journey to undertake."

Joe wondered why well-dressed folk never got straight to the point. Maybe because they did not have to face being out in the wilderness where there wasn't time to let a fellow traveler know. *"Grizzly!"*

"A man is meeting us with supplies, maps, lanterns, and horses," Gonzalez continued. "We will be returning to the north on our own."

"You want to go southeast, then north again," Joe said. "Why didn't your supplier meet you here? Coulda saved yourself some hours of daylight."

"We had understood, before we left Mexico to travel to San Francisco, that the Vallicita station was being run by a man named Brent Diamond," Sanchez said. "He was said to have connections with Confederate guides. We had intended to make this inquiry of him."

"Yeah, that fella got tossed out by his former slaves," Joe said. He was sure the men already knew this. He just liked saying it.

"We learned this from *Señor*—from B.W.," the Mexican went on. "The Whip also informs us that *you* are a man with detailed knowledge of this region, the terrain."

"Quite considerable," Joe agreed.

"Excellent," Sanchez smiled, relaxing a little. "We have need of such a man." The Mexican stepped forward, pulled Joe over, to the back side of the stable. Gonzalez looked around then came with him.

"Friends, what the heck is this?" Joe demanded impatiently. "Secrets, moving me around—"

"Joe, what we have to tell you cannot get out, not at

other stations, to the driver, to anyone," Gonzalez said. "We are agents of the Mexican Republican Army."

Joe gave each man a dubious look in turn. "You can prove this?"

"I left my *shako* in Mexico City," Sanchez said with more than a trace of sarcasm.

He was referring to the stovepipe hat worn by Mexican soldiers. The answer came quickly. The question had obviously been asked more than once in his career.

"We have papers, in Spanish," said Gonzalez. "They are in Sanchez's bag and we will show them to you. But we haven't the time now for that, *señor* . . . Joe," he corrected himself. "We also have gold to pay you. We need someone to take us north by land, to San Francisco, and not upon this Butterfield trail."

"There's travelers that you don't want to see."

"That is correct," Gonzalez said. "We are searching for a man. He may not himself be on the trail, he may be at sea. However, there may be others. And you are correct. We do not wish to be seen."

"How did you get up to Frisco to come back down here?" Joe asked. "I mean, you didn't go up on the stage. We'd've seen you."

"We went by sea," Gonzalez informed him.

"Why?"

"We were looking for this someone—for some *thing*—likely following the coast," Sanchez informed him. "We stopped at each port-of-call, searched—we were not successful."

"Looking for who and what?" Joe asked.

"We are not free to reveal that," the man continued apologetically and with a courteous little bow.

"That's fair, but then why should I trust you?"

"Because we are committed to a project that will affect you more than it will affect us," Sanchez said. "And not in a good way."

"We suspect the man we seek waited in one of the harbors before continuing, or changed ships," Gonzalez said. "He may have doubled back to confuse the trail—we do not know."

"But he must be found and stopped," Sanchez said.

Joe regarded the two. His family—especially the newlyweds—could use more money, there was no question of that. But he was far, far from having a settled feeling about this thing. He was going to let this rope play out a little longer.

"The questions about my family," Joe said. "Being away . . . and helping them financially. Is that what you were fishing for?"

"That is part of it."

"And you won't tell me the rest," Joe said. "Mexico. That's not my country and what happens there isn't any of my business. How will it affect us?"

"We *cannot* say more except to repeat that this will *be* your business, your country's business, and very soon," Gonzalez said.

Sanchez motioned for his partner to say no more.

"Uh huh. I should trust you, but you can't trust me," Joe said.

"If you choose not to go with us, we would have to trust you to be silent."

Joe considered this. "That's fair. You don't really know me. But here's where the road gets bumpy for me. How do

I know I won't be helping you or your countrymen to invade?"

"Because we have had enough of war," Sanchez assured him.

"This is worse," Gonzalez suggested.

"Worse than war," Joe said. He kicked a horse patty that sent a covering of flies into the air. The pests flew in all directions for a moment before buzzing back to their booty. "What the hell is worse than war? And how do I know that what you're doing is any kind of legal? You could be smugglers."

"We could be, but we are not," Gonzalez said.

"Gentlemen!" B.W. called out. "Where are you? We're near ready!"

Gonzalez did not answer. He continued to press his case with Joe O'Malley.

"I understand that you have only our word and, of course, you are to leave whenever you like. Some of the gold will be left here. Now." He patted the satchel.

Joe liked that answer.

"This fella you're seeking—he *is* a he, right?"

"That is the information we have received."

"He knows you're after him?" Joe asked.

"Given what they are transporting and why, he and his *compadres* have to presume so," Sanchez said.

"You'll know them by sight?"

"Not the people, only what they carry," the Mexican replied.

"Do they know you?"

"We do not believe so," Sanchez said.

"One more thing," Joe said. "You ain't wearing sidearms. If these folks're dangerous—why not?"

"It is essential that we capture our quarry, not shoot them," Gonzalez said.

"No one says you have to *kill* them."

"We must be able to capture and interrogate them," Gonzalez told him. "That is not your concern."

"I take it, then, that if we meet anyone else—it's part of my job to protect you two?"

Gonzalez lifted one side of his jacket. There was a four-inch knife in a sheath hooked to his belt. "I got too close to a knife, one time," he said, touching his scar lightly. "I was alone. I was able to turn it around and cut the throat of my attacker. I need no protection."

"Then I beg your pardon," Joe said. "I'm just trying to clear up what my duties would be. Shooting folks leads to complications, especially out here. Just got finished with some business like that."

"Of course," Gonzalez said, his own personable manner returned.

"The gold will help Slash and his bride, I think," said Sanchez. "But the question about your family pertains more to whether you will agree to be away from them for several weeks. Can they take care of the station without you?"

Joe chuckled. "That depends on who you ask. Inside, I'm told I get in the way."

That was true for Sarah. To Gert it was more so. Joe was too openly critical of her friends, her Indian friends, who she was fond of visiting and whose ways she enjoyed learning. Joe knew that some of the remedies she learned were useful. Dick Ocean had benefitted from that when he was shot in the leg. The scents in the root cellar, Gert said, helped him heal faster. She had learned those from Serrano Indians. Joe himself had learned how to cure certain foods from the Cheyenne during his frontier days. Both he and Gert had learned the ways of the tomahawk, which was useful where the noise of guns or the hilt of a knife was not. The same weapon that could scalp could also club.

It wasn't the knowledge that bothered him. It was the fact that she did not understand who the Red Men would side with if it ever came to war. It was not with the settlers. And what would happen if she fell in love and produced a child. Half-breeds were spurned by all peoples—if the Indians allowed them to survive at all.

"Joe?" Sanchez asked.

The lanky plainsman looked up. "Yeah."

"Your answer?"

B.W. shouted, "*Hey,* y'all! We are *ready* to roll out!"

The collies echoed B.W.'s cry. Joe's attention returned to the matter at hand.

"I'll talk to Jackson about it," Joe said. "Without Slash here, he's the one who'd be affected most."

"Of course," Gonzalez said with a trace of disappointment. He unshouldered the satchel, undid the leather straps, pulled back the flap. There was a small white canvas bag inside. He removed it and held it toward Joe. "We must know now whether we are coming west or going north on our own. Perhaps this will help you to decide. There are twenty dollars in California gold, Indian head. We will give that to you after we meet our supply wagon and come back here. There will be another eighty when we finish our trip to San Francisco."

The amount was more than Joe had ever earned for a job. It was half of what they earned from Butterfield every year.

"I collect whether you succeed or fail?" Joe asked.

"You will be paid in San Francisco, regardless."

Joe looked at the sack. Reality always made temptation *more* tempting. That was one reason he never stayed long in a city.

Joe's hands remained rigid at his sides. "Keep it till I see you again," he said.

"Then you agree?" Sanchez asked.

"If I don't, I'll get you on your way, no charge—at least as far as Oak Grove. That's better'n leaving from Vallicita through the foothills."

Gonzalez smiled crookedly. "I like you, Joe."

"We will come back this way in a day or so, allowing for any delays with the stage or our supply cart," Sanchez told him.

"Sure," Joe said. "I'll be right here."

Sanchez hesitated. He regarded Joe critically. "*Señor* Joe," he said, reverting to formality to stress the gravity of this request. "We need your help. I hope for a favorable response."

"Your proposition will get my full consideration," Joe promised. "I am neither an over-cautious or over-reckless man, but upfront gold always scrubs away all-overish doubts."

The men said nothing more. The gold was replaced and the satchel was closed and shouldered. The Mexicans bowed slightly and walked toward the stagecoach, escorted by Blood and Mud. In less than a minute, they were thundering out the front entrance onto the Butterfield Trail.

Slapping his hands on his trousers, Jackson wandered over.

"What'd they want?" he asked.

"Not sure," Joe answered.

"Oh? They seemed interested enough in talking to you."

"They was," Joe agreed. "They asked me to lead them north to Frisco."

"Did you tell them they could take the trail they came in on?"

"They don't want the trail," Joe replied. "They're searching for someone. Didn't say who or why, exactly."

Jackson looked toward the dust cloud, which was all that remained visible of the stage. "You turned them down?"

"Not yet," Joe answered.

He walked to the end of the stable, watched as Slash and Clarity walked around the yard, holding hands. They looked precious, together like that, their cart all decked and ready for a new life. While Joe had been talking to the Mexicans, the couple had added some ribbon and bows. That would last about a mile of bumping and wind, but the sentiment would last them far longer.

"They could use the gold the Mexicans offered," Joe said. "We all could."

"A man and his family can always use gold," Jackson said. "But we need you more."

Joe smiled. He loved his boys.

"I guess I'm suggesting that the reason for earning it has to make sense," Jackson said.

"Yeah," Joe agreed. "Thing is, I never had much gold or sense."

"That ain't true," Jackson said and put his hand on his father's shoulder. "You know you've got my backing whatever you want. We can talk about it if you like. But what you need right now is some cherry wedding pie."

Joe nodded, smiled contentedly, and followed his son to the back door of the station.

The sun was using the windless backyard as an anvil and the flies were losing interest in the stable and its patties. They were hovering in a flock about the well, and would have migrated to the outside table—if the O'Malleys had used it. The melting heat made that impossible.

Except for the buzzing as flies went by and the occasional whinny of an unhappy horse or chicken in the stable, the spread was quiet. Blood and Mud had been trained to stay outside or in the stable so as not to bother the stage passengers. Most of the time they obeyed. Having cleaned all the washed-off scraps from around the well, the dogs had retired in lazy strides, their tales drooping, to the stable where there was at least shade.

For Joe, as he entered the station, it was nice to have a moment of quiet. The kind he remembered from his prairie days. No people, no coach, no sound but whatever he made. Things had been unusually restless the past few weeks. A fortnight ago, the O'Malleys had never heard of Clarity Michaels or her brother Merritt. Now, Charity was family. The preacher was just settling down inside to share the nuptial celebration. Clarity and Slash having finished their walk—or maybe wanting to make an impression— were the last ones in, beaming nearly as bright as the sun and walking hand-in-hand.

"You didn't carry her across the threshold," Jackson said.

"Ain't officially our house," Slash replied. "We decided to wait on that."

"I like it," Sarah said.

"Too much to remember," Joe said. "Do it, get it done."

"Is that what you did, grandpa?" Gert asked. "Carry your wife across the campfire?"

Joe scowled. "That's impertinent. We had bedrolls—nothing else. I guess we stepped over them at some point. I don't rightly recall. I had other things on my mind."

The others laughed, except for Merritt who was vaguely embarrassed by the discussion of intimacies.

As Joe washed his hands in the kitchen basin, he fell into a contented silence. Even with the usual bickering banter—maybe even because it was so distinctly O'Malley—Joe was warmed to see everyone gathering around the big table. Talk of his own wedding day made him realize how, very soon—too soon—Slash would be where he is, fussing over something his own grandkids said, like some new cut of clothing or hairstyle, or maybe going to school with Injuns. Those would come, as surely as the seasons, because the world didn't sit still and Americans least of all. He regretted that he would not be here to see how Slash handled it.

He'll probably sit in a corner, whittling, telling them, "You don't know how it was . . ." Joe thought.

Joe also regretted that his Dolley was not present, in the flesh, and hoped she was somehow witness to all of this. Joe's religious beliefs grew a little at times like these, birthdays and anniversaries and births and such. It seemed to him that life had no purpose if the kindest and most loving people just vanished. He remembered—made a *point* to remember—looking at the body he had loved and cherished and knowing that his dear one was not present in that poor husk . . . but also knowing that she was not gone.

He felt that strongly then, and he felt no less today.

Joe took his place at the head of the table. Sarah sat at the opposite end, nearest the kitchen. Joe watched the bride and groom as they laughed about their short courtship, the attempted kidnapping of the Serrano shaman that had brought them together, and the fact that between them they had a complete mastery of weaponry pretty well in hand.

"Gun, knife, tomahawk," Slash said, pointing from Clarity to himself to Gert. Then he held his entire hand toward his grandfather. "All of the above."

"I thank you," Joe said, "though I only got a little of what you all got a lot of." He regarded his son. "Jackson—is bear traps a weapon?"

Clarity said, "For a bear, yes." She regarded her new father-in-law. "Was that a speciality?"

"Once it was," Jackson remarked. "I could set them quiet with a bear not ten feet from me."

"You want a new rug or mountain coat, you better be quiet," Joe quipped.

"I remember pa wouldn't take me out when he set them," Slash said. "Just in case the bear was smarter'n he thought!"

"That's why I'm glad we've got Clarity in the family now," Jackson said. "No need to get too close."

"Yeah, but ya gotta be careful where you hit," Joe said. "Lest you want wind whistling through the backside of your cold weather fur."

Slash laughed as he rose and raised a glass of wine to toast his bride. "To the woman who will provide me with winter wear!"

"And my husband can dress a b'ar faster than any man

since David Crockett!" she returned the toast from the seat beside him.

There was real love and respect in both those statements, Joe thought. The youngsters were lucky.

Everyone drank—even Reverend Michaels, just a little. And when Gert and Sarah brought over the wild turkey Slash had caught, Joe took knife in hand to carve. It was a regular holiday-style feast on the happiest day in memory.

Slash began to cut the bird. Sarah asked people to pass their plates and dished out potatoes, which she grew in her garden. The Mexicans hadn't noticed the vegetables were missing from today's plate. Gert passed around warm corn on the cob and then the crock full of freshly churned butter.

"Forgot the gravy," Sarah said, then went and got it from a hook in the fireplace.

"Mother Sarah, you are going to have to teach me everything you know," Clarity said as she accepted the bread plate from Gert, pausing to smell the loaf before it was no longer full. "I can bake, but not like this, and Slash can't hunt every day."

"There's always time to hunt," the young man disagreed.

"Oh?" Joe chuckled. "How long did it take you to catch this particular bird?"

"That's not fair, gran'pa. He was smart," Slash replied. "I spent a lot of time out by Civil Gulch figuring him out. Problem was, he was figuring me out at the same time!"

"You showed him who was smarter." Sarah smiled as she returned and sat.

Now that everyone had filled their plates, knives and forks scraped and stabbed, talk was boisterous, and laughs were easy and plentiful.

Only Clarity was silent. Joe noticed.

"Everything okay, granddaughter?" he asked her.

She looked over. The reality of living in the unsettled West was not something she had considered deeply—until now. She turned to her husband.

"Do you only hunt out there?" she asked. "By Civil Gulch?"

"Out there and toward Vallicita," he said. "Animals tend to shy from where people are. Gotta roam a bit to get the rabbits and quail."

"What's wrong?" Joe asked her.

"I didn't think—well, that's nearly a full day just to get supper," she answered. "I've been so busy these last two weeks, everything so new, I hadn't really considered it."

"It will be all right," Gert assured her. "You'll have chickens for eggs, a cow for milk, and a deer will last you over a week. Those woods are only a two-hour ride there and back, to the west. You should come with me to the Serrano camp. The women have a way of smoking bear meat to make it last an entire winter."

"Pa, time for you to get the old traps from the loft, the ones that ain't rusted!" Slash said.

"They're in pretty good repair," Jackson said, then added pensively, "Bear! Now there's a taste I haven't had since—"

He stopped. Slash also froze, then snapped his head toward the open window that overlooked the trough.

When Slash smelled the fire, his first thought was not what was burning but why the dogs weren't barking.

Joe had smelled it too. The back door was open and he could see the first wisps of smoke dancing past, away from the stable and toward the well.

"Water!" he cried as he jumped up, knocking the chair

back. Joe grabbed a blanket from the rocking chair and Jackson took off his good jacket, not yet having replaced his wedding suit with his travel clothes. Both men ran quickly to get outside and see where the fire was.

Joe burst into the bright sun, shielding his eyes and looking around. His chest tightened when he saw that the wagon with the newlyweds' belongings was ablaze. Slash went to rush by but Joe stopped him with a rigid arm. He took a moment to scan the grounds before rushing over. It was an old Indian trick to start a fire to lure settlers into the open. He didn't see anyone, and he was on good terms with the Apaches—the only hostiles in the region.

Ambush or not, he couldn't risk sparks flying to the station or the stable. The canopy was still standing and a spark had already caught the fabric. He watched it go up in a flash leaving just the four poles.

Joe ran forward, using the blanket to swat the tatters of the canopy into the ground before they could drift away. Slash hurried to the well, and Jackson limped to the well, followed by Sarah, and Gert. Merritt tried to restrain Clarity, concerned for her safety. It took her a moment to wrest herself free.

"Slash! Be careful!" she cried.

He glanced back and waved, saw Clarity go inside with familiar purpose.

On her way out, Gert had grabbed the wooden bucket they used in the kitchen. It was half-full, and she hurried to her grandfather. Joe took the bucket and hurled the contents at the rig. Black smoke sizzled and plumed in all directions. Joe passed the bucket back to his grand-daughter, who hurried to the well and hooked it to the rope. She passed Slash, who was rushing over with a full bucket. His expression was somewhere between confusion and rage, falling more and more on the side of the latter.

Joe took off his Sunday jacket and began swatting the fire, averting his face to keep from breathing the thickest smoke. Strangely, from what he'd glimpsed, the fire was burning from the bottom up, licking the rails and burning through the flat boards below. The wagon, and not the baggage itself, had caught fire.

Slash arrived and doused the entire rig. The inferno hissed louder and a grayish-white smoke rose from the burning wood, leather, and fabric.

Joe used the blanket to wave the smoke away. Another bucketful, and the fire was mostly out. As the clouds dissipated, he saw badly charred possessions and a wagon with a blackened underside.

Slash stood panting beside his grandfather on the station-side of the wagon.

"Blood! Mud!" the young man cried. The dogs did not respond.

Both men were perplexed and, except for Jackson, Joe ordered the others to stay back. The three men were shoulder-to-shoulder, a wall of quiet fury. Slash broke from the others and began walking about.

"This was set," Joe said angrily.

"By who—why?" Jackson asked.

"Maybe the Mexicans had enemies closer'n they thought," Joe replied.

"Look," Slash said. He was on the other side of the wagon, looking down.

The other two came over and glanced at the dirt. There were footprints in the dry ground, larger than those left by

Slash and Clarity. They came from the direction of the stable.

Slash threw his jacket down and ran ahead, ignoring his grandfather's calls to wait.

"It's all right," Slash assured Joe as he ran around the wagon. "Clarity's getting the guns. Someone's gonna pay."

"There's no need for weapons!" a voice cracked from the dark entrance of the stable. "And no, I'm not here for the Mexicans."

Slash stopped to peer into the darkness. "Who are you and what the hell did you do *this* for?" he demanded, gesturing angrily at the wagon.

The stranger replied, "I wanted to be sure nobody left."

Chapter 5

The speaker stepped from the dark stable. The sun struck him hard from directly above though he didn't seem to notice. He was dressed almost entirely in black, from his cravat to his boots. His face was long, his cheeks scruffy, and his eyes were hidden under the shadow of the only garment that wasn't black. The slouch hat was white, the brim pulled low.

The stranger carried a shotgun pointed down, and he wore a pair of Colts. They sat a little forward on his hips, suggesting to Joe a cross-handed draw.

Despite the stranger's admonition, Joe accepted the carbine Clarity brought over. She kept one for herself. Joe and Clarity both stepped apart from the others. When Joe stopped, Clarity continued walking. If the stranger was packing scattershot, she wanted someone to be out of range. She did not put the gun on her shoulder but did not point it toward the earth, either. It was held hip-high, aimed forward. She cleared the dripping ruin of the wagon. Wearing Sarah's wedding dress and a look of dark and hostile displeasure, she was the vision of an avenging angel.

The man in the stable didn't move.

Joe jabbed a thumb toward the wagon. "I figger this is your work," he shouted.

"That's correct."

The man's accent was Southern. But to Joe's keen eye he did not have the lost and beaten look of so many of the former Rebels who had come out here. If he had been to war, he might have been an officer—a high-ranking one, judging from his overall health and bearing. Since there was no pension to be had from the fallen Confederacy, those boys became lawmen or something akin to that.

"Who are you, dammit!" Slash cried out.

"Quiet, boy," Joe cautioned in a strong whisper.

"Grandpa—"

"I said *quiet*!"

Slash fell still and silent, but Joe could feel the anger raging a few steps away. Not that he blamed him. Except for the clothes they were wearing, the boy and his wife had just lost everything they possessed. But rage wasn't going to help whatever was going on here.

"What'd you do to my dogs?" Joe demanded.

"They are resting," the newcomer said.

"Doesn't answer my question."

"They ate raw beef with the god mushroom of the Mazatec of Huautla de Jiménez," he answered. "They will awake in just a few minutes."

"All right," Joe said. "Now tell me why."

"I needed to be free to do what I came for."

"And that is?"

"The woman to your left murdered a citizen of Murray, Kentucky, name of Bill Roche," the man said. "She will be returning with me to face a judge."

Slash erupted like a twister. "Like hell!" he shouted and started forward.

Clarity had not given him a gun. He moved to grab Joe's. His grandfather wrenched the rifle to one side and cautioned Slash with a look. The stranger cautioned him with words.

"I wouldn't start anything, Slash," the man said. He raised the gun slightly. "I *will* shoot you."

"Slash, stay where you are!" his mother screamed.

Once again, Slash stayed where he was.

The hot air was already still but now it was uncommonly quiet. Sarah, Gert, and the reverend remained where they were, gathered behind Jackson. He was the only one of the three men who had not moved.

Joe still didn't raise the gun. He began walking forward to keep a barrier between the man, Clarity, and Slash.

"You a lawman?" Joe demanded.

"I am Detective Leonard Tatham, North-Western Police Agency," the man replied. "I have the badge in my saddlebag, back a way down the road."

"Why ain't you wearing it?" Joe asked. "Law says you're s'posed to."

"Sun's moved a little behind you," the man answered. "You might've seen the reflection."

"And stopped you from burning the worldly goods of the newlyweds?" Joe asked.

"I truly regret that such was necessary," the detective said. "Couldn't afford to have a renegade riding off—"

"You will *watch* what you call my *wife*!" Slash yelled.

"It's all right, Slash," Clarity spoke calmingly. "It's just wind."

The detective continued to look at Joe. "I did not think

that you, sir, would be entirely unreasonable," he said. "I didn't know about the others."

"First *sensible* thing you've said!" Slash shouted.

"How did you know I'd be reasonable?" Joe asked.

"Mr. O'Malley, I'm afraid I don't have time to discuss my methods."

"You're gonna make time," Joe said. The frontiersman was still walking forward. "You police ain't official marshals, I hear. You're guards, mostly. Gold shipments and such."

"That is true," the man said. "But I was hired by the sheriff of Calloway County, through my office, to come and get Miss Clarity Michaels."

"O'Malley," the woman reprimanded the speaker. "I am Mrs. Clarity O'Malley."

Tatham tipped his hat. "Congratulations, ma'am."

Joe stopped halfway between the family and the man in the stable door. "Detective, what happens if we choose not to turn the lady over to you?"

"I will leave and then return with the U.S. Cavalry."

"I see. That's where you heard about me," Joe said. "You seem pretty sure they'll come."

"Very," the detective informed him. "You folks got away clean with the killing you did a few weeks back. I stopped at Camp—Fort Yuma," he corrected himself, the old name having only recently been changed. "General Guilford gave me the rundown, said you all claimed to have acted in self-defense. I get the feeling he didn't want an investigation of the matter, but that's between him and you and the federal marshal. I explained my situation to the commander, showed him the documentation, and he assured me of his support if such is required. Should I fail to return, with the prisoner, he will send a party after me."

A sense of finality and hopelessness seemed to settle on the group in quick succession. Slash sidled over to his wife and put his arm around her. She seemed utterly unaware of his presence. Her look was rigid with hate, not just at the man who had come for her but those back in Kentucky who had sent him.

Clarity's brother stepped forward. "Detective, I don't understand why this matter cannot be handled here, in California. I understand there is a judicial seat—in Needles, I think."

"That's true," Tatham said. "But the family of the deceased has insisted that she be tried in Kentucky," the man replied. "My orders are to bring her there, if possible."

"And if not?" Merritt asked.

"Then the matter is remanded for disposition to the local military commander, who is General Guilford," Tatham said. He regarded Joe. "I should think you would prefer Kentucky."

"What I would prefer is that you return to the horse you say you have and leave," Joe said. "Since I'm not counting on that, I want to see this paper you say you have. I give you my word that no one will leave here while you are gone."

The detective considered the request. "I accept your assurance and I will be right back with my documentation."

"And your badge," Joe said.

Tatham nodded.

"Y'know," Joe added before the detective left, "you coulda just knocked on the door instead of setting a fire.

Despite what you may think, we try to be civilized out here."

"I had a different story from the general," the detective responded. "He heard that you fired on the last party that came calling for a prisoner."

"They came to kidnap a passenger, not a prisoner," Joe informed him.

"He was an Indian, and they were lawful Indian agents, I'm told."

No one in the group had an answer to that. On the surface, it was true. The detective had apparently not been informed that the agents were also allied with rebels to start a western war.

"Mr. O'Malley," Tatham went on, "you and your family will be reimbursed for the loss of the wagon and for what was on it. I will see that funds are sent on the earliest possible stage. I am not a savage and I hope there will be no reason for me to become one."

"You were gonna show me some things?" Joe said.

The man vanished into the stable, leaving behind a threat that hung like a circling hawk. Joe turned to his grandson and the new bride. He never again wanted to see a look like the one he saw on the face of his grandson. There was murder in the boy's eyes, the kind he had never seen in a man.

Still holding the rifle, Clarity turned and hugged him. "I'm so sorry for this," she said into his neck.

"We'll leave," Slash said. "Now."

"Slash, I don't believe that is the best course of action," Joe said.

"What do you mean? Grandpa, you can't be thinking of letting Clarity go!"

"I don't see as we have the luxury of choosing."

Slash stared wide-eyed. "You can't *mean* that!"

"Boy, nothing that man said was improper," Joe replied. "Even burning the wagon, heartless as it was. I seen the Texas State Police do something similar to rustlers once. Let's see his paper and—Reverend Michaels, you're used to picking your way through scripture. Maybe there's something in the document that we can use to prevent this."

"Yes, of course," the pastor said, trying to throw off his own air of despair.

"To what end?" Clarity asked Joe.

"I won't hear of it, any of it!" Slash said.

He tugged on Clarity's hand. She took a few steps before stopping.

"Slash—we can't."

"What are you saying? We'll lose ourselves somewhere we cannot be found. Mexico or the northwest up Canada-way."

"You will *not*," Joe said very firmly. "I have given my word that you will stay here, and there is the rest of the family to consider. What happens if we abet a fugitive? Pardon me for use of such a rough word, but that is what the wanted posters for *both* of you will say. While you're running, we will lose the Butterfield contract, possibly our freedom. *All* of us!"

"But this is *wrong*!" Slash said. "This man—the charges!"

Clarity faced her new husband, put her free hand to his cheek. Her expression softened. She removed a necklace he had given her as a wedding present, one that had belonged to his grandmother Dolley. The bride put it around his neck.

"Keep this until I come back," she said.

"No—"

"You must," she said. "Right or wrong, it was always just hope to imagine this would never happen. What you suggest . . . that was the plan Merritt and I had for San Francisco. But you know—it was never a good plan. The Roches are a well-connected family. Something like this was bound to happen sooner or later."

"Clarity, we don't even know that this man is what he says!"

"We'll find that out soon enough," she said.

Merritt walked up to Joe. "Sir, your concerns are valid," the pastor said. "But here are mine. In a more just world, this would be a question of the law or writs. In this world, it's a matter of how much influence a family has to corrupt the law. My sister acted justly. I fear, however, that she cannot get a fair trial in Calloway or any other Kentucky county."

"That may be," Joe agreed. "And maybe—you said something about Needles. That may be a possibility. What we have to do right now, first, is to see if everything the man said is true. We also have to cooperate so's one of us can go with the detective and your sister."

"That will be me!" Slash said. "Who else?"

"Someone who might not be tempted to try and hit Tatham on the head with a rock," Joe said. "Your pa, maybe Merritt."

"You can't mean that," Slash said. "For better or worse—those were the words I said not an hour ago! My place is at her side!"

"You haven't asked me what I want," Clarity said. "Do you think I want to go through this seeing the pain in your face—pain I caused? How will I be able to look after myself if I have to worry that any word, any action someone takes may set you on fire?"

Slash stared at her open-mouthed, then turned away. He stomped the ground hard, then again, then spun and hugged his wife so tight she did not breathe for the duration.

Sarah began weeping and Gert looked only a little less angry than Clarity had been. Jackson, slope-shouldered, said nothing. He went to the wagon to see whether it or any of the belongings could be recovered.

While the newlyweds stood there, the other members of the family went back inside—save for Joe who went to see about the dogs. When Slash finally released his wife, she held his face with both hands and looked at him.

"I'm sorry to spoil the day," she said with a tearful smile.

"I married you," Slash said. "It's not spoiled. We are in this together." He shook his head. "But honey, my gut tells me that what grandpa wants to do is wrong. I don't believe this tin star who burned our wagon, and I also don't trust General Guilford."

"What do you mean?"

"He wanted to hurt us over that last affair, but couldn't," Slash said. "He will find a way this time. He'll get at us through you."

"Which is all the more reason I have to cooperate," she said. "And flight—what kind of a life is that? Even if your family were not hounded by the law, when would you see your family? When would they see their grandchildren?"

"When will *any* of that happen if we go back to Kentucky?" Slash asked. "Going, without a fight, to where that family has power—that's just foolish."

Clarity shook her head, her defiance giving way to

tears. "I have to go. I have to be rid of this, and there is no time for flight. That detective will be back soon—"

"To hell with him," Slash said, renewing his defiance. "He's not taking you. I will cut him down."

"You will not," Clarity said. "I took the same oath as you did, to cherish and protect you. If you hurt him, the cavalry will come for us *both*. I won't allow that!"

"I still don't see what business this is of the cavalry, other than Guilford having made it so," Slash said. "And based on what? A piece of that calls you—"

Slash stopped speaking and stared at his wife.

"What is it?" Clarity asked.

"—a fugitive," he said.

"I—I don't understand," Clarity said.

The young man was looking at her with a hint of hope in his eyes. "Papers can be counterfeited, Clarity. Would you know what a proper document or a proper badge looks like? I wouldn't."

"An imposter?" she said with surprise. "Why?"

"Not an imposter, exactly. That's not what I'm thinking. But remember what grandpa said? He said 'fugitive,' which is what the law would call you. That Tatham—he said 'renegade.'"

"I still don't understand."

"That's what bounty hunters call their quarry," Slash said excitedly. "Don't you see? Maybe the Calloway County marshal has already looked into this, settled the matter in your favor. Maybe the family's not happy with that. Maybe—"

"They hired a bounty hunter who has a kit full of fabrications."

"Lies, I call 'em."

Clarity nodded. "It's possible. The Roches have more money than scruples."

Slash started back to the stable at a run. "Go inside," he called back to her. "I want to see this detective fella when he comes back."

"Slash, please—*please* don't do anything we'll all regret!"

Either the young man did not hear or, she thought, more likely he was going to do what he had to do regardless of the consequences.

"I cannot blame you for that," she said softly. "That is, after all, the Slash O'Malley I love."

The dogs were lying on their sides just inside the shade of the stable. Joe took a water skin from a peg and used it to dampen the faces of the two collies. They were breathing steady but not moving. He hoped the water would help rouse them.

Joe heard his grandson's hasty footfalls on the dry hay.

"Grandpa!" Slash said excitedly. "I think I got something—"

"I know," Joe said calmly.

Slash stopped suddenly. "You know what?"

"That Tatham ain't the law, he's a bounty hunter," Joe answered. "That's why I came out here to think."

Slash beamed. "You figgered the same thing I did, from the words he used?"

Joe stood, gave the dogs some room. He set the water back on its hook. "Before that," Joe said. "This fella came prepared with something to still the dogs. That's part of the bounty hunter trade. That didn't mean he wasn't hired by the police—'cept lawmen carry warrants *with* them.

Hunters leave them safe in their bags until they have to show 'em at some government outpost, local or federal. Otherwise, they're just killers. An' then there's no reward. Plus, that business with the badge. He knew where the sun'd be when he came for us. He had to have been watching. He had this planned. I never known a lawman who did more than ride in and make his claim."

Slash was speechless first, then overjoyed.

"Then Clarity doesn't have to go with him!"

"Just the opposite, boy," Joe said. "This man positioned himself for resistance. He had the stable, we had nothing but open air. Fact is, if there's a warrant for your wife then there's something we have to find out."

"What's that?"

Joe said gravely, "Whether it's fer dead or alive."

Slash stopped breathing for a moment. That thought hadn't occurred to him. But people of influence like Clarity described could have pushed any abomination through.

"Dead," Slash said suddenly.

"Son?"

The young man's good mood sobered at once. He stared at the ground, barely noticing when Blood and Mud started to come awake.

"Thank you," Slash said suddenly.

"For what?"

"Thinking, when I didn't," he said. "Looking back— the man was trying to provoke us . . . me. He *would* have shot my Clarity. You putting yourself between us, staying calm . . . you saved her."

Joe noticed the dogs begin to stir. He went to them,

stroked them with both hands as he squatted between them.

"If killing her is his game, we are far from out of the woods," Joe said. "But you know that I don't like to see things get whipped up as a rule."

"Yeah, and if you weren't there, that's exactly what would've happened."

Joe patted Blood, then Mud, on the head, then stood.

"What's past is past," Joe said. "We have to consider what's next."

He looked out the back end of the stable. He heard, then saw, Tatham's horse coming along a narrow dirt path that roughly followed the turn of the Butterfield Trail.

"I heard everything you said before and now," Slash said, "but if he's not the law, then why don't we just jump him and figure this out after?"

"'Cause he may have been telling the truth about General Guilford," Joe reminded him. "I don't trust that hornswoggler, boy, not as far as Blood can spit. That's why it's vital that we be careful and that Clarity not go alone."

Watching Tatham's slow approach, Joe thought, *There was another sign that the man is a bounty hunter.*

The man came in cautiously, like someone who was accustomed to watching out for ambushes. His face was in shadow under his hat, but Joe was willing to bet the station that his ears were attuned to both sides while he watched the two men and dogs silhouetted against the western side of the stable.

He's looking to see if the dogs go to anyone other than us, Joe realized. *He dropped them in this spot because they're a weather vane to who is here. And he's trying to stay protected by the stable in case someone's back at the house with a rifle. Especially the gal he's come to take away.*

Again, it was a careful plan by an experienced man.

Tatham dismounted on the far side, in the sunlight. He left his horse outside, tied to an old pine. That, too, was no surprise. Nor was the fact that he stayed with it.

For a quick escape along a route he knows, Joe thought.

The man went to his saddlebag and removed a folded document. Tatham made no move to come inside, so Joe went out to meet him.

"I'll stay here," Slash said. "I shouldn't put myself in strangling distance."

"I won't try to change your mind," Joe said.

The frontiersman walked over, followed by the dogs. It started to burn him, too, that such a happy day took a turn like this, but he did not dare to let himself get bitter.

"You afraid of getting bushwhacked inside?" Joe asked.

"Should I be?"

"You left some upset O'Malleys back there," Joe admitted, simultaneously warning himself to watch his mouth.

Tatham let the comment slide. He had fished a badge from the pouch and handed it and the paperwork to Joe. The dogs busied themselves with the horse while Joe examined the objects.

The older man unfolded the paper first. His eyebrows rose a little.

"This paper is not from Kentucky, it's from Fort Yuma," Joe said. "It's an arrest order."

"They are the local authorities," Tatham said. "I wanted everything to be right legal."

"Maybe you did, but that ain't what you told us. You

never used the big word that's printed right here on top. Arrest."

"What's the difference?" Tatham asked. "One way or another, she goes with me."

"Where's the warrant you said you had?" Joe asked.

"I said I had documentation," Tatham said. "The warrant itself is with the general."

Joe didn't like that answer. It meant, he was sure, that Clarity could be jailed anywhere Tatham—or Guilford—saw fit. He examined the badge. He wasn't impressed by that either. It was a silver-finished shield with a heavy pin for piercing leather. It was engraved with a six-pointed star between the words North-Western cut in a rainbow arc on top and Police Agency straight across on the bottom.

The badge proved nothing, other than that Tatham had one. He could have bought it from a retired officer or snatched it from a dead one. But none of this changed the risk of openly defying this man or the United States Cavalry. Not at this point.

Joe turned to the stable. "Slash, go an' get Clarity and your pa and Gert."

Slash was looking at Tatham, his fingers open at his side. Despite everything they'd talked about, if he had his knife Joe knew he'd use it.

"*Do* it, boy!' Joe shouted. "Tell them what we talked about and tell them no guns."

With a frustrated growl, the young man spun and ran back to the house.

Tatham turned a searching expression from the stable to the man standing before him. "What's this about?" he asked. "Everything's proper."

"To be honest, Mr. Tatham, 'proper' ain't good enough

for me to let a member of my family ride unescorted with a man I just met to a destination a half-a-day's ride from here."

"You have no reason to be concerned," Tatham said.

"Yet, that's *exactly* what I am," Joe said. "You can either accept a chaperone riding with you or behind you. Choice is yours."

"All right," Tatham said. "Who?"

"As the lady's new pa, my son Jackson seems the best to chaperone her."

"Not you?" Tatham asked. "Not the woman's devoted husband?"

Joe couldn't tell if he was being serious or trying to provoke a fight or both. "Jackson is the most rational and patient of us, and I want him to hear from the general that things are as you say they are."

"I cannot promise him an audience," Tatham said.

"I'm betting you can," Joe said. "As for me, I've got business and Slash—he should not be anywhere he can cut your throat."

"I invite him to try," Tatham said coolly.

"Something I learned on the plains," Joe said, "is when you think too little of crossing someone's territory, that's when the Injun gets you."

"I appreciate your concern for my well-being," Tatham said. "I won't draw to prove you wrong. Someone from the house might use it as a reason to shoot me."

"Oh, they don't need a reason," Joe said. "It's only because of me that you're alive—Guilford and his cavalry be damned."

Tatham grinned. "The offer I made about Slash—it's open to anyone."

The frontiersman had enough of this man and his shiny-gold vanity. He wished right now that he had some of Jackson's good sense. He was losing his. He changed the subject by gesturing vaguely to the east. "You didn't come through Apache territory on the way here."

"I went wide around on the general's advice," the man said.

"Well, Gert is going to stay here with her ma but you can go more direct with some names she'll give ya," he said. "She knows those folks there and will get you through."

Joe did not mention that several of them knew Clarity too. He was curious to see what would happen when a stranger rode in with her as his prisoner.

"How do I know Gert won't tell them to kill me?" Tatham asked.

"For one thing, my new daughter'll be with you. For another, if you don't return, I'll have the cavalry on me like wolves at a deer—didn't you say?"

"Mr. O'Malley, you're testing my good nature, as the general said you would."

"What else did the general say?" Joe asked.

Tatham said nothing more. Not verbally. But the look he was wearing—secretive, like a dark cave—said otherwise. His strong jaw was set with displeasure, though Joe wasn't sure whether it was for him or for the fact that he would not be traveling alone with his bounty. The only reason Tatham didn't object, Joe suspected, was because he had made a point of telling Slash to leave the guns behind.

Joe handed back the paper and the badge. "How do you intend to get Clarity east?"

"Same way I came west," Tatham said. "Boat and rail-road."

"That horse, then," Joe nodded ahead. "Cavalry?"

"Yes."

"Bought or loaned?"

"Loaned. Why you asking?"

"I got a curious nature," Joe said. "You can't know what's under a rock till you lift it."

The men fell to a very intentional quiet, then, each wary of the other. The more Joe learned, the more this whole thing stank like a buzzard's beak. The United States Cavalry did not just lend its horses as a courtesy. Joe knew that because B.W. had to go with a three-horse team a year back when one of his lead animals died not far from Fort Mason, up north. The whip driver was irate that the general there, Lars August, cited regulations that would not permit the loan of an animal. B.W. had to go at half-speed until he could get a horse from the Butterfield corral in San Francisco.

Joe was certain, now, that this was as much Guilford's plotting as it was Tatham's. The hunting of Clarity may be rooted in Murray, Kentucky, but it flowered at Fort Yuma. The plainsman still felt his measured approach was the right one, though. He had spent enough time in the high mountains to know you didn't go rushing across a frozen lake unless you were keen on a cold bath.

Sweat was beginning to dampen their clothes. Joe moved into the stable with the dogs and stood facing the house.

"What's keeping them?" Tatham demanded.

"Slash would've explained the situation," Joe said. "They're probably packing a few things, I suspect. Going through Gert's things, Sarah's things, to see what Clarity might borrow." Joe regarded the other man's horse. "You're traveling light. You leave your bags at the fort?"

Tatham said nothing.

"It's kind of the general to let you do that," Joe went on. "I was at a station managers meeting in Los Angeles. My employer, John Butterfield, printed this big book of do-not-dos, had one given to each of us. One of the do-nots was asking to use army property for civilian storage. Y'know, like extra bags. We could leave a mail overload, it being federal property and all. But not luggage."

Tatham still said nothing. He shifted his weight impatiently, clearly tired of the sun and of his companion.

A few minutes later the entire family emerged from the station. Jackson was moving very purposefully despite his limp. A canvas bag was slung over his shoulder. It contained all the money Sarah kept in her sewing kit, as well as the money Merritt and Clarity had brought west. Gert was to his right and Clarity was to the left of her husband. Merritt trailed behind. Joe was surprised to see Jackson and Slash talking animatedly. Joe wondered if one of the men had thought of something he had not.

He hoped so.

When they arrived, Joe told the others that Gert would remain with Sarah after providing the names of Apaches to Tatham.

"They're going through the settlement," Joe said. "It'll save a day's wear on the party."

Gert regarded Tatham. "When you arrive, whoever meets you, tell them you ride under the protection of Wind Rider. I am known there."

"Are you?" Tatham said.

"Not everyone announces themselves with fire," she said.

Reverend Michaels came over to Joe. He did not try to conceal what he had to say from Tatham.

"I am going with my sister," he announced.

"I agreed to one person riding with us," Tatham said.

Merritt looked at the speaker. "I will follow you if need be, but I will not leave my sister without blood kin or religious comfort."

Tatham did not debate further. His expression lost some of its stern resolve. The same idea had apparently occurred to him at the same time as Joe. The frontiersman's strong fingers gripped Merritt by the arm and led him aside.

"I think you should go," he agreed. "But you have to be careful—this varmint may try to bring you in as an accomplice."

"I welcome the chance to travel with my sister and defend her," Merritt said defiantly.

"Then I'd get your mule ready, pilgrim. You've got some riding to do."

The pastor smiled. "I have been doing little but since I got here."

Joe patted him warmly on the shoulder. The man left, and Joe turned to Jackson. The two O'Malleys did not need to speak. Joe knew that his son did not need a talking-with. He had been a brave but responsible bronco-buster, and he was an even braver more responsible man and father. They exchanged a hug.

Slash, meanwhile, had broken away from the others when they arrived. Joe noticed that he was wearing two of his knives. One stubbier blade for throwing, one longer knife for hunting and skinning. The boy had gone directly to one of the stalls.

"The boy's going somewhere?" Tatham asked Joe.

"I haven't a mortal foggy notion," Joe answered truthfully.

Tatham entered the stable, came closer to Slash.

"I warn you, son, not to interfere with my duties," the detective warned.

Slash finished saddling the animal. He settled his black hat on his head and stepped to just a few feet from the man he wanted to kill. Joe was behind Tatham now. The older O'Malley came a few steps closer.

"I got business that is none of yours," Slash replied.

"Be sure of that," the detective answered.

"I'm sure, and I'm sure of this too. You got what you came for. Get the hell out of my stable."

Tatham turned, purposely presenting his flat back to the boy. The shotgun was in its holster on the horse but his hands were both very near the handles of his sidearms.

The detective watched Joe watch his grandson. The older man's expression was guarded, then relaxed. Slash was not going to do anything rash.

But what are you doing, boy? Joe wondered. His riding out had not been part of the plan. Except for blowing off steam at Tatham, the boy was acting like every second mattered.

Like he was in a hurry to get somewhere and *do* something.

That was of no immediate concern to Tatham. He waited, smoking well away from the stable, while Clarity, Jackson, and Merritt readied their two horses and a mule for the ride east.

Tatham gave the three what time they needed. The group would ride until they reached their destination. It did not matter when they started.

Once they departed, all Tatham had to do was get Clarity O'Malley to the fort without her husband ambushing them. Tatham was confident the boy would not do that. Joe had given him an order that seemed to carry weight. Wherever Slash had gone, whatever he was doing, he would not disobey. If he did, if Slash watched them or tracked them, the boy would risk his father's displeasure, he would endanger his wife and his brother-in-law, and one thing more.

He would face the guns of one of the fastest, deadliest shots east of the Rockies.

Chapter 6

After an extended period of rocking, with howling winds pushing against the vessel from all sides, *The Dundee* settled somewhat. But not entirely.

Neither did its captain.

Lying in his bunk, Alan Swift slid in and out of sleep. The movement of the ship didn't jar him. He was used to that. He woke every time the tightly pinned bandage that was wrapped around his skull pulled at strands of hair. He knew it was afternoon from the way the light fell on the ceiling. And he was still dressed. The bunk felt different, less inviting than when he was wearing his long wool nightshirt. But he knew nothing else about his condition, other than each time he woke he tried to rise, only to have his arms wriggle like a loose galley stove pipe.

The last time he tried, after hearing the door creak open, he moaned aloud and saw lightning flashes inside his eyes.

"Don't try that again," said Russell Puckett, the ship's surgeon, as he came closer.

"Aye-aye, cap'n," Swift said.

"Oh, still got your sense of humor, eh?"

"Not really," the captain said.

Puckett held open the man's bloodshot eyes in turn, looked at them, took his pulse, examined the bandage, then stood.

"It's a concussion, but you'll survive," Puckett said. "*If* you stay in your bunk."

"Not going to move," the captain promised.

The short, swarthy physician, aged in his mid-fifties, was stopped and stood off to the side, near the chart cabinet.

A native of Portsmouth, England, Russell Puckett was an expert on tropical diseases. The skill had come to him before he was even a medical doctor. A young seaman shipwrecked on the shores of Sierra Leone, he ended up walking the coast, studying the ways of any villagers who would have him. He was fascinated by the primitive medicines. He collected samples and tested them to great success when he returned to Europe and enrolled at the College of Physicians in London. Puckett had only recently come to America, after his work with cadavers came under the unhappy scrutiny of the Pathological Society of London.

The eternally curious, adventuresome man did not mind being an expatriate. Especially here. The fresh, blue coast of California bestowed an invigorating quality he had found lacking in the gray winds of the Atlantic, along both the African seaboard and Europe.

The physician had sailed with Swift for nearly a year and, as the two oldest men aboard, they got along like brothers.

Swift was on his side, his face mostly buried in his pillow. He turned very slightly, his body straining to overcome his pained, screaming skull. The conflicting desires called a truce and he froze in mid-turn.

"You promised to stay still," Puckett said.

"I can't," the captain replied.

The captain cracked his wrinkled eyes. The room seemed to move. He groaned once again and shut them.

Puckett shook his head, his thick, ruddy cheeks swaying. He moved back to his patient's bedside.

"I'll help you move a bit, but don't try that on your own again and don't attempt to open your eyes."

"I must . . . talk," Swift said. "That's all."

"About what?"

"Danger," he said. "I fear . . . we are in peril."

"The winds? We've been through storms before," Puckett replied. "We'll get through this one."

"It is . . . not just the weather," Swift said.

"What is it, then?" Puckett asked.

Swift did not try to move again. The tension in his shoulders and arms left him entirely without energy, and he lay deflated on the bed. Breathing heavily, he turned his mouth up slightly.

"How long have I been here?" the captain asked.

"Not long," Puckett said. "A quarter-hour."

"It seems longer," Swift said. "The squall?"

"Still too early to tell what it'll be," Puckett informed him. "The first mate moved us closer to shore—we are getting backwash."

"Was that Francis Sullivan's order or our passenger?"

"Mr. Martinez? Why would he give an order?"

"The owners granted that power," Swift told him.

"Did they? Odd," the medic said. "Well, whoever is in charge, neither man seems terribly concerned. We are not taking on water. Mr. Martinez is below."

"Armed now, no doubt," Swift said into the pillow.

"I do not know," Puckett confessed.

The physician came forward. The cabin was alternately

in dark and light as the sun fought to assert itself through the gathering gray clouds, only to be swallowed again. Puckett steadied himself by leaning on the wood over the bunk.

"If you can tell me, briefly, what is this about?" Puckett asked.

"What . . . what do you think happened?" Swift asked.

"To you? As I said—"

"No," Swift interrupted. "No . . . I mean how. *How* it happened."

"You struck your head. On the pillar. Mr. Martinez was holding a cloth to stop the bleeding when I arrived."

"That isn't what happened. I did not . . . strike my head," Swift said. "Our passenger clubbed me."

"Captain, delirium often accompanies—"

"It is what *happened*," Swift cut him off again. He winced once more from the force of his own indignation.

"All right," Puckett said calmingly. "All right, let's say it happened. Why would he hit you?"

"Because I attempted to find out what is in that chest we carry," Swift said.

"The small one in the hold?" Puckett asked. "What do you think is there?"

Swift rolled his head very, very slowly and opened his eyelids a crack. He wanted to see the physician, to focus on staying alert. He saw the bleary figure of the doctor looking down. There was pain, but not so great that the captain could not keep his eyes open.

"Martinez . . . was afraid of chains."

"I don't follow you," Puckett said.

"They rub. They . . . spark," Swift said. "He wanted *rope* around the chest."

"For what reason?"

"Have you heard of a compound called nitroglycerin?"

"Blasting oil?" Puckett said. "The liquid that blew up when the Central Pacific was using it."

"Yes, that's it," Swift said.

"It was in the newspapers," Puckett said. "They were trying to put a tunnel through the Sierra Nevadas. It blew up before it got there." The physician suddenly looked alarmed. "Do you think that's what we're carrying?"

"I feared it from the start," Swift said. Urgency helped him to find strength, to find his voice. "There have been rumors . . . that the California Pacific owners would try to transport it again, not by land this time. You didn't see it carried aboard."

"No, but now that you bring it up—I heard the men talking," he said. "They were saying the boys handled the crate like it was a flower that must not lose a petal."

"Exactly so," Swift said. "It was set down carefully, the crate held in place while it was secured."

"Rope," Puckett said thoughtfully. "That would also give the crate some play. There would be minimal jarring. Is Martinez with the railroad?"

"I don't know . . . but it doesn't matter."

"True," Puckett agreed. He was contemplative. "So you fear that rough seas—"

"Will cause the compound, if that's what we carry, to detonate," Swift said. "Better to drop it overboard before then."

"But captain, weren't you afraid that by the very act of attempting to force open the crate—"

"Yes, of *course*," Swift said, ignoring the pain now. "But then I and *The Dundee* would be the only casualties. There would have been time, and relatively calm waters, for the crew to abandon ship."

"And now," Puckett said, "the ship is rocking . . . and the cargo with it."

"If we try to remove it, the crate may be dropped before it can reach the side. That is why I acted when I did."

Puckett was still thoughtful. "Yet Mr. Martinez seems unconcerned. You might be wrong about what he's brought aboard. It could *be* a potted plant with delicate flowers, for all you know. Remember the *Bounty* and its cargo of breadfruit."

"That would give me enormous joy, worth the blow on the head," Swift said as he gently lay his head back down. He closed his eyes again. "But let me ask you, Russell. Does Martinez look like a man with agrarian interests?"

The physician chuckled. "I can't say he does."

"It's a sinister face, and I cannot believe his mission is a good one."

"What did the Ritchies say?"

"Only to obey his orders—another cause for concern," Swift said. "When have you known them to cede authority to anyone?"

"If it is the railroad, they stand to land a great deal of business, transporting supplies and building material," Puckett said. He considered the situation a moment more. "Nonetheless, there is nothing you can do now. The mate seems at ease, as does the crew. It may be best to let this slide, especially if Martinez is armed, as you say."

"This ship . . . should be run by its captain."

"We are in agreement," Puckett said. "But that is not possible right now. And the captain himself has said that the crate is best left alone right now. Is that not so?"

Swift nodded slightly. After determining that the captain

needed neither water nor his chamber pot, Dr. Puckett departed.

The captain would let this be because neither he nor the weather was in any shape to pursue it just now. But one way or another, if the ship survived, the scoundrel they carried would answer for having struck him.

And Swift, as he lay there, knew just how to do that.

Assuming they survived.

Chapter 7

Slash breathed as hard as he rode. It was as if the panting horse and its rider were one chimeric creature.

Part of Slash's vigorous passage was the result of anger toward the detective—if he was one—for having shown up like some corrupt, impossible mirage. And on this day, above all.

But Slash was also angry and ashamed of himself for having given in to his grandfather. Not just given in: Slash barely put up a fight. The young man had disagreed with the old plainsman many times over the years. He respected Joe O'Malley's cool wisdom and a lifetime of adventure and challenge. Only a fool would disregard words that came from that kind of experience.

But those were mostly about small things, Slash reminded himself.

Where to dig the new well. Whether to break a horse when it was spirited in the morning or tired in the afternoon. How to cook a wild turkey on your wedding day—indoors in its own smoke and juices or spit-roast with fat sizzling back from the burning wood. Slash had wanted to build a fire pit but everyone in the family was lined up against him.

The two O'Malleys had never fought over how to stand up as a man. There was not, *could not* be, a disagreement about that. You defended your family. You defended your land. You defended your name. In that order, set in stone as surely as God's own Commandments.

They had not disagreed about that until today. If Grandpa Joe hadn't been there, Slash would have cut the stranger's hamstring and been gone with his bride, forever. They would have found some way to clear her that did not involve surrender.

You are letting this swaggering tormentor take her away! he chastised himself and Joe both.

What Joe should have been doing was distracting the self-proclaimed lawman so Slash could get close enough to cut him. Maybe General Guilford would have sent a party after Slash and Clarity, but there would have been no cause to accost anyone else.

The young man couldn't decide whether he was angrier at his grandfather or at himself.

You caved like a dry thatch roof, Slash bitterly chastised his own behavior. *You put grandpa's desires over what your new wife needed.*

As he rode, Slash began to think differently, now, of his own father disagreeing with Joe over the years. It was never loud, never more than firm language. But Slash had always wondered why his pa always gave in . . . even when he was in the right.

Because Joe commands respect, Slash knew. From B.W., from the Mission Indians, from random strangers like that cracked-head newspaperman with the big mouth who came by on the stage that first brought Clarity. Only the women ever talked back to him, sassed him, but even that was with love.

Stupid, Slash said, once again thinking of his own actions. *You were just upset and listened to a calmer voice.*

But it was also Joe's careful, outwardly unemotional reasoning that brought him to this place, to this new mission. One that did not require running away like rabbits. One that was risky, but still farmed within the plow lines that had been laid out.

That was the other reason for the young man's hard breathing, the urgency of this ride. He *had* to get to those he needed to see. He was tortured by the thought that he might miss them on the road, or they might take a different path.

He wished he could stop thinking about everything that could go wrong. He wished, for a moment, that his grandfather was every bit as wise as he seemed, that the old man somehow *knew* things would work out if they did what he'd said.

God, grandpa, I'm trusting my wife, my life, to your instincts, Slash thought. *Please let you be right and me be wrong.*

Slash cut through Civil Gulch, a relic of the War Between the States. It was here that a swapping of gunfire was about to begin between Union Rebel hunters and Confederate Yankee haters. As the men had assembled atop the facing cliff sides, and folks from all around gathered to watch, word was brought by a brave civilian rider holding a newspaper that the strife had ended three days before. General Lee had surrendered to General Grant.

Another piece of paper that changed lives, Slash thought.

According to the newspaper, President Lincoln had decreed that the men who were on the verge of slaughtering each other were loving brothers once more.

That rider who came running to stop the carnage was Dick Ocean, the stagecoach shotgun rider. A Colored man. He had been at the Vallicita Station when he read the newspaper they themselves had brought for owner Brent Diamond. It was that Southern refugee, who was connected to the Rebel population out here, who informed B.W. and Ocean about the impending battle.

Little did the driver, the O'Malleys, or any of the other locals know that Diamond would later use those Rebels to his advantage. He would recruit them in an effort to start a war of extermination out here, a policy not sanctioned by Washington, a wave of organized killing with powerful new Spencer repeating rifles. All of it was being run by General Guilford and General August up at Fort Mason up north.

Quietly, of course. No slips of paper there. No written orders. Just a doctor running messages and money being paid out from Cavalry funds.

When the O'Malleys helped to expose and defeat the scheme, Diamond fled. His two accomplices from the Bureau of Indian Affairs—the ones Clarity had fired at, as Tatham had said—went deaf and dumb. And the two senior officers were never implicated. The only visible scar of their criminal acts lay here in Civil Gulch. It was where one of the former Confederates used black powder in an effort to bury Joe O'Malley and Clarity Michaels. As Slash rode through the jumble of rocks that blocked the northern half of the pass, he suddenly—and with wrenching guilt— found himself both humbled and grateful to Grandpa Joe for his quick thinking. If Joe hadn't saved Clarity right here, Slash should never have met his bride.

Slash pushed the palomino onward, into the hot afternoon. There was a creek ahead and he would stop to water the horse there. Hopefully, his objective would not be far beyond that.

During the rest of his ride, Slash considered what his father had been telling him when they walked back toward the stable. That was when he suggested a plan—this different course of action.

"This might not just be about Clarity," Jackson had said. "You got your mind set on shadowing this Tatham and your wife, and I understand. But there's more than that to be done. We need eyes on the fort, in the fort."

"How?" Slash had asked.

That was when Jackson suggested enlisting the help of Malibu and Sisquoc. The Indians had a great deal to lose, helping men who were looking to undermine something the general may have planned. But Jackson believed they would put honor above fear.

"Their loyalty will be to men of good character," Slash's father had said. "It must be."

Slash believed the same, and he would soon find out. As it happened, the Mission Indians were at the same cool, shallow waters that were his own destination. They had heard his hurried approach, and Malibu had scaled one of several oaks that lined the shore. It was uncommon to find anyone riding hard and fast out here who was not being chased. Malibu descended quickly when he saw who was coming.

"What is the hurry?" the Indian asked, his face and voice reflecting concern.

Slash reined the horse to a stop. "I need your help," Slash told him breathlessly. "I need it very much."

The young man dismounted, and after leading the horse to the pebbled bank, he recounted the events that followed their departure. Neither Indian reacted until Slash had finished.

"I saw this man you tell about at the fort," Sisquoc said. "He walked to the general's quarters as if he were a general."

"Is that all you saw?" Slash asked.

"Yes. Thought no more of him until now."

"I am sorry to hear this news," Malibu said. "What can we do?"

"He is coming along after me, with Clarity and with my pa—maybe the reverend. They are supposed to stop at the fort. I think, my grandad thinks, that the general may be using this Tatham and his warrant to harm my family."

"That may be truth," Malibu said. "When we returned to the fort after the rescue of the Serrano medicine man, the general asked if we had seen O'Malleys shoot anyone. We told him we did not. He did not smile, hearing this."

"I'm afraid, very afraid, that he's smiling now," Slash said. "He'll want to hurt us for stopping his plan to kill Indians."

"You are asking us to stop him?" Sisquoc asked.

"No, I don't want nothing that will get you in trouble," Slash said. "I'm going to camp beyond the fort, by the river. If something happens while they are there, I need to know. That's all."

"It will only be what we see," Sisquoc said. "We do not go where officers go."

"I understand, but what you see is worth what ten men hear," Slash said.

"And with that information you will do what?" Malibu enquired.

"My friend, I have no idea," Slash admitted. "My interest— well, maybe Grandpa Joe was right about this too. My interest is whatever is next, not what may be in the future. And what's next is making sure they try to hurt my wife."

Slash pulled himself back in the saddle. Sisquoc looked the horse over.

"You have nothing to make camp," the Indian said. "We can bring you some things."

"I'll be okay," Slash assured him. "I don't know that anyone'll be staying put very long, and I'd rather not have to waste time setting something up or taking it down."

"You have no gun," Malibu observed.

Slash slapped the knives on his hips. "You know me, I got what I need."

"Tatham had what he needed too," Sisquoc noted. "I saw many guns."

"If it comes to that, they won't help him from behind, in the dark," Slash said. "Thank you, my friends."

"The Cavalry is our home, but the O'Malleys are our family," Malibu said, putting a fist to his heart and then holding the hand palm out, a Chumash sign of devotion.

Slash bowed his head at the men, then pushed his hat firmly on his head and turned to the east and Fort Yuma.

General Rhodes Guilford was writing letters for the Fort Yuma mail carrier to take east that afternoon. A lantern sat to his left, an ashtray to his right. Though it was daylight and the shutters were thrown open, his eyes were not what they once were. Every bit of illumination helped.

Guilford always wrote his letters after lunch, when his body was contented and his mind was relaxed. He was smoking a cigar, occasionally brushing ash from the 1st California Cavalry Battalion stationery. At least whoever received these letters would know they had not been forged. Everyone knew Guilford's strong cheroots. They came from his brother-in-law's tobacco farm in Connecticut, a concern that had trebled its size during the war. The cigars were a particular favorite of Ulysses S. Grant, and as the victorious general went, so went other smokers.

Guilford was just now writing a letter to Secretary of War Edwin Stanton notifying him of what had been the sudden, very quiet transfer of two agents of the Bureau of Indian Affairs from Fort Yuma to Fort Delaware.

"It is my hope," he wrote, "that being tried proximate to the seat of our government, the exposure and trial of these individuals Douglas Kennedy and Jessup Hathaway will serve as warning to others who might sow uprisings or even sedition for profit or power."

This letter would not be rewritten more legibly in sec-retarial hand, as was the general's usual custom. A person-ally drafted and written note carried more weight. He also wanted the contents to be private. He had written slowly, to make sure he got the sentiments exactly right. Those two cowards, inept and reckless, might seek to turn on the general, name him as a participant in the plot. Guilford wanted to be certain that he had powerful men like Stanton at his back should that occur.

Privately, of course, he blamed the two for their colossal failure and wished them a long stay in prison. Had an

Indian uprising been stirred, had the cavalry crushed it, Guilford would have seized the opportunity to create a glorious new nation, the Western States of America.

But Kennedy and Hathaway had failed. And they had been helped along in that debacle by the meddling of the O'Malley family—Joe and Slash O'Malley in particular. And that ridiculous newcomer, Clarity Michaels, the woman with a carbine.

Guilford reread the letter, huffed approvingly, signed it with a modest paraph under the name, then set his pen down and puffed on the cigar. Helped by ventilation from east and south-facing windows, the smoke filled the small, log-built room. The general's uniform jacket was draped over the back of his chair for easy access. He sat in his white shirtsleeves, though the breeze also kept the heat from being too oppressive. He listened to the sounds of commerce on the Colorado River, military supplies and commercial manufacturers mingling in a chugging, ringing, clattering symphony.

It was to have been the southern lifeline of his new nation. He resisted the desire to pound his desk. If he began, he might not stop.

The officer thought back to the O'Malleys. Guilford had been in battle, many times, boy and man. He had never hated an enemy. He only saw them as obstacles. The general felt that if he could sit at a bar with most of the men he fought, he would have more in common with them than with the bureaucrats in Washington. He did not even hate Indians. It was unfortunate that they were trying to survive on land coveted by the federal government. They were brave and capable but they, too, were obstacles.

He didn't even hate the two Indian agents. They were only men, and, unfortunately, they were the wrong men.

But hated the O'Malleys. They weren't warriors. They were wild, undisciplined *bobcats*.

A perfect plan spoiled by ignorant frontiersmen, he reflected bitterly. He could not even give them credit for ingenuity. They had stumbled onto the plan, and then they did what their kind were expert at: stayed with their prey till it was captured or dead. No planning, no thought, just animal sinew and endurance—and, by stupid luck, a woman sharpshooter.

A woman sharpshooter, he repeated in his head. *What a wretched band to have undone a proud new nation.*

Guilford was looking forward to their arrival. The bounty hunter could have his Clarity Michaels. He could take her back to Kentucky for trial and hanging or he could take her to Needles, if the judge was sitting, and hang her there. Guilford didn't care. The warrant said "Dead or Alive." He would even help to get her to Needles, just to pain the O'Malleys.

Most of all, though, the general wanted Joe and Slash O'Malley.

Guilford read his letter again, signed it, and blotted it dry. He tucked it in an envelope and wrote the name of Secretary Stanton. The general took a stick of wax and his seal from the desk and closed the envelope. His secretary and aide-de-camp, Lt. Bernard Anthony—whom he trusted with most of his secrets, but not this one—would address it.

The general crushed the stub of his cigar in the copper tray. He stared at the smoking ruin.

Done correctly, men are only a little less easy to break, he thought.

Before this current matter was finished, Guilford would have the old plainsman and his reckless grandson behind iron bars, the woman gone or dead, and he would consider some other way to achieve his goal.

Chapter 8

As soon as the Butterfield coach had arrived at the Vallicita station, Isaiah came out and took the team to the stables out back. Ordinarily, this would have been done at Whip Station where the facilities were larger and repairs could be made to the rigging. But the wedding interfered.

Isaiah was grateful that Jackson had taken the time to come out and show him how it was done. The former slave had a great deal of experience on rivers, very little with horses.

"A most interesting and enlightening journey," Rafael Gonzalez said to the whip as he stood in the shadow of the stagecoach. "Is it customary to tip the driver?"

"There's no rule says you can't," B.W. replied as, grunting, he hauled the first of their four bags from the rear boot.

"Then one for you and one for the shotgun rider," Gonzalez said.

The Mexican reached into his satchel and removed two ten-franc gold coins from a purse. When B.W. had finished unloading the bags, Gonzalez dropped each in turn into B.W.'s waiting, calloused palm.

B.W. took a moment to turning the gleaming specie over in his hand. "French, eh?"

"I have no use for those nationals or their currency," the Mexican stated with open disdain.

"Well, I got no such objections to their gold," B.W. said. "You are most generous and kind."

Gonzalez acknowledged the remark with a small bow as B.W. carried the bags toward the station.

It was usually Dick Ocean who retrieved the luggage. But he was still weak in the leg where he'd been shot. Instead, he went inside to collect the two passengers who would be traveling from here to St. Louis. They were an older couple, Theodore and Marie Graham, and they were heading east to see their grandson.

"This is very exciting," Theodore Graham told B.W. "We have been here since '49. It's our first time back home to Ohio."

"I'm guessing from the date you came for the gold?" B.W. asked, referring to Murphy's Diggings.

"We did, and we found it," the man said. "Blessed country. Blessed."

Gonzalez smiled. "It is a good thing to be grateful and content, my friend," he told the new passenger. "May you and your wife have a safe and happy journey."

Mr. Graham thanked him and, with his wife, they examined the conveyance that would carry them as far as St. Louis. It was the first big, proud Butterfield stagecoach they had ever seen and their excitement was evident.

Gonzalez joined Sebastián Sanchez inside. Bonita Sunday came in the back door to tell the passengers that the wagon they were expecting had just arrived. It was in the shade around back, where the horses could also be watered. Young Joshua Sunday was going about that chore.

Since none of the Mexicans was a stagecoach passenger, the driver of the wagon paid the boy for his help. He also gave Bonita coins for a meal and drink before continuing with Sanchez and Gonzalez and B.W. on their journey.

B.W. followed Gonzalez in with two of the Mexicans' bags, then went back and retrieved the other two. He set them down heavily, then walked over to the Mexican who was standing at the back door with Sanchez.

"Mind if I ask you about the situation to the south?" B.W. asked his recent passenger.

"In my country?" Gonzalez asked.

"Uh huh."

"Please do," Gonzalez said.

"I send my earnings home to family what needs it," B.W. told him. "Now, Dick reads newspapers, I don't, and I don't trust what he says they say. What're the chances that things will spill over here, us being so close to the border."

"None, I would say." Gonzalez shrugged. "There is enough trouble fighting each other without fighting the Americans as well."

"Did everyone have to take a side, like in our recent war?"

"We took sides, but it was not the same," Gonzalez answered. "It was for or against an invader. What I disliked, along with many of my countrymen—and along with your Mr. Lincoln and now Mr. Johnson—was the presence of the French and their puppet Emperor Maximilian. Sadly, his execution last month did not end the unrest. Now it's the Liberal Party and the Conservative Party."

"So now it's like our Civil War."

"There are similarities," Gonzalez admitted. "But you

were fighting to restore unity. In Mexico, we are fighting to prevent a dictatorship by the peasantry and their allies. We are fighting to prevent economic and social chaos. It is a fight which will remain, and which should remain, among Mexicans."

The explanation seemed to satisfy B.W. more than the newspaper articles. He walked away considering what was said, and comforted that it would not likely affect his route or his livelihood.

"He doesn't get to talk to people very often, does he?" Sanchez said as his companion walked over.

"I suspect not." Gonzalez smiled. "I wish I could have told him the truth."

But the Mexican had dared not say more. The hatching of the Conservative countermeasure, *Plan de la Noria,* was not known to the public—only to those, like himself, like their leader General Porfirio Diaz, who objected to the radical and unconstitutional reforms. He and his allies objected to mob rule that relied on the integrity of serfs and not the wisdom and experience of masters to govern Mexico.

And the nobility and their military partners had reason to believe that the struggle would very soon be coming to America. That was why they were here, to prevent that. But for word of it to get around could also imperil his mission.

The two Mexicans finished their drink and walked over to their driver Rodrigo Álvarez while he ate his meal

"Have you rested?" Gonzalez asked him.

"I let the horse drive himself a little," the man replied from under his drooping moustache. "I am all right."

"You've been out there two days," Sanchez said.

"Sitting is halfway to sleeping," he said. "When I have eaten, I will be fine." He grinned wryly. "I have been up longer defending ramparts."

"That was when your life depended on it," Sanchez pointed out.

"It is true, it focuses the attention," Álvarez acknowledged. "But this is important too."

Gonzalez lay an appreciative hand on his shoulder and went out to examine the wagon that was to take them west and then north. He wanted to make sure it was provisioned as it was supposed to be for the hard, long journey. A journey he very much hoped that Joe O'Malley would take with them.

B.W. had already carried the Mexicans' four bags out back and found room for them on the cart. Then he went to help Isaiah in the small, ramshackle stable. There were holes in the roof and birds of all kinds flitting in and out. Brent Diamond obviously had not intended to run this place for very long since he put no money into much-needed repairs.

"Not that it's my business," B.W. said to Isaiah, "but have you put in to Butterfield for a loan for repairs and improvements and such?"

Isaiah gave him a strange look. "Didn't know I could."

"Most definitely. There's money available to all station owners," the whip said. "What Butterfield does then is hold back money and interest until it's repaid."

"Interest?" Isaiah said.

"That's money you pay to borrow money," B.W. informed him.

"So it costs you more than if you save up," Isaiah said.

"Sure, but then you don't have birds flying around like you do."

"I got no objection to them," Isaiah said. "Cheaper to shoot 'em than to pay this interest."

B.W. shrugged. "I reckon. But y'only got four stalls. You got your own mule outside. You need to expand."

Isaiah went about swapping the harnesses. "Brother, we'll be lucky to see a penny here after we get finished buying essentials like feed and fabric for clothes. It's how many months till the next station managers meeting?"

"I dunno—four, five."

"Uh-huh. That means we will be eating what we grow or hunt and wearing whatever Bonita can patch back together until then. Heck, I still got no idea how the other owners'll take to me."

"Why, 'cause o' your color or slave status? Hell," B.W. said, "they got a woman, a half-breed, and up near Frisco they got a couple o' Nipponese who got shipwrecked. This is the West, Isaiah. They ain't exclusive."

"I can affirm that," Gonzalez said from outside their little huddle. "Except when it comes to Indians and Mexicans. Americans seem to prefer Indians on reservations and for us working the fields or south of the border."

"Say, now that's not entirely true," B.W. protested. "We're generally very welcoming folks out here. In my own stage I've carried Germans, Swedes, French, Russians. My shotgun is a Caribe. No, sir. Anybody willing to cross mountains and rivers and seas to get here is welcome. Even Rebs, for that matter, except those who still want to fight a done war."

"My experience up north was different," Gonzalez said.

"In Frisco?"

"Yes, sir."

"Was you spending money? On drink and women, I mean."

"We were not."

"Well that was yer problem," B.W. said. "What you encountered is just business. Y'ain't buying, then you're in the way of someone who is. Mr. Gonzalez, what we *object* to is folks trying to kill us. Starve us, take our homes, attack our women, butcher our cattle. There's enough room for everyone, enough food and water and timber for all people. Those who let us live, they get to live."

Gonzalez smiled politely and turned back to his wagon. "I beg your pardon for having intruded on your conversation."

"No intrusion," B.W. called over. "We're free to talk all we like here, whoever we are and whatever we say."

While Isaiah went about changing the horses, B.W. walked toward the Mexican.

"You don't agree," B.W. pressed.

Gonzalez turned and regarded the man. B.W. suddenly felt like one of those peasants the man had mentioned and he didn't even know why.

"I do not, sir," Gonzalez said. "As you know, I have just traveled south from a place as degenerate as any I have seen or even read about. Yet I found myself unwelcome at a number of Barbary Coast places frequented by some of the lowest seamen. My companion and I spent money on a hotel room. On local transportation. On meals. We were still treated with disrespect. To what should I ascribe that?"

"Why did you go to San Francisco?" B.W. asked.

"I'm afraid I cannot discuss that."

"Well there you have your answer, y'see?" B.W. said.

"Folks was fearful. They're afraid of secrecy there, of well-dressed folks who won't say what their business is. In particular, they'd be worried about you offering sailors better wages than they was getting from their current bosses. You came by sea, you said."

"Yes."

"I know some of those barkeeps and hoteliers," B.W. went on. "They're paid by shipping interests to watch for 'snatchers,' as they call 'em. True or not, you look like you could be some *hermano* who might wanna hire men to come south and harass the Mexican Navy."

Gonzalez had heard of the practice, though it did not occur to him that resistance was institutionalized. The irony was that he did indeed represent those interests. Had he not been on another quest, such a task might have fallen to him. It still might, some day.

"Mr. B.W. Lafayette, I thank you," Gonzalez said sincerely. "I thank you for the education. I mean that in earnest."

"I didn't think otherwise," B.W. answered, which was true. The driver took everyone as they appeared to be. Sometimes it turned out bad, as with the Indian agents Kennedy and Hathaway, but mostly people were good. Or at least obvious, the way Brent Diamond had been.

Gonzalez left to check that the water barrel on their wagon and the water skins were all full. That was essential to their journey.

B.W. went back inside to eat his own supper before driving off. As he sat, he felt himself envying Willa. The Grahams had returned to get out of the sun and the eighty-year-old was telling them stories from the last century that had them engaged and laughing.

Just my misfortune to have my life fall in a century that everyone remembers, B.W. thought as Bonita gave him a plate of beans with some spiced chicken cooked in. *I'll never be able to impress no one.*

Returning to the station, Gonzalez found Sanchez and Álvarez just getting ready to join him. The men changed into riding clothes and packed their finer things in a chest on the wagon. Gonzalez did the same. The Grahams were thanking Bonita for having hurried back from the wedding to provide for them. Willa was singing a hymn quietly to herself from her place at the end of the table. Dick Ocean seemed to be enjoying it. He was sitting on a stool nearby, his wounded leg stretched comfortably before him.

"Fair gleams the glorious city, the new Jerusalem!" she said in a high, soft, wavering voice.

The logs of the station absorbed the sound so that, even if one had been disposed to silence, her breathy voice would hardly have intruded. Outside, Joshua was using a stiff brush to clean the leather seats of the coach. On hot days like this, passengers preferred dirt and insects to choking heat. Racing along, the open window snared as much dead brush as it did air.

"I think we'd best get going," Sanchez said to Álvarez. "Water cask filled?"

"I checked it," Gonzalez said.

Sanchez nodded and Álvarez rose. The driver was a man in his middle twenties, of medium height and build, distinguished by a long, drooping moustache and black hair that reached to his shoulders. He was dressed in white with a black sombrero. When the hat was on his head, the long hair protected his neck from the sun.

Álvarez paid for his food and thanked Bonita for serving it.

"I got no idea what you said," she replied, smilingly to the man who spoke in a heavy Spanish accent. "My ears is used to Alabama an' the way they all talk. But I like the fact that you came over and said it."

Álvarez and Sanchez rode on the high buckboard. Gonzalez had made a seat for himself, facing front, with the four bags. Packed tightly around him were nondescript sacks containing weapons, ammunition, a cashbox, medical supplies, and tools for repairs.

The three left the station and went to the wagon, where B.W. wished them well on their trip. Gonzalez and Sanchez thanked him in passing—not to be rude or diminish his wishes but because they were already focused on what was next to come. The journey back to Whip Station and, hopefully, the company and guidance of Joe O'Malley.

The three men and their one horse passed neither Slash nor the Mission Indians. Though the way to Fort Yuma followed the Butterfield Trail east, riders tended to take a shorter route through foothills and across the Gila River.

Because the men had not wanted to speak in front of the Sundays, the stagecoach crew, or the passengers, Sanchez and Gonzalez had no current information on the status of events in Mexico. Sanchez had asked about that as soon as they were away from the station.

"When last we heard, Tomas Martinez was *south* of you," Álvarez said. "He was headed north—but he was not north, as you suspected."

"He sailed north, then south, then north again?" Sanchez asked.

"*Si.* It seems he was studying the route before transporting his goods. At least, that is what *Coronel* Cantú believes."

Vicente Cantú was the famed one-eyed field commander against the French, now aligned with the forces against

Juárez. He was based, with a small force, in the Magdalena de Kino region in the north.

"I still don't regret going," Gonzalez said. "We have learned both the sea route and the land route. We will get him *this* time."

"If he is south," Sanchez said pensively, "then there is a chance to stop him. Did the *Juaristas* know or did they suspect our mission?"

"We do not know," Álvarez said. "We know only that they were *watching* some of our people." He shrugged. "Their numbers are far greater. They can afford to have eyes everywhere. *Coronel* Cantú said we must be very careful."

"Of course," Gonzalez said. "Watching our people does not mean they suspect anything. It is a precaution. If we had enough people, we too would watch their key men . . . and women. But if they know, it could only be through a spy in our ranks."

"Either way, we have to assume that some part of this mission was observed," Sanchez said. "We cannot risk ignoring the possibility."

Gonzalez agreed. "That's something we must consider when we return to San Francisco," he said. "It isn't likely that anyone will find us before then, not with Joe O'Malley leading us."

"Not in that wilderness," Sanchez agreed. He regarded Álvarez. "How are you, my friend? How was your journey?"

The man looked at him with soulful eyes. "I am all right. But my wife—she is tired of listening, always listening, at the *cantina* where she works."

"We are grateful to Maria," Sanchez said. "She has heard much valuable information."

The wagon driver made an apologetic face. "She fears she will be discovered by the *Juaristas*. They will not be kind to her."

"Her family farm was turned into communal land," Sanchez said. "Every estate will become another *ejido* if we fail. If we succeed, her lands will be restored."

"She knows what is at stake," Álvarez said.

The three fell to reflection. Only the clattering of the wheels and the hooves of the horses broke the silence. There was nothing, however, to break the heat. The fire of the sun was like scalding water, rippling against their skin any way they turned. The stagecoach, at least, created an artificial breeze as they moved. The cart was heavy and pulled by just one horse. It moved slowly.

Sanchez and Gonzalez were not wearing coats and rolled up the sleeves of their shirts. They kept angling their hat to protect their faces, and their clothes became saturated with hot sweat. Flies and hornets came at them, some dislodged from the horse by the constant sweep of its tail. Announced from many hundred yards distant, the odor of dead and sun-rotted carcasses was present more often than not. He thought back to what B.W. had said at the stable, about the West being open to all.

Gonzalez was from Mexico City. He could not imagine who would choose this life over civilization. Even Sanchez's place in Vera Cruz had chickens and a well and servants. Álvarez had been one of them, content to live and work there with his family—until they were killed by *Juaristas* under French command who burned the place.

But then, the comfort of men like Gonzalez and Sanchez was part of what had fueled the unrest in Mexico. Most Mexicans had no choice where they lived, in what hovel, in what village. They were concerned about survival—until power-hungry Mexicans and French told them they should be resentful of those who could afford a hacienda with a cooling fountain, or rooms above and facing away from the foul-smelling street in a city.

Most peasants had never left their little towns, let alone seen an estate, Gonzalez thought. *Each poor citizen of Mexico, and they were everywhere—each would be like the Grahams examining the stagecoach at the station. They wanted what was new and comfortable, and they would not spend years panning for gold. They had revolted to take it now.*

The tragedy was there was not enough wealth to go around. They would discover that it was a stupid, pointless, bloody struggle that displaced a few nobles with a few leaders, like Juárez. For the peasants, nothing would ever change. How could it? They did not know how to live, only to survive. Gonzalez had seen it already. No sooner were seized farmlands divided and handed to the workers than they fought amongst each other for seeds and water, over the need to cooperate to kill foxes or wolves. Those who had no monetary or food reserves fought for hares and birds when bad weather or drought or insects ravaged their crops.

Mexican men are now free, Gonzalez thought. *They are free to die.*

And, ungoverned, they were also free to be misled into the kind of hellish insanity he and his comrades were trying to prevent.

How strange that those "men of the people" like Juárez, who claimed to be so concerned about life, should be so willing to destroy it.

"Do you still believe that Joe O'Malley should not be told the purpose of our journey?" Sanchez asked suddenly.

It took few seconds for Gonzalez to return to the moment.

"I do," he replied. "You saw the interaction of the O'Malleys. You heard what he told us. If this man ever suspected that his involvement might lead to retribution from across the border against his family, he would immediately withdraw."

"I wish you would reconsider that position," Sanchez said. "If we lie to him, and he discovers this, we will be on our own."

"First we have to make sure Joe is with us," Gonzalez said. "Then, I promise, I will think about it."

It was rare that Joe was alone with his daughter and granddaughter. In fact, he could not remember the last time it happened. He himself or Slash went to the general store in Vallicita. Jackson rarely went with them. His poorly healed leg made travel difficult. Joe worried how his son was going to make the journey to Fort Yuma and back.

But being alone with the ladies? He remembered Jackson and Slash going hunting together, once, and leaving them behind. That was at least seven or eight years ago, when Slash still needed someone to go out with him.

Given the rarity of Joe being alone with Sarah and Gert, it was even rarer that they were alone—and never for very long. He didn't like the idea of them being without a man or someone like Clarity. It didn't have to do with chores. In all truth, since Jackson's accident, Sarah had done more and more man's work—lifting, chopping, and drawing well water—than her husband. She did not resent that but made a point of doing the most difficult jobs when Jackson was in the stable or in San Diego buying horses or picking up shipments of clothing or tools. Sarah never wanted her husband to feel any kind of shame.

Chopping wood had left her extremely capable with an axe, which is one reason Joe did not feel uneasy about leaving her. And Gert—

Well, he had to admit with reluctance, *her skill at throwing a hatchet with the best of the Indian squaws could come in useful.*

The young woman had two hatchets, both of them gifts. They were crossed over the hearth. To an unwitting observer they would have seemed ornamental. To anyone trying to bust in, they would be something else.

Joe and the women had taken everything from the burned wagon and salvaged what they could. The women washed and hung the clothes they were able to salvage. It wasn't much, mostly a gown, undergarments. There were also high-laced shoes Clarity had brought from the East, intended for San Francisco social wear, and two of Slash's shirts and a neckerchief. The boy had lost his only pair of trousers, apart from the one he was wearing, and a pair of dress shoes. Clarity's hairbrush and hand mirror survived, though the glass had suffered a crack.

There was no lamentation. Both women were accustomed to hardship and loss in the West. Whatever the cause, this was not something for lamentation or bitterness. The ruin had to be dealt with and put behind them.

Dolley taught both him and their daughter well.

"You can't do nothing about yesterday," Dolley used to say.

"That may be so," her husband would answer. "But you can do something about the person who made yesterday unhappy."

She had proved him wrong, of course. Death was above

chastisement. Since Dolley had been taken, Joe had tried to keep himself from hating all people whose purposes were opposed to his own. That would leave him a constant desire for vengeance, bloodlust that would never be satisfied.

Detective Tatham made it difficult to uphold that policy. He was a stern, unfriendly cuss. But Joe wondered what he would be feeling if it was Slash that Clarity had killed and run away. If he couldn't have hunted her himself, and he had the means, he might have done what the Roches did. Either went to the law or, if they wouldn't cooperate, he may well have hired someone to hunt her for him.

The problems you don't have when you are alone in the plains, he thought—not with regret, because he loved his kin, but with an honest yearning for a simpler time.

Joe had time to reflect as he waited for the Mexicans to return. He had decided to go with them, not just for the gold but because he knew he would be restless if he sat around waiting for word from Slash or Jackson. He also knew that rather than wait for her, he was likely to ride out in the direction of Vallicita and Fort Yuma.

That would just add too many squirrels to the tree, he told himself. Even if Slash was impulsive, Jackson was not. He would keep a steady hand on this thing, make the right decisions. Merritt was also a reasonable man, and reasonable men were what was needed now.

The frontiersman took some care preparing his grip and horse for the trip north. He changed from his buckskins to lighter, whiter clothes. It would be hot out there, dangerously hot to the east of the Butterfield Trail where there were no mountains or trees to shade the riders.

He also took along jerky enough for a three- or four-day

passage through the plains. Most of the big, meaty animals did not come out till night there, and he didn't feel like hunting field mice for a nibble during the day. He didn't even want to travel when the sun was up. He did not know when the men intended to leave, though it would be dusk at least before they arrived—probably later, given the heat and the unwillingness of any horse to work hard in the furnace heat of afternoon. He would suggest an immediate departure to take advantage of the cooler evening.

When he was done, Joe went to his daughter and granddaughter who had moved from the bedroom and were on their knees, checking tomatoes and peas growing in the garden, their slender hands moving among the thick leaves and propping bent stalks with broken bits of tree branch. They didn't do this until late in the day when the setting sun and things were cooling off.

"Why don't you two sit for a spell," Joe suggested.

"Because uneaten cherry pie is not a vegetable," Sarah said. "Contract calls for a side of—"

"I know, I know," Joe said. "But you got two days before the next coach. Happy Morrison always brings you corn from the Arizona Territory."

"You mean maize?" Gert teased.

"I mean what I said," Joe told her. "I'm speaking English, not Injun."

Sarah looked up. "She was just goading you, pa."

"Yeah," Joe said. He looked across the blanched plain beyond then down at the teenager. "I'm a little sorry, Gert. I'm not myself. I didn't like leaving your pa and brother and I don't like leaving here now."

"We're all, none of us, ourselves," Sarah said, sniffing back sudden tears.

"We can handle things till someone gets back," Gert assured him.

Joe smiled crookedly. He squatted beside his grand-daughter. "I truly am sorry about what I said. I know I give you a hard time, but when it comes down to it—"

"I know, grandpa. You love us." She smiled. "And I promise, I will scalp anyone who gets out of line."

She looked as if she were kidding. Joe didn't think she was.

"I don't have any idea what to expect north, east, or here," Joe admitted. "I don't like that. And I been thinking about Slash riding out the way he did, in a determined kinda hurry. I think—I hope—I know what he's planning."

"Nothing sensible, if I know my brother," Gert said.

"In this matter, honey, there *ain't* nothing sensible," Joe said.

"What do you think Slash was off about?" Gert asked.

"There were just two things a head start would get him," Joe said. "Beating Tatham to the fort . . . and looking for help from either Isaiah Sunday or Sisquoc and Malibu. Maybe all of the above."

"I don't want him out there alone," Gert said, "but I am sad to think of others getting involved in our troubles."

"I know," Joe said. "I feel the same. But it's what we would do for them. In all the years I been out here, I seen folks who never worked together learning how. That's the breed of man—and woman—we've made out here. And I'll tell ya this. If the Apache and Cheyenne and Pechanga ever learned that kinda cooperation, they would never have been forced onto reservations."

"Or they may have been exterminated in the war General Guilford was planning," she replied.

"There's that too," Joe admitted.

Sarah was still on her hands and knees, but Joe noticed that she had momentarily stopped working. She was looking down with a thoughtful expression. She was not the talker her daughter was. But Joe knew well the look of a woman who was chewing on some other thought.

"You're wearing your mother-in-law Dolley's look," Joe said.

"I earned it on my own, dealing with O'Malley men," she answered.

"What's on your mind?"

"You are, pa," she said without hesitation.

"What'd I do?" he asked, offering the same measured response he always gave to Dolley. It wasn't conciliatory but it wasn't challenging, either. It was almost like a question.

"It's what you're about to do, again," she said. She looked up, wiped tears from her cheeks leaving a dirty smear. "The years I have known you, and they are many now, I was always used to you being away. It came with being the wife of Jackson O'Malley, and it comes with being your daughter by marriage. It was necessary, we all knew it. But it was difficult. Very, very difficult."

"I was a frontiersman," he said. "Still am at heart, and always will be. You know that."

"I do," she agreed. "But it's been just two weeks since you rode to the north where you might've died. I thank God in my prayers each night since that Slash gunned-down the Rebels who were chasing you. Slash isn't here now and you're getting ready to go north again, for farther and longer, with men you don't know."

"Sarah, I almost *always* scouted and guided for men I don't know—"

"Not from a country that is still filled with revolution and is within a day's ride of here. We're already involved with a situation among our own kind. Why do you want to put you, and me, and your granddaughter, in the path of some secret business from the south? For gold?"

"Not for gold as such but for Clarity and Slash," he said. "Maybe for legal costs. I been thinking hard about this."

Sarah had no answer for that. She went back to tilling soil with her fingers around the youngest of the tomato plants.

"Sarah, I can't lie and say there's no danger," he answered truthfully. "Heck, I admit it. That's part of what keeps me going. What else would you have me do? Watch the cactuses grow here?"

"I am sure Mr. Butterfield, perhaps the railroad, would have some less mysterious jobs for you."

"Done all those, and got bored with them," he told her. "You go out with a surveyor, you plant the seat of your trousers on a rock ledge and look out at the golden eagles and envy them their freedom, 'cause that's something you ain't got. You sit there, dripping good sweat into ground that don't care, until the man finishes his readings and making his maps and walking his measured steps and only calling you when he sees a bear or a snake." Joe shook his head. "And it don't even pay well. It'd take three years to earn what these Mexican boys offered in gold. Gold that will be left here before we leave."

"And possibly recovered or stolen by a band that's riding after them," Sarah suggested.

"Now that's just gloomy," Joe said with a little smile.

Sarah pointed past him. "Mexico is that way, a half-a-day's ride. They have scouts too."

"And if such as they come here, you will tell them everything you know," he said. "Send 'em our way. We'll be ready. And Jackson will be back. Or Slash."

Sarah shook her head. "I am not afraid for us."

"I know," Joe said. "And I love you for it." He kissed her on the back of her head. "My Dolley looked at the dark side of things too. Mostly, though, things turned out okay. B.W. would say God was looking out for us. Maybe He is. Maybe Dolley is. I don't know."

Both fell silent. Joe rose. He pinched the front of his cotton shirt, loosening the white laces that crisscrossed the front. Then he rattled the garment to air it.

"Sarah, I'm gonna tell you something I haven't told to anyone else," Joe said. "I'm kinda just realizing this myself. You know it was at my urging we took this place, but I feel mostly useless here. Everything that earns money—caring for the horses, growing the food and feeding the passengers—all of that is done by you, Jackson, and Gert. Slash does the hunting. He's keen of eye, spry, *better* than I ever was. I'm proud of the boy, but I don't feel like I earn my keep. With this trip, I got a chance to do that now and I'm gonna take it." He paused. "I *have* to take it."

Sarah smiled up at him and stood. He always seemed so strong and self-assured. Just now, she saw the determined little boy he must have been at the turn of the century, new and young like America. The nation had suffered its war. Now it was time for Joe O'Malley to wage his.

"Thank you for saying that," Sarah said and hugged her father-in-law tightly. The move came unexpectedly and his arms went wide with surprise before closing around her.

"You are funny," Joe said.

"Why?"

"'Cause even in this moment, you are being careful not to put yer dirty hands on my nice, white shirt."

She slapped her palms on his damp back and held him

tightly. Joe's eyes found Gert over Sarah's head. She was still on the ground, smiling with a warmth he was not used to seeing.

Probably because me or the guests are usually saying things that sting like a passel o' hornets, he thought.

He wondered if he could change the way he thought about her, about Indians, about a lot of things.

That was something he would have plenty of time to think about on the long, long ride ahead.

Chapter 9

It was dusk before Tatham and his party reached the outskirts of the Apache settlement. There was a smell of burning hickory in the air, of cooking meat, of tobacco that was grown in the struggling South and sent west.

The place smelled to Tatham like it belonged to another time, to a race that should have long vanished from the plains. What he should be smelling out here was coal being burned in locomotives, in forges, in the belly of civilization.

He could not wait to be done here and return east.

The trip had been distinctive only in the lack of camaraderie among the four travelers.

Jackson had gone on long rides with his father and son over the years. Before being crippled, when there was still the possibility of Texas ranching in the O'Malleys' future, he would visit ranches throughout the near southwest and camp with other cowboys and wranglers, often in search of new herds of horses. Whether or not you liked or knew the person you were with, you could not help but get to know and understand them, even just a little. If they were from another country like Argentina or another part of your own, you had to make sure you understood what they were saying. If you suffered a snakebite, a horse fall, encountered a suddenly swelling river, even a lightning strike or fire—your life could depend on them, and theirs on you. It was a bond like family, only narrower and in some ways stronger.

Jackson missed that. He had not expected to find that here, nor did he desire it. But he had never met anyone as stubbornly aloof and profoundly disinterested as this Leonard Tatham. If the ground suddenly split and swallowed the man, Jackson was not sure he would throw him a rope.

Not only did Jackson, Clarity, and Reverend Michaels remain disengaged from Tatham, they only spoke to each other to make sure they were drinking enough water and not falling asleep in the saddle—another hazard that beset long rides under a furnace-hot sun.

Clarity knew that being in the saddle for any length of time was challenging to Jackson. Slash had told her that the muscles and bones in both his left knee and hip had been damaged in his horse fall, and the injured leg ached bad from the hip to the knee and often up the back. Clarity, who was riding behind Tatham but in front of Jackson, would often glance back and see him listing to the right to take the pressure off his left side. Her heart ached for that good, good man.

But she would not ask Tatham to stop. She did not know Jackson very well, but she suspected a request made on his behalf would probably shame him. And Tatham's refusal would infuriate her.

Even without that particular provocation, the solid, rigid back of the man in front of her was a tight bale of hay she yearned to use for target practice. There were times when Clarity wanted to ride her horse straight at the so-called detective and chance the consequences. He had ruined the best day of her life, upset her brother and new family, destroyed just about everything she owned, and also put her freedom and possibly her very life in jeopardy. If it weren't for the threat of General Guilford's retribution against the O'Malleys, she was thinking now that she should have gone along with Slash's offer to "vamoose," to use her husband's word.

Captivity with dignity does not seem preferable to flight with your husband, she had decided.

She also wondered, almost constantly, how Slash was doing. Because she had not been alone with Jackson, she did not know what they may have discussed or planned. She was worried for him, but the fact that he was out here, somewhere, maybe watching her at this moment, also gave her strength—and hope.

The nearness of the Apache lands also gave Clarity heart. It meant, for one thing, that they could stop riding long enough for Jackson to ease up in the saddle. For another, it showed her that Tatham was willing to risk the passage among hostiles rather than to seem afraid. If he showed fear to them, it might encourage his prisoner to turn on him.

Finally, and to that point, Clarity had been thinking about whether she should use Gert's friendship with the Indians to turn against Tatham. Clarity herself had one friend here and she wondered whether to call upon him when they arrived. She had gone back and forth on what to do more times than mating dragonflies had knit past them since four or five miles back, when they took the passage that brought them here instead of around the settlement. If she did not act, there was no possible salvation between there and Fort Yuma.

But if she tried, and the Apache came to her assistance, it might cause Tatham to start shooting at everyone around him, including Jackson and Merritt. Squaws and Indian young might die as well. The man from the East certainly had the weaponry.

The Apache did not have lookouts, other than dogs. The animals had begun to bark when the riders were quite some distance away. Three braves rode out, four spotted coach dogs accompanying them. The horses of the new arrivals were spooked by the presence of the dogs. Tatham and the others halted to calm their mounts.

There was still sunlight beaming from behind Clarity and she easily made out the faces of the Red Men. All were hearteningly familiar to her from the young woman's last ride through Apache territory. That was with Joe, when they had gone looking for the renegade ex-Confederates who had ridden to Whip Station in an effort to kidnap their guest, a Serrano shaman.

The three Apaches galloped wide around the new-comers and went behind them. Tatham broke from the line and turned to face them. They rode up intending for one to be to the right or left of each rider. The dogs were distracted by animals in the surrounding woods, and the horses calmed.

One brave broke rank and doubled back so that he was beside Clarity. He held up his hand and the other riders stopped near Jackson and Merritt. Clarity did not speak to the Apache. She had learned, quickly, the way of these people. A White woman did not speak first to a brave.

"I remember," he said.

"Hello, Baishan," she replied.

He regarded the woman and her horse. He seemed perplexed. "Where gun?"

"Back at the station."

"Where Joe?"

"Also at the station."

"Hurt?"

"No. He is well, thank you." Turning to the two family members behind her, she said, "This is Baishan, trusted brave of Tarak, War Chief of the Apaches. This man behind me is Joe's son Jackson. I have married his son Slash."

"I remember Slash. We must fight."

"I'd prefer you didn't," Clarity said. "The man at the rear is my brother Merritt."

"Blood?"

"Not blood brother," she replied, discerning his meaning. "Of our mother. He is a preacher."

"Shaman."

"In a way." She faced front. "That man," she pointed ahead, "is a snake belly. He is the reason I do not have my gun."

In saying that, Clarity realized she had moved in a direction that could be dangerous for everyone. There had been nothing else to do. The words just emerged.

Baishan had grunted out a laugh at the name. Clarity was still looking forward. Even in the amber-hued darkness, she could see the rage in Tatham's otherwise still posture and expression.

Baishan signaled one of the other braves. The two rode around the group so that Tatham was between the two Apaches. Tatham did not show whatever fear or concern he felt. He also did not move his hands anywhere near his revolvers or shotgun.

"Why you chief of her?" Baishan asked.

"She killed a man," Tatham answered in a firm voice. "I am law."

"I kill many men. Law want me?"

"Not this lawman," Tatham said.

The Apache sniffed at him. "Here, I am law."

"Get him away from me, Clarity, or it will go hard on you," Tatham said.

"I can't tell him what to do in his own land," she replied.

"It'll go harder on you, I think," Jackson said from behind Clarity. "You don't get prickly with Apache."

Tatham did not change his ramrod posture, or his disapproving expression. He did, however, stop talking.

Baishan rode back to Clarity. "Where you go?"

"To the fort," she replied.

"You want to go?" the Indian asked matter-of-factly.

This is it, Clarity thought. The moment when she could go free and, if Tatham were foolish enough to try and stop them, he would not die well.

"She wishes to go," Jackson replied. "Miss Clarity wishes to clear her name."

Baishan continued to look at her. "Brother say for you?"

With great reluctance, with a warrior's soul that was fighting hard against her better judgment, she replied quietly, "He does."

Without hesitation, Baishan said, "You may pass."

The Apache moved away and said something to the other two braves, who rode ahead. Baishan called to the dogs, who came running from the woods. The Apache warrior turned and followed the others, leaving the three alone in the darkening field.

Tatham kicked his horse ahead so fiercely that Clarity thought the animal might buck him. He pulled hard on the bit and stopped beside the woman. For a moment, Clarity believed that he was going to strike her. He sat there simmering and glaring at her for a long moment.

"You will regret what you have done," Tatham vowed.

"What I've done? I stopped him from killing you," she replied.

"How will she regret this, detective?" Jackson demanded. "You are bound by oath to act within the law."

Tatham looked up. His eyes blazed blood red with the last of the setting sun.

"You would be surprised, Mr. O'Malley, just how much leeway I have to act."

The detective whirled again, the horse stomping up black clouds of dirt as the man resumed his place at the front.

Jackson leaned forward on his horse. "Clarity—what were you *doing*?"

She turned without the horse breaking stride. "What I have always done. Fighting back. We gain nothing by being soft. What more can he do?"

"Let's not find out," he urged as they continued toward the settlement.

It was nearly nighttime before the wagon with the three Mexicans arrived at Whip Station. A lantern at the entranceway and another over the front porch showed the way. Álvarez did not have to direct the horse to the half-filled trough. Once through the entranceway, the animal went directly to the water on its own.

Barking, Blood and Mud came out to greet them. The horse and the men in the wagon ignored them. The sun had drained them of any concerns that did not involve comfort, and the cramped ride had sucked away whatever human touches were left.

Gonzalez was the first to climb from the wagon. He was

eager to stretch, to walk a bit. They had only stopped three times since Vallicita, and briefly, during their journey west. One of those was in Civil Gulch, the only place where there was any shade. However, the heat was intensified by the rock walls and they did not stay long. Gonzalez had not smoked a single one of his cigars. He had weighed the idea of the flavor and a relaxing aroma against the proximity of heat . . . any heat.

Sanchez followed his partner down. He twisted at the hips and arched his back and touched his toes. The driver just lay back on the buckboard, his knees up.

"I prefer the sea," Gonzalez said.

"I will ride in back when we leave," Sanchez said.

"No," said Gonzalez. "The sun was the worst of it—we will be traveling at night."

"Where the only danger is falling into a chasm or losing our way," Sanchez said, not entirely in jest.

The journey gave Sanchez and Gonzalez a deep, deep respect for what lay ahead. Without Joe, they wondered if a trip through the plains would be manageable. A wrong path might put them against a valley or cliff that might require turning back or detouring—losing time and, perhaps, their lives as supplies ran out.

Standing unobserved by a window, Joe had watched the men. They themselves were the only consideration that might keep him from going. If they had showed any great experience with a long ride in a crude conveyance, he would have doubted that they were members of the nobility. It was clear these two had never ridden anything other than a horse or a carriage.

Joe stepped out under the lantern, closing the door quickly so the moths would not enter. They had lost enough clothing today. Stepping closer, his eyes accustomed to picking out details in the night, Joe saw at once how much the sun had stolen from the two men. They had lost their shoulders-back posture, not to mention their jackets. Their shirts were opened against all modesty—another hallmark of the Mexican upper class. Gonzalez shivered slightly being exposed to the cooler night air that chilled the sweat on their bodies. Having walked about, he retrieved his jacket. Even their step was unsteady as they walked toward the porch.

"You're the first folks I get to ask," Joe said.

"What is that?" Sanchez inquired.

"I been told that rattling across uneven terrain is worse than travel by sea."

"Decidedly," Sanchez said. "Without the benefit of a sea breeze."

Joe nodded. "Hard ground don't generously soak up the sun. It throws it back at you."

The two men became animated as they swatted at the bugs that swirled round the light, their perspiration, and their heads.

"Them fleas like the smell of hair," Joe said of the relentless gnats.

"I am impressed with frontier wisdom," Gonzalez said admiringly.

That was another indication the men were who they said they were. Now, among the peasantry, the man's dignity and composure were returning somewhat, like groundwater rising.

"Come inside," Joe said. "I'll get cool water from the well an' you can lie down on—"

"No thank you," Gonzalez interrupted. "We must go on." The man's tone was harder than it had been just a moment before. He was a man used to giving orders.

"Tell me, Joe," Sanchez said. "What have you decided?"

"You got a half-an'-half chance of making the trip on your own," Joe said. "I know I cain't talk you out of it, so I'm going to take you north."

"Thank you," Gonzalez said in apparent earnest.

Depleted like he was, Joe did not think the man had the strength to put on airs. The frontiersman now turned his mind to the fact that he *was* going . . . and leaving Gert and Sarah behind. The man who did not pray much thought, *May You look after my girls, Lord.*

Joe used his hat to swat at moths as Sarah opened the door.

"As for going now, are you certain o' that?" Joe asked. "You may not want to rest, but the horse—"

"We can, all of us, rest when the sun is up, the horses included," Sanchez said. "I hope you will accommodate that desire. We must get to San Francisco, and we cannot afford to lose even a nighttime."

Gonzalez added, "We have lanterns to light the way."

"I saw," Joe said. "Very well. This is your hoedown."

Joe followed him, taking a moment to glance back at the wagon. In the light, he saw several carbines and handguns packed among the supplies. He was gratified that he did not have to remind the men about the gold. Sanchez reached into the wagon and withdrew a leather bag. He undid the strap, handed Joe a purse from inside.

"Thank you," Joe said. "While I get the water, you okay with coming inside for a brief sit-down?"

"Very gratefully," Gonzalez confessed. They followed Joe in, bowing to Sarah and then to Gert.

"Your driver?" Sarah asked at the door.

"He requires a *siesta* more than water," Gonzalez said.

"More than breath," Sanchez added. "He has been traveling for two days without a stop."

Sarah and Gert welcomed them to the table while Joe got fresh water. The women did so without serving any food. They were no longer paying customers on the route. That changed when she saw the sack of gold on the counter beside the inside wash basin. Joe had put it there on his way out the back door. He had left it open so she would know what was inside. There wasn't time to prepare a warm meal, but noticing the uneaten pie, she offered some to their guests.

The men sat, accepted the water but declined the pie. Joe returned and poured the bucket into a clay pitcher.

"This is from this morning," Gonzalez noted as Sarah set it on the table. "I remember admiring it."

"We didn't get to celebrate," Joe informed them as he poured water into their glasses.

"I was about to remark—the others," Sanchez said. "Where is the rest of your family?"

Joe explained briefly. Even though the Mexicans had not been part of the wedding party, they seemed genuinely indignant and hurt for the O'Malleys.

Joe went to his small room off the one central corridor on the western side of the long stationhouse. He retrieved the grip he'd packed. He donned his holster and Colt, took his shotgun from its slot on the wall, and took only a few loose shells. The rest of the ammunition he left for the women. He took his brass compass from a rickety wooden night table. He hadn't had one for most of his life, and shouldn't need it now, but it was a long trip. And if he was disabled or killed, at least the others would not be helpless.

When he returned to the main room, the Mexicans had

already gone outside. Joe walked over to the sack of gold, took a coin and put it in his pants pocket.

"The gentlemen are well-armed," he said quietly to Sarah. "I'll pick up more shells in San Francisco. You keep what we have." He grinned. "May end up being a useful shopping trip. Get Clarity and Slash a few new things there."

Sarah nodded, a catch in her breath as she and her daughter both hugged Joe in turn.

"When was the last time you were in San Francisco?" Sarah asked.

Joe thought as he took his buckskin jacket from the hook on the wall. "I was there for the gold fever," he said, "so—near eighteen, nineteen years."

"I read that it has changed, grandfather," Gert said.

Joe smiled. "What hasn't in nearly a score's time?"

Gert replied. "You, I think."

Joe's smile widened. "That's sass I can't fault you for, girl. Not when you're probably right."

He moved toward the door and Sarah touched his elbow. "Be careful," she said.

"You got the gold, so all anyone can take from me is some skin," he said, making a fist.

Sarah scowled. Joe knew it would remain there until she heard what she wanted to hear.

"Of course, I'll be careful," Joe said, brushing aside the hair that had spilled across her brow and kissing her forehead. "See you in about two, three weeks." He took a moment longer to add, "Both of you—be strong for the men. And be patient with Slash. They'll need that."

The women did not express the darker fears that were

in their hearts, about which men might and might not return from that trip.

Joe was still smiling as he went out the back door to the stable to get his horse. And then the reality of the larger situation once again took hold. Slash, Jackson, and Clarity were still at the mercy of a questionable lawman and an openly vengeful general.

He hesitated a moment.

"You should be here if the men need you," he told himself before he mounted.

But there was also the reality of having given his word to help these men, and the danger to which they alluded— something that could also affect the family.

He left the stable, joined the wagon, and led them toward the back of the house. They followed the Butterfield Trail for roughly a mile until they reached the low foothills that would take them to one of many unmarked courses to the north.

The Apache settlement that had been announced by its rustic smells was now visibly defined. Spread across the flat plain, the encampment was lit by campfires burning proudly at the crossroads between the dozens of tepees. Because war parties and nighttime hunts required stealth, the Indians rarely lit fires beyond the settlement. This, however, was home. The Apache allowed no darkness here, and permitted no one to bring it.

Tatham continued to ride at the front of his small column. He was aware of Clarity and Jackson chatting, but could not make out what they said—nor did he care.

If they did anything to try and change his plan, one or both would be shot from their horses.

The Easterner did not know much about Indians, other than what he had been told at the fort before departing. But he suspected it would be a mark of cowardice to put a woman or a lame man at the head, as shields. It was also too late to go around the settlement. To backtrack and go south, then east, would cost him at least a day. It would also likely embolden the woman to try something Indian-like and escape.

Not the Indians, not the men in the column, only Clarity O'Malley interested him.

The camp was busy with the preparation of the evening meal, and none of the squaws stopped what they were doing. A few looked up and several braves came over, on foot, standing near but to the sides as the three began their passage through the camp. A few whooped. It did not sound, to Tatham, like a welcome. It seemed more of a provocation, the equivalent of tweaking a man's nose back East.

Clarity felt it strange that she should feel more comfortable here, with these half-dressed savages, than with a supposedly civilized man from east of the Rockies. Stranger still was how much she thought she knew just three weeks ago, when she was still in St. Louis awaiting passage west, compared to what she knew now.

And what I will learn in the future, she thought, trying to tamp down the fear she suddenly felt. This was her last sanctuary. And it tempted her greatly, since there was something else on her mind.

Tatham turned halfway around.

"I don't see your friend," he said to Clarity.

"You won't, I don't think."

"Why is that?"

"I believe that in his view you are beneath concern, his and mine."

"He cannot believe that." Tatham actually laughed.

"Were that not the case, he would likely kill you on principle for stealing my gun. He tried, once. Joe stopped him."

"Maybe he just doesn't want a shootout here, with all the women and children about."

"No," Clarity says. "He believes you to be a coward."

"My being here proves otherwise."

"Hardly. You are under my protection. What he saw back there is that I insulted you and you made no answer," Clarity said. "That showed him you fear me."

Tatham laughed again. "You are ridiculous and so are these Red animals."

"I would not say too loud," Clarity said. "They may not know English, most of them, but some do. And others know contempt when they see it. They don't like that from the White Man."

"Would they go to war with the United States Cavalry over you?"

"The better question, one that I have just been considering, is whether the cavalry would go to war with them over *you*?"

The conversation ended, and Clarity was grateful for all Gert had learned and shared about the primitives and their ways. Even as she spoke about the tribe and its ways, Clarity felt stronger than she had before they ran into Baishan.

The detective has guns but no power, she thought. *Baishan understood that. It is something to remember.*

The passage through the camp took several minutes and passed without incident, after which Tatham fell back alongside Clarity.

"Be careful," she said. "Baishan is probably watching."

"I don't doubt it," the detective said. "I have no need to do anything that might upset him. I only wanted to tell you this." He glanced over his shoulder. "I want you all to hear this. For what you have done and what you just did—one way or another, Clarity O'Malley, I *will* see you hang."

Chapter 10

It was, in the end, just a brief coastal squall that rocked *The Dundee*.

The vessel rolled and tilted but sustained no damage, other than the few seabirds that had been dashed into the masts and dropped bloodied to the decks. Even they were washed away by the wind and rain.

Captain Swift had remained below. Dr. Puckett had returned at the height of the storm and given him a generous dose of potent, undiluted laudanum to dull the pain, discourage trying to get up, and induce sleep. Puckett knew that since the time Swift was a boy, he had always regarded sea air as a cure-all. But since Swift was in pain, and would have had trouble reaching the deck, and difficulty remaining there during the storm, he had reluctantly accepted the medic's ruddy, foul-tasting solution.

Puckett left to see to any other injuries that might occur during the blow. Though the opium extract dulled the ache in the captain's head, it brought on delusions rather than sleep. Every slap of a wave on the hull sounded like an explosion, and each one caused him to start:

The chest has blown up! The ship will go down. . . .

Yet in the few moments of pain-free lucidity he enjoyed, Swift managed to think of a way he could thwart the ruthless *Señor* Martinez. One that could not be countermanded by a knock on the head.

The problem would be getting to First Mate Francis Sullivan in time. Swift did not know where along the coast they were, what time it was, or when the doctor would be coming down again.

He lay there, impatiently waiting for the loud, echoing sounds and alternately fuzzy, double images to pass. The part of him that was a man, and a commander, wanted to take back control of his ship.

Swift did not know how long it was before Puckett came to check on him. The injured captain was lying on his left side. Puckett crouched and gently raised the man's eyelids, looked into his eyes in turn.

"What—what is going on above?" Swift asked very softly.

"There's nothing to report, as far as I know," the doctor said quietly. "You know that I am never told very much." He chuckled. "The first thing out of any seaman's mouth is, 'I have a pain here . . .'"

"I want," Swift said loudly, wincing as the sound of his own voice made his head hurt. He continued in a whisper. "I want for you to send Mr. Sullivan to see me."

"Why, captain?"

"Because . . . I am ordering . . . it."

"And I am asking for medical reasons, 'Why'? Are you inquiring about the ship or is it something else? Is this still about Martinez?"

Swift knew that asserting his rank would avail him nothing. Puckett was a friend and a sailor, but physicians had their own, special authority.

"It is . . . about Martinez," Swift admitted. "Would you . . . do that for me?"

"You seeking to get hit again?"

"If that . . . is what it takes to regain command of *The Dundee,* then so be it," Swift replied.

"Captain, you have noticed that we didn't blow up as you feared," Puckett said, still whispering. "Maybe you can let this sit?"

"I think you know me better," the captain replied.

Puckett shook his head. "Knock on the head didn't put sense in. It may've took some out. All right. I'll do what you ask."

"Thank you, doctor," Swift said.

The doctor left, and Swift exhaled, happy for the respite from having to be alert. Following a symphony of sloshing and shouts from on-deck, the first mate knocked on the door. Swift answered but the mate did not hear him. After another knock, Sullivan opened the door and looked in.

"Sir?"

"Come," Swift said. "Forgive me . . . I'm not able to talk very loud."

"Of course, captain," Sullivan replied, stepping inside and shutting the door behind him.

The first mate was an oak with a dark face that looked almost graven, like a totem. It was capped by sandy blond hair with a short, curly blond beard below. The thirty-seven-year-old tightly filled his blue-and-white striped jumper and blue trousers, and had doffed his peaked, patent-leather cap with a gold band. Sullivan was a veteran of the Union Navy where he had been a chief engineer.

"Doc says I shouldn't stay long," Sullivan said as he approached.

"No need," Swift said. "How far are we out of San Diego?"

Sullivan thought for a moment. "About fourteen leagues northwest from the port, I can figure out distance from the county line if—"

"That puts us some twenty-one leagues from Los Angeles and San Pedro," the captain interrupted.

"We haven't cargo to leave or pick up there, sir, so I was going to pass 'er by as your original—"

"I understand . . . let me think," Swift interrupted. "Feels like the prevailing winds are southwesterly."

"Yes—"

It was difficult to concentrate. He shut his eyes and thought aloud. "We won't gain time whichever way we turn," he said. "Best to go with the nearer port. "Turning about would save time, even though he would know."

"Who would?"

"Our passenger," Swift said. "Bloody Martinez." He opened an eye and looked toward the first mate. "Franny, I want you to head back to San Diego, and do not change our course unless you hear directly from me."

"Yes, sir," the mate said behind a two-finger salute. "May I ask why, captain?"

"I've no ship's secrets from you," Swift said. "I am doing it to seize command of this ship from our passenger. He's the reason I'm here."

"He did that?" the first mate pointed toward Swift's head.

"Aye. And I may need Rog York's help at the harbor to make sure he is held for the sheriff." The captain's blood-shot eye turned up slightly. "You'll see to it?"

"Of course, sir," Sullivan replied. "And what do I say when Mr. Martinez asks about it?"

"It's none of his business, but you may tell him . . . those were my orders and leave it at that."

"It'll be done, sir," Sullivan said, saluting again before leaving the cabin.

The Mission Indians had always intended to ride through the night to reach Fort Yuma.

Sisquoc and Malibu were devoted and attentive members of the Cavalry. They owed their lives, hearts, and industry to the people who had rescued them and brought them to salvation at the mission. Leave had been granted for the wedding, provided the two returned to their post by sun-up.

But there was more to each man's life than a cherished uniform.

Malibu belonged to the Chumash Indians and Sisquoc was Yaqui. The two had been raised at the Mission San Luis Rey outside of San Diego. That was where they had met the O'Malley family, who attended services there on Christmas.

Over twenty years earlier, the Indian youths had been orphaned in separate incidents and carried off by the U.S. First Regiment of Dragoons. The Dragoons had not been party to the killings—the tribes had fought with one another—but had been scouting in California when it happened. The army's action was not one of charity. The two boys were old enough to know the language and some of the ways of their people. Like other disenfranchised young Indians, they were taken to the local missions. The goal was to raise them to work with the army against the native population.

The program, which was ongoing since they rode from

Fort Leavenworth in Kansas in the fall of 1849, was still very active. It had achieved remarkable success in creating effective and loyal scouts. Given a choice between the life of a lone wolf on the prairie or food, shelter, money, and occasionally drink, the Mission Indians selected the ways of the White man.

Sisquoc and Malibu had something deeper than a sense of duty to the United States Cavalry. And that was their affection for the O'Malley family. Joe, Jackson, and Sarah had been welcoming in a way no settler, no shop, no food establishment, no church, no individual soldier had been to them. The Indians' uniforms could not hide their skin color. To most people out here, that swarthiness meant they were not to be trusted. They were the enemy.

Joe did not have a high regard for warring tribes or the natives who overhunted neighboring lands. Yet individually, he regarded any man as an equal. The two Mission Indians saw that today with the welcoming of the freed slave Isaiah Sunday and his family, with the Caribe shotgun rider, with people who were partial to the North and to the South during the recent war, with the two Mexicans who were guests at the station during the wedding.

The O'Malleys were uncommon people, and the two Mission Indians cherished their friendship. More than that, they treasured the people themselves. Which is why both men were deeply troubled when they arrived at Fort Yuma. The story Slash had told them could make General Guilford, their commanding officer, an opponent.

That prospect weighed on each man like a storm cloud as they rode the winding path that went to the hilltop ridge of the fort.

It was just before dawn and the fort was quiet, as usual.

The Colorado River was beginning to show its usual morning muscle as shoreline activity rose with the sun. Animals were roused to pull carts and cargo that would soon arrive, while others were loping in along well-marked roads that followed the river to the short piers. Breakfast, along with morning assembly and drilling, was still at least an hour off.

General Guilford typically did not enter the open compound until that time. But he was out there now, talking with Woodrow Landau—the assistant provost marshal of the battalion. The officer's job was to oversee the arrest and incarceration of deserters and other accused criminals within the ranks. Absent a federal marshal, the provost was also charged with maintaining order in the region until one could be summoned.

That task was supposed to be independent of the judgment and influence of the military commander. The marshal's only guidelines were local and federal civilian law.

Upon seeing the men together, Malibu and Sisquoc exchanged looks. The looks said: the general is up and about early. He is talking with the assistant provost marshal on the morning that Clarity O'Malley is due to arrive.

Both Indians felt a gravity that had been abstract before, but was very real now.

The general did not notice the arrival of the Mission Indians and they did not linger near the flagpole where he was standing. They went directly to the stables, each man considering what they should—and could—do next.

Away from the stable boy, the men talked while they unsaddled their horses.

"Do you think the general knows where we have been?" Malibu asked in a low voice.

"I have been wondering that," Sisquoc said. He looked over the wall of the stall to the stable door behind him. There was no one but the stable boy. If Guilford were waiting to talk to them, someone would have been watching for their arrival and reported it. The sergeant had been the only one who needed to know their whereabouts. "Rostov would have had no reason to tell the general nor the general to him. The sergeant would not know who Tatham was or why he was here."

"If the general finds out, we must tell him we were at the wedding . . . nothing more," Malibu said.

"Tatham will verify that we were not present," Sisquoc said.

The men went about their work quietly, in thought.

"If the general is helping this detective, then her return to Kentucky is assured," Sisquoc said when they were nearly finished.

"Unless she is tried here," Malibu said. "They can wait for the traveling judge or send her to him," he added ominously, given what they had just seen. "That is the decision of Marshal Landau."

"It is likely the detective will be paid however this ends," Sisquoc said, echoing the fears that Slash himself had expressed.

Malibu moved over to Sisquoc's stall. "What can we do? If she is put in a cell, it will be a firing squad if we attempt to free her."

"We can ride out again to warn her," Sisquoc said. "But if we are seen and stopped—"

"Desertion is not a solution," Malibu decided.

Sisquoc's expression reflected the limited nature of their options. "We cannot do *anything* without putting our own freedom at risk. I would give my life for the O'Malleys, but that does not help the girl. Slash asked us to get him information. That is what we should be doing."

The grim expressions of both men reflected not the risk they mutually faced but their unhappiness at being inside the fort—yet relatively helpless observers to what was likely to occur. But they also knew that if anything were to happen to them, the O'Malleys would have no eyes or help inside the fort.

Together, they finished up and left the stable to report to First Sergeant Rostov and check the duty roster for the day.

Slash was not a patient man.

His mother was fond of telling how, as an infant sharing a cradle with his sister, the baby boy had managed to rock it hard enough to move it across the floor and close to the front door of their small cabin in Texas.

"He could not wait to get out and take on the world," Sarah said.

She was right.

When Sarah was schooling Slash and Gert on reading and writing, he was barely engaged until they got to the silent k in "knife."

"That's 'cause a knife is silent," the seven-year-old had observed.

Gert informed him that that idea was stupid. "The k is also silent in 'knight' and they clang."

She was right too.

Slash spent the entire night, under a candle, going through the few books they owned so that, the next day, he could say:

"Gert, you should be silent, too, if you seek 'knowledge.'"

Finally, Slash was right.

Sarah was impressed by his tenacity. She commended him for the hours he had spent searching to find that word. For his part, Slash never understood why his mother and Gert seemed to feel that hours spent hunting for a particular word was somehow better than spending hours hunting for a particular turkey, but Joe had an answer for that.

"Everybody has things that's just important to them," he told his grandson. "One day, you'll understand."

That happened twice to Slash O'Malley. Once was over a decade past, when he got his first Bowie knife. He did not want to part with it. Not at bedtime, not when he bathed in the river, not in the privy—never. When he was told he could not bring the knife to the dinner table, it was important for him to leave it somewhere he could see it.

The second time he felt that need, stronger than any other, was today.

It was ironic that on the one day he had finally found tranquility, with no desire other than to be alone with his wife, the world had brought these troubles to him.

Arriving at the banks of the Colorado when it was still before dawn, Slash had ridden along the dark river, far enough from the fort so he would not be recognized. There was scant torchlight and he had ridden, as he sometimes did at night, by sound. He could not see the waters of the racing river but he could hear them. He knew when he was getting too close. So did the horse, who somehow felt the activity of the water through the air or the ground—maybe both.

Tired, his mind wandering in the dream-like dark, he found himself wishing that he were an eagle with knives for talons. How easy it would be to fly up to the fort, silently hover until he saw the general, and then attack.

Slash did not know where the sun rose here, exactly, at this time of year. When he found his eyes wanting to shut, he dismounted, splashed them with water, and walked slowly until he saw first light streak the horizon. He sought a spot where he and his horse would be a silhouette that the Mission Indians would recognize and where he could see them come to and, more important, from the main gate. He could also see the Butterfield Trail from here. He would be able to see when Detective Tatham arrived with his wife. While he yearned for just that glimpse of the woman he missed so dearly, he sincerely did not know what he would do.

Be glad you're tired, he told himself. *That limits your options to—how did his ma once describe it? "Your impulse to fix something by breaking something else."*

She was right. Even without the sight of the detective, his palm sweat with the desire to feel the hilt of one of his blades in it. His heart screamed with pain that only Clarity's freedom could calm. His soul screamed with the need to drown this man in his own blood.

He could *fix* the situation by *breaking* Tatham.

That is not what you came to do, he had to remind himself. Even if Tatham had been lying about General Guilford's promise, murdering any man would most assuredly empty the fort in pursuit. That would not help Clarity in any way.

Slash stopped where there was a turn in the river, a place with shade trees and migrating fowl. He hadn't seen ducks and geese in years and was happily distracted by their frolic and disinterest in his presence. Most of the animals he encountered fled. These birds didn't know any better.

Slash tied the horse to a low branch that allowed it to reach the water. Then he sat. He hadn't eaten, and hadn't brought anything but water, so he looked around for a food stand. Several people were setting up tables closer to the pier and he wandered over. He always kept coins in his saddlebag and used one to buy an apple. He sat back down, his back against a boulder. He peeled the apple with his knife, giving the skin to the horse.

It felt dangerously good to hold the blade. Slash had to put it aside for now, and quickly. He wiped it on some shoreline scrub and sheathed it. Eating the apple, he wondered how long he could keep from doing something. *Anything.*

Instead of watching the gate, he turned his eyes westward, watching the Butterfield Trail as the sun set the tawny dirt and pebbles ablaze with ruddy then yellow fire. Each of the now-and-then horses and carts that came around the gentle turn in the road caused his gut to burn with anticipation. He tried to calculate how long it would have taken the party to make the trip. Did they stop to rest or push on through?

He had his answer as the riverbank swelled with activity and the sounds of bugles and the voice of a drill sergeant rose from behind the log walls of the fort.

Then, as light played through the leaves behind him, Slash saw them. He saw *her*. They were too far to be able to see Slash, but Clarity was a bright light, like an angel, riding behind the Devil himself. Slash's father and Reverend Michaels were behind her. Slash hurt for his father.

Jackson was shifting constantly in the saddle, trying to get comfortable.

"Thank you, pa," he said in a voice that was low and like a prayer.

The pastor was slumped, obviously exhausted inside and out.

His eyes quickly snapped back to Clarity, his beloved. After all the time thinking about her, there she was.

So near.

Stay, he cautioned himself, as if he were talking to Blood or Mud. He snuggled back into the shade of the tree. Like a hunter, he examined the terrain. He had not been here for two years. That was when he and his father came to help evaluate new ponies the Cavalry had received from a Confederate roundup right after the war. The animals were lean-looking but battle-tested. More so than many of the recruits who had done their war service out here. Slash remembered, then, briefly meeting and being impressed at shaking the hand of a general.

The fort was not like others he had heard about. There was no surrounding wall. It was a series of structures on the top of a hill. By the time hostiles scaled the slopes, defenders would have had enough time to muster and shoot down at them. A fence ran along both sides of the one road that ran directly along the riverbank. The Colorado was the fort's major supply line.

Fort Yuma was not a station stop, and the stagecoach did not typically enter. Those approaching by land along the Butterfield Trail had direct access to the 'S'-shaped dirt path that rose to the fort. At the top of the road, a small gate made of upright posts was manned by two sentries. The gate was closed only when the cavalry was working out new and secret maneuvers or unloading new cannon. It was the army's policy to assume that today's innocent eyes could be tomorrow's revolutionaries, just as had happened in Mexico.

Slash was able to watch as the four traveled along the front of the fort from west to east, then up the turning path to the fort. They stopped by the gate, some two hundred feet above the Butterfield Trail. Without dismounting, Tatham conferred with one of the sentries. The guard left through a door in the gate, and the four riders remained where they were.

Clarity was looking straight ahead, as unbowed as when he had left her. He could only see her straight, proud back. As the moments passed, she turned casually, almost furtively toward the river. Was she simply watching the activity or was she looking for him?

She stopped suddenly, nearly turned around. She was facing in his direction. His wife might have seen the horse and recognized it. She had ridden her several times. Slash leaned forward slightly, out from under a leafy branch and into the sun. If Clarity saw him, she made no sign of it. Yet he felt the bond—fleeting, but it was there.

And then she looked away, perhaps fearing that his father would follow her gaze. Tatham might also look back and notice. Not that the detective would care. He had the U.S. Cavalry to back him. That would make any man brave.

The sentry returned and, with the other man, opened the gate. He pointed to a spot in the compound, and the four rode in.

Look back, Slash implored inside.

With Jackson and Reverend Michaels between them, Slash tilted his head as they vanished behind the gate—

He caught Clarity's glance, briefly, as she turned. He smiled for the first time in a day. It made his heartbeat rise and his desire for her increase.

Now impatient *and* lovesick, he sat back to await a new development, word from either Sisquoc or Malibu—something that would allow him to help his wife.

And destroy the son-of-a-dog who did this to her.

Chapter 11

It was not an easy night for any of the four men in the party that had headed north from Whip Station.

A wind from the west had come in after sunset and it poured relentlessly across the plains ripping up dust and grasses with it. The storm increased in ferocity as darkness settled across the land. Joe and Álvarez were the only ones who had kerchiefs. Gonzalez hunkered face-down in the back of the wagon, his arms crushed flat at his sides so he could fit. Sanchez turned up his collar and faced away from the wind, his ears stinging as grains pelted them from behind. The gale was too strong for anyone to wear a hat, and sand prickled their scalps like pins.

A lantern hanging on a pole by the driver's side of the buckboard was the first casualty. It rocked back and forth, the flame whooshing out and leaving them in darkness.

The horses were most vulnerable, struggling to turn their sides from the onslaught. As soon as Joe found a pile of rocks that afforded shelter, he motioned for Álvarez to follow him. The two men got the horses sheltered and then all but Gonzalez sat against the boulders, their backs to the windstorm. He remained in the wagon, partly because he was protected, but also to keep the loose contents like water skins and bundled maps from blowing away.

"How long will this last?" Sanchez asked, having to yell over the whistling howl that was all around them.

"No telling! Don't you have dust storms down south?"

"Not on the coast," he answered, spitting out sand that blew back at him in a crosswind.

"These dusters usually blow themselves out after two hours or so!" Joe replied.

"How do the stagecoaches get through?"

"Butterfield put their trail through valleys and hills," Joe said. "Took me years of sitting these things out to map it safely. Still, this time o' year till early next, there's no way to know when they'll hit or how hard! They're temperamental that way!"

The winds actually blew for less than an hour, lasting another twenty minutes or so. They died suddenly, as though someone had dropped a mountain in front of them. The men could actually hear the pattering rain of granules as they fell from a considerable height, for a considerable time.

When that was done, Joe stood and shook off his hat and stomped to knock the dust from his clothes. He knew the dusty smell would remain in his nostrils for hours.

"You still want to keep moving?" he asked.

Gonzalez pushed himself from the floor of the wagon. Dirt flowed from his back through the slats in the wagon floor.

"We do," he said. "There is no point in having gone at all if we arrive too late."

While Sanchez relit the extinguished lantern, Joe went to his horse. He poured a palmful of water from his deer-skin and rubbed his eyes clean. Looking at the wagon, he blinked out the muck.

"I noticed before you're riding heavy," Joe said. "Part of that's the water barrel up front but what in hell have you got weighing you down in the back?"

Gonzalez said, "We tested it before leaving," he said. "It?"

The Mexicans were silent. Joe shook his head with more than a little disgust.

"Gentlemen, there is nobody—not even a stray Injun—out here who I could possibly tell anything to," Joe said. "You trust me with your lives but not your secrets? That just don't make sense to me."

Gonzalez was still looking at Sanchez, who nodded. Jumping down from the wagon, which produced a fresh cloud of dust, the Mexican walked over to Joe.

"What we have in two of those crates are bulletproof vests," Gonzalez told him.

Joe regarded him strangely. "You serious? There's clothes that can stop a shell?"

"They will stop a pistol shot at ten paces, a rifle shot at forty rods," Gonzalez said.

"How can that be?" was Joe's disbelieving response.

Gonzalez got the lantern from the buckboard. He walked over to one of the padlocked crates, stomping off more dirt with each step. He took a key from his pocket, opened and removed the lock, then raised the lid. Joe came over, still blinking out wet dust. He looked inside.

Within the crate were black vests that looked like something out of a picture book of medieval knights. They were very tight blue cotton with a line of brass buttons down the center and a slightly rounded quality. Gonzalez rapped lightly on one. It clanged.

"There are two light steel plates sewn inside," Gonzalez said. "The metal hooks over the shoulder for added support. Under a jacket, it cannot be easily distinguished from a regular vest."

"Unless you walk into a tree," Joe said. "May I?" He extended a hand toward the crate.

"Briefly," Sanchez said. "We must be going."

"It'll take a minute more for the horses to clear their own eyes," Joe informed him.

He ran his hand across the strangely starched fabric, then slipped his fingers under to heft the garment slightly. "About ten pounds?"

"Twelve," Gonzalez said.

"That'd tire you out right fast," Joe said.

"You just named the reason they were not very popular in your Civil War," Sanchez said. "Added to some fifty pounds of gear a soldier had to carry, it would have been exhausting on a long march."

Joe withdrew his hand and stepped back. Gonzalez locked the crate. Sanchez walked over to the buckboard. Álvarez had dusted himself off and joined him.

"You said we ain't going to war," Joe said. "Why do you need these things?"

"Because the person we are pursuing has something that I would not care to approach without it," Gonzalez said. "Something he stole. Something powerful, new, and deadly."

"You talking about a gun or a bomb?"

"Neither, as you imagine them," Gonzalez said. "But that is all I am comfortable saying right now."

There was something unsettling in the Mexican's tone, something like the way a preacher talks when threatening children with hell. It added to Joe's sadness to think that he lived in a world where armor like this and the bullying arrest of a new daughter-in-law were now a part of life, of his life. He found himself wishing for the old days, when it was just him against whatever familiar and even unfamiliar dangers the plains, mountains, and waterways might throw at him.

"But come, Joe, please," Gonzalez said. "We must be on our way."

Joe took a moment to dust off his horse. The animal did not mind the coating, but the rider did not feel like being enveloped in a dirty cloud every time the animal took a step.

The four men continued north beneath a suddenly starlit sky. There was no moon and the terrain was dark, but Joe knew it well. The underlying rock was too tough for gophers, and the hills they were about to cross were sparsely treed.

For at least a few hours, they should have a trouble-free passage.

Gabriel Martinez was in his cabin, changing clothes after getting splashed and slipping several times on the rough seas. Though he was damp, he was encouraged. He had checked the crate and it was dry.

The contents, which he had examined before leaving Europe for the return to America, were as safe as he had been told. That was going to change the face of warfare, among many other things.

The lodgings onboard *The Dundee* were small compared to that of the captain. There was only enough room for a bunk, a small writing desk, and a closet in which his personal trunk sat upright. The only reason he did not store the crate in there was because the box was too wide to have fit through the cabin door in its current, flat position.

Everything was very carefully arranged inside. He did not want the box tilted.

The salt water had begun to dry on his clothes, causing them to stiffen quickly. He couldn't help but wonder if there was a military application in that. Perhaps a new kind of saddle for Marines to carry ashore, lightweight to transport and then drenched at the disembarkation point. Or possibly as a skin for observation balloons to keep the fabric from tearing and leaking.

He smiled. Martinez loved these kinds of thoughts. When this mission was ended and the final triumph of the *Juaristas* secured, he hoped to have time for exactly this kind of work. War was the ultimate challenge for any man, and knowledge like this gave him an edge. That thrilled him, almost as much as weak-minded civilians like Captain Alan Swift offended him. He remembered, over four years ago, during the French bombardment of Vera Cruz, a sergeant commending Martinez for his willingness to take on dangerous tasks back-to-back.

"Time enough for a soldier to rest," the older man had said, "and we call it death."

Martinez embraced that sentiment. He had seen a great deal of death. If it came for him, he did not want his last thought to be that he should have tried harder.

The forty-seven-year-old had been chest-deep in conflict for most of his life. He had joined Santa Anna's army when he was fifteen, as a way to escape poverty in the humid, constantly flooding jungle of Jalapa, Mexico. He not only discovered the world outside his small village, he had fought in the war against the Texians. After that humiliating defeat and the resignation of Santa Anna, the disillusioned young man had joined Benito Juárez as one of the activist *liberals*. Because of his diminutive size,

Martinez was able to squeeze into fortifications, move through tightly corralled horses, spy from hay lofts or on rooftops. Martinez rose in the organization and, just eight years ago, was in charge of carrying out the Law of Nationalization of Ecclesiastical Wealth. Either the Catholic Church handed its properties over to the government, or those structures and its clergy would immediately cease to exist.

The Church and the wealthy and the conservative generals did not like the new ways. When the retired old men took up arms—individually at first, on their own lands—they were hunted down and eliminated. In 1862 the French saw an opportunity to extend their influence to Mexico. Five years of war followed, in which Martinez was sometimes knee-deep in fallen soldiers.

Now it was over, Juárez firmly in power.

That is, except for a few strong, still well-financed pockets of resistance. They were dogged, those men. And these entrenched, old foes must be silenced. To do that required the people of the United States to turn against them. The newspaper editorial writers, the military, the ordinary citizens. Europe as well. Without support for the purchase of arms, without transportation, without manpower provided by American mercenaries, the resistance to Benito Juárez would disperse like sea mist.

Martinez finished dressing. He would get his clothes quickly laundered in the next port. There would be Chinese women at the pier ready for that. For now, his flannel shirt and butternut pants would do. He pulled on his stiff riding boots, his only other footwear, and stood.

Martinez remained still for a very long moment.

Something wasn't right. The boat was moving but it was

listing to port. Martinez remained there for a few seconds more, trying to figure out what was happening—

"Damn you!"

Martinez's cabin was forward the hold, in the crew compartment. He raced around the hammocks, a few of which contained sleeping sailors, to get to the ladder that led to the bow. It was not quite dawn. Lit by the lights that hung from various parts of the deck, the bowsprit was in the process of moving from north to south, dragging its tip across the western sky. The sails were raised and billowing full, swinging the ship around.

The Mexican braced himself on the rail as the schooner turned. His eyes, afire, sought and found the first mate aft, by the wheel. Martinez grabbed the rail so tightly that his fingers paled. He followed it to where the captain's lackey stood beside the broad-shouldered helmsman.

"What is your intention?" Martinez demanded. Though he had the authority, he knew it would be pointless to countermand whatever the mate had been told.

"Captain Swift ordered me to put in at San Diego," Francis Sullivan calmly replied.

"And me?"

"There are no other orders, sir," the first mate answered.

Martinez did not waste further time in discussion. He stalked toward the captain's cabin. He arrived to find the door locked. He pounded it with the side of his fist.

It was a moment before a voice answered, close to the door. "Who is it?" a voice said softly.

The speaker was Russell Puckett, not Captain Swift. Martinez did not bother to engage with him. It would not be long before they reached the port.

"I want the captain to reverse course *immediately*," Martinez said.

"He is unable to do that," Puckett said.

"Why not?"

"He is asleep."

"Open the door! I will *wake* him!"

"In medical matters, you have no authority, Mr. Martinez," Puckett replied. "I have given the captain a powder. He is asleep."

The Mexican checked himself from pounding the door again. That was no solution.

His mouth a straight, resolute line, Martinez spun and purposefully made his way back to his cabin. The only thing that prevented him from persuading the first mate at gunpoint was that Martinez and his co-plotters had worked out the timing of this effort. Given the ocean and land crossing, they had allowed him leeway in case of a delay.

As he walked, he did some quick mental calculations. Had the vessel continued its course, Martinez would have had a week to arrange things in San Francisco. He believed he could still do it in far less time, even with such a great distance left to cross.

He had gold, enough to buy whatever he might need. He took the fat purse from a locked compartment in his trunk, placed it in a pocket of his wet jacket, and put the garment back on. He looked around, thinking about what else he might need. There was a rolled map of the California coast. He folded it and put it in his jacket pocket.

His pistol. He put that in his belt. He spilled the cartridges into his shirt pocket. He would not be able to buy supplies in San Diego but there were other towns along the way.

I will not fail, he told himself as he went to the hold with fire still burning in his eyes and hate in his soul.

The compound that comprised the bulk of Fort Yuma smelled, to Clarity, like compost.

It was a musty mix of men, horses, chipped wood around the flagpole and under the elevated walkways, food smells that clung to the wood, cigar and pipe tobacco—air that clogged her nostrils and weighed oppressively on her skin. It seemed as solid as she imagined the salty ocean to be—a sea she had hoped to finally visit. The uninviting atmosphere made the compound *feel* dangerous. Just inhaling the odor made it seem as if she were riding into a den, not a residence or open-air outpost. It was a lair in which the bears or wolves or bobcats were everywhere in wait. Threading through it was a smell she knew well, that she could pick out on the open plain: the smell of gunpowder, both stored and used.

This is how and why men go to war, she could not help thinking. *They live within the fumes of cannon fire and decay.*

And there was a deadly air about each man she passed. Tatham was a loner, but these men were a feral pack, like wolves. The uniforms they wore were like a common fur— instantly tribal, inescapably dangerous. Unlike a church congregation that builds civility and the higher aspects of a human being, this place encouraged the lower, bestial qualities.

Perhaps that was necessary to make war, but Clarity did not think so. It was necessary to butcher mindlessly. She was a warrior. She used a gun to kill, and she did it quickly, instinctively. But based on a threat, not a more organized form of mob violence.

With every step of the horse, the place caused Clarity's despair to deepen. It took all of her self-control not to turn the horse and bolt. She went so far as to glance back at the door that had been shut. Even so, she could ride out the back, around the outside of the compound, follow the wall that sided the road—

Stop, she told herself.

What she felt was not just about now. It was the same desire to flee that had come over her when Billy Roche tried to drag her with him in his sudden need to escape Murray, Kentucky. Then, as now, it was the same sense of being trapped and desperate.

Please, God, get me out of here, she found herself thinking—and she was not a prayerful woman.

She concentrated on things, not feeling. The man in front of her, whose back she had continued to regard with an imaginary target, blended right in to these surroundings.

She had to look away and turned around again. Dear Jackson was tired and in pain. Behind him, Clarity's eyes met those of her brother. She knew his expressions and she knew that he smelled the taint of this place too. The unhealthiness, the danger. He rode like a sleepwalker, stiffly and by rote.

Clarity realized just then how tightly she was gripping the reins, how taut her legs were around the sides of the hard-breathing animal. She relaxed. And at that moment, coincidentally—or in answer to her prayer?—there was a wisp of hope.

To the right, fussing with hammer and nail on a loose plank on the walk, she saw Malibu and Sisquoc. The Mission Indians had left shortly before the rest of them, yet they did not seem surprised to see Clarity and the other men. She realized that they must have been the reason Slash left in such a hurry. Were they hiding him? Simply observing for him?

Whatever it was, that brief moment of encouragement and raised spirits was abruptly terminated.

The line stopped moving when Detective Tatham did. They were near the towering flagpole, its long, morning shadow cutting across them. A tall man in a smart uniform walked toward them. Clarity wasn't knowledgeable about the emblems of rank and knew only that he was an officer. He looked too young to be a general, too rigid to be in command. He moved to impress someone higher, not to lead.

Tatham dismounted and shook the man's hand.

"Is there only one prisoner?" she heard the newcomer ask.

The question, the word, shot fire through her belly. It also brought Jackson alert.

"Prisoner?" Jackson said. "There is no prisoner here." He rode to Clarity's left side. "Don't do anything," he cautioned.

"I won't be locked up," she whispered back, her fingers once more taut on the reins, her eyes on the back of the compound.

"They will pursue you," Jackson said, leaning close. "Possibly firing. Please. We are here to help."

Jackson made sense. Clarity tried to relax, felt as if she was tumbling helplessly like a shot grouse. To be strong without her gun was something new. She did not like it, did not know if she could do it. Looking for support, she turned back to the Indians and noticed that they were gone. Despair filled that vacant spot in her soul.

Clarity's brother rode to her right side and remained

there. He took her hand in his. Together, the three watched Tatham and the officer talk. Finally, the detective walked over. He stood in front of the reverend's horse and looked at Clarity.

"Would you dismount?"

"Why?" she asked.

Tatham replied with a frankness that bordered on cruelty. "So that Assistant Provost Marshal Landau can spare you the embarrassment of being pulled from the saddle."

So it was to be bullying. Clarity regretted having come instead of listening to her husband. But here, now, Jackson was right.

She turned stiffly to her right. "Brother, would you give me room, please?"

"With great reluctance," he said.

Reverend Michaels reined the horse away several paces. Clarity slowly dismounted. Her hand ached for a weapon. Her heart was slamming hard against her ribs, her head so full of rushing blood she almost fainted.

The newly arrived officer stepped forward. He was wearing a blue hat and did not remove it.

"Will you come with me, Mrs. O'Malley?" he said. It was an order, not a question.

Jackson looked down from his horse. "As soon as you show us this warrant you're supposed to have," he said.

Landau seemed puzzled. He turned to Tatham.

"Put her in the stockade, Provost Marshal," Tatham instructed.

"Warrant first," Jackson warned. He added in a louder voice, "That is what we agreed on. Unless you want to wrestle a young lady to the ground with all these fine soldiers watching, you will keep your word."

Tatham glared at Jackson, then turned and stalked toward the general's headquarters.

Provost Marshal Landau stood there, the very model of a proper officer, looking toward the gate and not at the new arrivals.

Jackson stepped his horse closer. "Provost Marshal, do you know that man?"

Landau looked up and seemed to consider whether he should answer. He took orders from superior officers, not civilians. But as it said in the regulations that he knew so well, he was here to serve the civilian population. As far as he had been told, this man was not a subject of the warrant.

"I have only known him since he arrived," the young man said. He added, "That was three days ago. About this time."

Clarity's riderless horse seemed restless and she grabbed the bridle, patted the horse on the neck.

"Do you know that this is my sister's wedding day," Reverend Michaels said.

"I did not know that," the provost marshal replied. He looked over at the woman. Her open face and fair features moved him. "If it's any consolation, Mrs. O'Malley, I was fighting in Antietam on my fifth anniversary."

"When the war was over, you were able to go home to your wife?" Clarity asked.

"Well, yes, ma'am. I was fortunate."

Clarity smiled sincerely. "I'm glad. That, Mr. Landau, is how our circumstances differ. I believe that this man wishes me to hang." She looked around. "Where do you build the gallows, Mr. Landau?"

The question surprised everyone, including Clarity. She was getting defiant again.

"I—I have not seen one raised in the two years I have been here," he said. "And ma'am, I want you to understand that I am a soldier, not a judge."

"That holds for everyone here, does it not?" Merritt asked.

"It does," Landau confirmed. So saying, the officer turned his rugged face to the ground.

There was a lengthy, awkward silence in which the only local sounds were beyond the courtyard. It was more than breakfast being served in the mess hall. It was as if anyone without business here had retreated. Perhaps they were watching, listening. Clarity could not tell since the sun was now bright, and everything under the eaves was in opaque, black shadow.

There was sudden movement at command headquarters directly ahead. Tatham emerged from the darkness and was walking toward them. In front of him, by several paces, was a short, bearded man. On the shoulders of his blue uniform were the braided epaulets of a general. He also had the impatient demeanor of a man accustomed to being obeyed.

Clarity, Jackson, and Merritt all watched warily as Landau turned to face him. The marshal saluted.

"Provost Marshal Landau, were you instructed to arrest this woman and place her in the stockade?" the general demanded as he approached.

"Yes, sir, by this civil serv—"

"He is operating with my full authority," the general interrupted.

The arresting officer did not move for several moments.

Then he did an about-face and looked directly and with a stony expression at Clarity.

"Come with me," the young officer said, more insistent now.

Jackson moved his horse forward, not quite between the two but nearly so.

"Just a moment," Jackson said.

The general stared up at him as he reached the group. Jackson dismounted and limped toward the officer. The men stood eye-to-eye just feet apart.

"Who are you, giving orders to *my* command?" Guilford said angrily.

"Jackson O'Malley, and I'm this lady's father-in-law," he answered. "We were informed by Detective Tatham that there is a warrant for the arrest of Clarity Michaels, no O'Malley. We demand to see it and read the particulars."

"You make no demands in my fort," General Guilford replied.

"General, our cooperation was secured by the promise that we could see the documentation that brought us all here—"

"Detective Tatham does not make policy for Fort Yuma or its commander," Guilford brusquely informed him. "To read official documents, you will petition my office for a convenient time to visit. At that time, you may also request time to visit the accused, if you so choose."

"Accused of what and by whom?" Reverend Michaels asked. "We are entitled to know the details!"

"Murder, by the State of Kentucky," Tatham answered.

"We have only your say-so!" Jackson said.

"And now you have mine," Guilford replied. "Clarity Michaels O'Malley will be incarcerated until such time as a civil court can be convened. I will make sure you are notified of any particulars." He stepped a little closer to Jackson. "Now, you two gentlemen will either leave or schedule those appointments and then leave."

"This isn't legal," Jackson said. His eyes went from the dark eyes of Guilford to the darker eyes of Tatham. "You were sent to kill her, 'detective,' and you, general, have a vendetta against my family. This is about nothing that is legal."

"Sergeant Bissett!" Guilford yelled.

"Sir!"

One of the gate sentries hurried forward, double time. Upon arriving, he saluted.

"Yes, *sir*!"

"Escort these men from this fort and do not readmit them without my permission," Guilford said.

The sergeant saluted and stood back to give the men room to turn around. "Gentlemen, you heard the general." He regarded Jackson. "Mount up and follow me."

Jackson glared at the general. "You will not get away with this," he vowed.

Guilford's mouth turned up slightly beneath his beard. "You forget yourself, sir," he said. "*I'm* not the one who stands accused of murder."

Jackson looked over at Clarity. She seemed near to crying but refused to give the men the satisfaction. She forced a small smile at Jackson and her brother. Then, leaving her horse, she walked over to Landau who led her toward the rear of the courtyard, to a gate that must open to the stockade.

Guilford and Tatham turned and also left, and two men came running over to take charge of the horses of Clarity and the detective.

Jackson climbed painfully into the saddle. He knew that

Clarity would not look back, but he continued to watch until she was gone behind the gate.

Merritt sat frozen on his horse.

"Reverend, let's go," Jackson said.

"Yes," Merritt said. "I'm sorry."

The two followed the soldier toward the gate. He had one consolation as he left.

The men who had collected the horses were Sisquoc and Malibu.

Chapter 12

It was close to mid-morning before the sun was too hot and Joe and his companions were too exhausted to go on. They were in a shallow valley, well southwest of Oak Grove and the Butterfield Trail. The walls looked like they had been shaken down by some ancient tremor, or several, with boulders large and small piled high against sloping walls.

They were some seventy or eighty miles from the ocean. Yet, now and then, they caught a whiff of the sea. The Mexicans were accustomed to the smell. Joe was not. Farther south, the winds from the Pacific were met and pushed aside by gusts from the desert beyond the inland sea.

The small party was certainly alone. They had not encountered a soul at night, nor seen a campfire, nor did Joe hear any sound that might have been an Indian—or, more likely, his horse. This was dry terrain, without water for miles in either direction. Joe would not have agreed to go this way if they didn't carry the cask, which he checked with some frequency. The cart rattled, and he wanted to be sure the cask was well-secured to the solid side panels of the wagon. It was an old rum barrel, with a spigot and the smell of its former contents. Fortunately, that smell did not carry more than a few feet. No one would come seeking it.

As long as they didn't break a wheel and have to abandon the water, they would make it out of here without drying out.

Once halfway through the valley, Joe situated them against a rock wall with a little shade for them and dry grass for the horses. He unhitched the wagon and had a look around. As the sun rose higher, the shade would shrink. He selected a spot with the largest boulders.

"I suggest you put your hat on your face to ward off flies and try to sleep," Joe said. "That's what I'll be doing."

The three Mexicans concurred, stripping to their bare chests and using their shirts for pillows. Joe removed his boots, flexed his toes to air them, and sat with his back to a rock some ten feet high. He pulled his hat low and remained dressed. He preferred to sweat than be nibbled by insects or be awakened by a small lizard running across his chest. He didn't say anything to the others, however. Either the men would learn or they would be lucky.

Gonzalez learned almost at once.

"Madre de dios!" he cried, swatting at his chest and scraping his back against the rock wall at the same time.

Joe looked over from under his hat. He saw a tiny fence lizard airborne, courtesy the back of Gonzalez's hand. The other Mexicans came alert to see what the fuss was about. Joe remained with his arms crossed and his hat pulled low.

"That was fast," the frontiersman said.

"What do you mean?" Gonzalez said.

"I figgered the four-legged locals might not bother you, on account of the heat. I was wrong."

The Mexican just now noticed how Joe was seated.

Pulling on his shirt, Gonzalez sat and put his back to the stone, wincing where he'd scraped it. Then he had to recover his hat, which had gone flying. Álvarez put on his shirt but lay on his back in the dirt. Sanchez had not been disturbed by the commotion. He was already asleep.

"I do not know whether to admire a man who can live out here or to feel sorry for him being *loco*," Gonzalez said about his partner. He tried to settle in. It took several attempts.

"It's a special life for a curious breed of man," Joe agreed. "If I didn't have a family, I would never have left the frontier." He looked out at the sun-bleached dirt and rocks, at scrub that had barely a trace of green among the brittle hay color. "I love it here, my friend. And I love what it asks of me."

"What?" Gonzalez asked.

"Courage," Joe said. "An ability to blend in, like everything out here does."

"It can kill you with a bite," Gonzalez said. He pointed off where the reptile had flown. "That could as easily have been a rattlesnake or a Gila monster."

"No, sir," Joe said. "If I'd seen one, I'd've let you know."

"Is that why you looked around?"

Joe nodded. "You don't bother them, they generally don't bother you. That lizard you threw off? He probably couldn't tell you from a rock, was just making his passage. Even when they're hungry, they gotta figure you're hungry too—an' could just as easily kill them if they got too close. Depends how crazed they are."

"This place will make you *loco*," Gonzalez said again. Hat back on his head, he settled in again.

"What does happen if we fail to catch this fella?" Joe asked.

The Mexican looked at him. "Does that matter to you, Joe?"

"Not much," Joe admitted. "Though there are some things I don't want to be a party to."

"I will tell you, Joe, though you may find it difficult to believe." He shook his head. "I am not a cruel or violent man."

"I believe that," Joe said.

Gonzalez held up a hand. "Hear me out. We live in a strange world full of modern wonders. They can be beneficial. I give you the railroad and the repeating rifle which bring expansion and peace. But not if you are an Indian or the French. In both cases, they have done harm to you. The good or bad is in people, not in the tools they use."

Joe agreed, though in the hands of someone like Detective Tatham, there was no tool that would not bring destruction and misery.

"I can trust you, *si*?" Gonzalez said. It was less a question than an affirmation.

"Let me tell you something," Joe said. "While you were gone to meet your wagon, my new daughter-in-law was arrested for murder."

Gonzalez stared at the man. "Truly?"

"Truly. It happened right after you left, in fact. My son and grandson went with her to Fort Yuma to try and sort things out. The reason I am here is because I made a commitment to you. My word does not falter."

"Thank you," Gonzalez said. "And may I say that I am sorry to hear this."

"I have faith they'll get it sorted out," Joe said. "But I appreciate the sentiment."

"It is sincere," Gonzalez said with one of his courtly bows.

The Mexican used his hat to fan himself for a moment. It seemed to Joe that he was either considering what he was about to say—or else whether to say anything at all.

"You had some troubles in your life too," Joe said.

"I don't understand," Gonzalez replied.

Joe touched his own face in the same spot where the Mexican had a scar.

"Ah, *si*. A relic of my capture by drunken *Juaristas*," he said. "They said that noblemen were too 'pretty.' That we would think more like *el peon* if we looked more like them."

"I guess it didn't work," Joe said wryly.

"No," Gonzalez smiled. "Anger and revenge never win allies."

"You are not out here because you are angry or looking for vengeance," Joe said.

"No. I am, at heart, one of those people who wishes to do good. I have been forced into this life by those who do not." The Mexican inhaled slowly, exhaled quickly. "We have been informed, through our trusted spies in Spain, that revolutionaries have stolen something from Sweden and plan to use it to advance the *Juarista* cause," the Mexican said. "Something terrible. A weapon. It was on its way to be tested when it was stolen."

"What kind of weapon?" Joe asked.

"It is said to be a very destructive form of blasting powder," Gonzalez told him. "Destructive because it is safe to transport. Safer than any other kind of explosive. It is placed in a small tube about the length of your foot and ignited with a fuse. It is called dynamite."

Joe repeated the word slowly. "Certainly doesn't sound so bad," he said. "A mite's a tiny little chigger."

"It's from a Greek word," Gonzalez said. "Scientists like to do that. But however it sounds, we are informed that just one of these sticks is enough to bring down the side of a mountain."

Joe brushed away a lean, hungry hornet. "Spanish, French, Swedish, Greek—this dynamite sounds like it was bound to end up here, among the other settlers. But tell me, why would a *Juarista* be traveling north from Mexico with something that he would want to use against his enemies in the south? Enemies like yourself, I assume?"

"Yes, I am opposed to the rebels," he said. "We intercepted a written communication between leaders in two *Juarista* villages. We allowed it to continue on its way, with a different messenger. It spoke of a plan to turn your country against those of us in Mexico who seek to depose the *Juaristas*. This dynamite is to be used to destroy the Barbary Coast and make it appear to be the doing of one of our leaders, Felix Maria Zuloaga."

"Destroy," Joe said the word slowly. "That's a big word."

"Joe, they mean to blow it up, every building," Gonzalez said. "It is believed he carries a crate of these tubes, more than enough to destroy structures and start countless fires in the process."

"You plan to stop him," Joe said. "While he has this dynamite stuff that can blow y'all to bits. Those metal jackets you brought—they don't protect all of you."

"We will find a way," Gonzalez assured him.

"I like a confident man," Joe said. "Y'also have to be practical. San Francisco is still a ways off, and you seen the hardships."

"They are more severe than I expected, yes," Gonzalez said. "But I will also tell you this. During the struggle, the *Juaristas* performed miracles of endurance. I personally witnessed one. They moved, by hand, a two-hundred-pound siege gun through a swamp to attack a French fort from its unprotected rear. A party of assassins crossed the Chihuahuan Desert with kegs of black powder to attack the French on May 5, 1862, before the Battle of Puebla."

"These *Juarista*s seem to like their explosives," Joe said.

"They were able to risk just a few men to achieve mass killings and injuries," Gonzalez said. "*And* create fear," he raised a finger in emphasis. "Fear among the troops, who suddenly had more to worry about than gunfire. They were no longer safe behind their stone walls. And fear among the population, who might be forced to turn their homes or foods over to the French. It was better to resist than to be blown up. Now—think of it—with just one man, they may be able to destroy a seaport. The United States has been supplying the rebels with arms for years. Now they might also provide troops to crush the old guard."

"They should be careful what they wish for," Joe suggested. "We got folks in Washington who would like a new southern border, one that dives a little deeper."

"We believe the *Juaristas* think it is better to have developers from the north rather than conquerors from across the sea," Gonzalez said.

"Politics makes me want to ride somewhere else," Joe

said. "What even makes you think you'll even be in time, stopping this guy? Whatever way he's going, he has a galloping head start."

"That has to do with the last part of his plan," the Mexican said. "We believe—we hope—that there is an event he will seek to interrupt."

"Something having to do with Mexico, I'm guessing."

Gonzalez nodded. "Who but one of *my* people, the land owners, the merchants, the old generals—who but our class would seek to disrupt a visit north by Benito Juárez?"

"Your president?" Joe said. "What if they kill him?"

"Even better," Gonzalez replied. He snuggled into the rock and prepared to cover his eyes with his hat. "Then he becomes a martyr. I have learned, these past many years, never to underestimate the derangement of our liberal revolutionaries."

Joe went back to sleep as well. He thought, as he drowsed, that Gonzalez told an interesting story.

He wondered how much of it was true. And how much Gonzalez might not know.

Civilization, power, paper regulations, Joe thought as sleep overtook him and his mind returned to his family's problem. *Yeah . . . you can keep every little bone of it.*

The height of Fort Yuma made it difficult for Slash O'Malley to see what was going on beyond the gates. Shortly after Clarity and the others had arrived, he walked briskly up and down the shore to see if there was a break in the surrounding bungalows, some spot that would allow him to see inside.

There was not, of course. The designers would have

planned it that way so spies would not be able to see very much.

Frustrated, and more eager than cautious, Slash decided to climb the tree. Someone at the fort might see him and wonder what a man was doing there. He didn't care. Fortunately, Slash had stalked prey from treetops since he was a boy. He was able to get up among the higher branches and the canopy of leaves without being seen from below— or, more important, from afar. From there, though they were small, he was able to see over a bungalow rooftop at the four horses and their riders.

Clarity was no longer mounted. There was a man in uniform talking to her.

Then he saw Tatham in the company of what looked like the general. Slash felt heat rise in his spine and set fire to his arms. He was getting good at making that feeling stop, by now. He did so again.

There was talk. Slash didn't know who was saying what to whom, and all that mattered was how it ended. So fast that he lost his breath, Slash suddenly saw his new wife marched away between Tatham and another officer. Then he saw his father and Merritt turn away.

"No!"

Slash's cry rustled his body, which rustled the tree, which scared his horse, tethered below, into neighing.

A few people looked over from outside the food tent, and Slash quickly half-climbed, half-jumped down. He threw himself onto the back of his horse, whirled it round, and galloped toward the eastern side of the Butterfield Trail. That was the part beyond the fort and the road from the river. He would have taken that route, but supplies were already being carted from the river. He did not have the patience to wait for oxen or mules. He also no longer cared who saw him or what they did. His was a mission of fire-red rage, mindless and all-consuming.

Before he reached the portion of the trail that intersected the "S"-turn, Slash found his way blocked by another rider.

It was not a merchant but his father.

"Stop!" Jackson yelled, turning the horse in a full circle, ready to move in case Slash tried to bolt in any direction. The maneuver hurt the older man, since it required pressure from his hips, but the old bronco-buster did it better than anyone when he had to.

Right now, he had to.

Slash saw Merritt Michaels arrive behind him. The young man stopped, though not happily—or with an apparent intent to stay.

"What happened up there?" Slash asked. "I saw them take Clarity away!"

"You stay calm and go back down and I'll tell you what happened," Jackson said.

"Pa, they—"

"Son, you can't do *nothing* but get yourself shot right now! Guilford is behind Tatham one hundred percent."

"I don't care—"

"I *do*, and so will your ma an' Gert an' your *wife*!" Jackson declared.

Mention of the women caused Slash to settle the horse and himself. Already, the two men had kicked up considerable dust and attracted attention from the sentries.

"Go down to the river, I'll follow," Jackson said.

Slash hesitated.

"*Now*, son, or by God I will pull you from that saddle!"

With a growl that added to his agitation, the young man spun the horse back toward the trail and the river beyond.

After nearly a minute the men slowed to a walk and Jackson came up beside his son. Slash just glared ahead as they walked through a field toward the rushing waters. The current did not have the settling effect a creek or river usually had on either man.

"Did you see the warrant?" Slash asked suddenly.

"No," Jackson admitted.

"Jesus," Slash moaned.

"There may be one, but Guilford had it in mind to make us obey on his say-so. Some folks is like that."

"I told grandpa from the start we never should have trusted Tatham," Slash said, practically spitting the name. "That bastard is a detective like I'm an Apache."

"He may well be a bounty hunter or a hired gun or the Lord knows what," Jackson agreed. "But boy—the O'Malleys have always respected the law and we did right to try and do so here. I do not regret that."

"Pa, this is not the time to remind me about our family ways," Slash said.

"A time like this is when you need it most!" Jackson snapped back. "Now if you calm down and listen, I will tell you where we are. But you have to *stay* calm. 'Cause there's a lot here you ain't gonna want to hear."

Again, the young man forced himself to relax. But he couldn't look at his father, who was beside him now. He just couldn't.

"First," Jackson said, "there was no discussing this matter with the general. Merritt will back me up. Guilford intends to hold her till a trial can be arranged."

Slash kept his mouth shut so his strangled cry would not escape.

"Maybe that's true, maybe it's not," Jackson said. "He may let Tatham take her just to cross us up. Merritt saw the padre as we were leaving—he turned aside so they could speak. The parson said he will see if he can get permission for Merritt—just Merritt—to come back in so they can talk about it."

"I came down just to tell you I have heard of this parson and he seems a good man," Merritt said. "If he can help, he will. I also wanted to offer you any help you might need."

"That—that's kind of you, brother. Thank you."

Merritt found a smile. "I'm going back up to see if I can talk to him now."

The parson turned and, with patience befitting a man of his profession, began the ride back toward the crowded path. Slash and Jackson watched him turn the corner and then Jackson regarded his son.

"We also saw Malibu and Sisquoc," he said. "They was the ones who took charge o' Clarity's horse."

That caused the boy to perk.

"They're still for us, boy," Jackson said. "That is why the O'Malley name matters. I assume you got to talk to them before they got back?"

"I did."

"What'd they say?"

"They'll help," Slash said. "They will figure out some way, I know it."

"Then we got allies," Jackson said, trying to sound hopeful. "I agree with you, son. This whole affair is rigged like a Conestoga wagon and—what I wanted to tell you first off—is we can't let Clarity stay there. We just have to figure out what to do and when. Maybe Merritt can find out more."

"I hope that's the case," Slash said, "because I made a promise to myself, pa, and I mean to keep it. My wife will not be spending the night in a jail cell."

Chapter 13

Gert was awakened by the sound of horses.

There were no metallic pings or the distinctive squeak of leather. The smell was unfamiliar, not the clinging smell of hay but the lighter smell of open-field grass.

The horses were not their own.

It was just before dawn and the young woman's window looked north. There was no light yet to see anything, though she knew the time from the distinctive cries of the morning birds.

The young woman's room was a small, narrow nook in the back of the station. It was situated just before the root cellar. Gert was the one who had populated it with vegetables and Indian herbs, and she was the only one who enjoyed the aroma. She said it helped her relax.

But it had been difficult for her to get to sleep this night, thinking about her brother and father off to the east and her grandfather alone up north on a long journey. Joe was a vital man, as tough as the cowhide and buckskins he wore. But he was also seventy—and no doubt as distracted as she was.

The situation with Clarity ate at her as she lay there until well after midnight, wondering if the O'Malleys, in a show of unity, had done the wrong thing by letting that stranger take her. Slash was impetuous but sometimes, *just sometimes,* he was right. Maybe Slash and Clarity should have ridden off while the rest of them figured this out.

Poor Slash, she had thought over and over. Guilty or not, Clarity had brought this on herself. Slash hadn't done anything but fall in love.

The young woman had finally found her way asleep. She was dreaming about something that immediately slipped away when several unmistakable *clops* and exhales of breath caused her to wake.

Her heart drumming, Gert pulled on a robe and picked up the hatchet that hung from the corner of the headboard. It was supposed to bring her ancient dreams, having been wielded by generations of Serrano Indians. That was not the only reason she kept it there. Unlike those in the main room, this was not for decoration. Joe had once told B.W. that whether a mountain lion or mountain man appeared at the open window, she would be ready for them.

Gert made her way around a small featherbed that had been set up for Clarity.

The door to her room was open, there being no one but her mother here. Walking silently in her bare feet, trying not to make the floorboards creak, she went into the hallway. Her mother was just coming to the door of the bedroom she shared with Jackson. The older woman was holding a carbine. Sarah wasn't a very good shot but, hopefully, whoever was outside would not know it.

The women could not see each other's fear in the dark but they could feel it. They did not speak. There was no need. Gert led the way. Even when the O'Malley men were here, Sarah was unsettled by confrontations, especially in the night. Gert was less distracted by the fear scudding up and down her spine. She had grown up with Slash. She had the backbone to stand up to trouble.

Gert did not yet know how many horses there were and whether there were riders on each. She only knew that they had to have come in through the front entrance. They could be travelers—folks did pass through, maybe once every week or two—but then why were they still mounted? She had been listening for footsteps and had heard none. If the newcomers wanted to know who was here, someone would be stalking around, looking in windows, listening for breathing or snoring.

And they wouldn't have ridden in with their horses. They would have left them outside the stone wall.

She had the frightening thought that it could be Slash or her father, or Joe, wounded and unable to dismount. But then, they would have called out or made some kind of sound.

Gert felt a brief, girlish chill as she recalled a story her grandpa once told her about a Hessian soldier who had lost his head to a cannonball during the War for Independence and rode around looking for it. She wondered if it might be spirit animals outside. She had spent enough time in Indian camps to have heard and seen things that were not entirely natural.

In which case the hatchet and rifle won't do us any good, she thought with a shiver. *And if they were animal or heathen spirits, Bible verse probably wouldn't be much help either.*

The nineteen-year-old did not know which she preferred: something living or something undead.

Suddenly, she held her hand back to stop her mother. She bent a little to sniff ahead. Her mother could hear, if not see, what she was doing. Sarah smelled as well. She didn't know what her daughter had picked up. All she could smell were the ashen remains in the hearth.

Gert knew that her mother had not been around enough campfires to know the clinging smell of smoke from wood and peat. Apart from cabins like this one, there was only one place she had encountered that smell around here.

No longer fearful, Gert straightened and strode into the main room of the station and lit a lantern.

"Gert!" her mother hissed with open alarm.

"It's all right," the younger woman replied.

Gert walked to the front door, lit the lantern hanging just inside, pulled back the dead bolt, and held the light high as she opened the door.

Three Indians were at the front of the station. She did not know them by name but she recognized the one in the middle, and slightly ahead, from her visits to the Apache camp.

"You Joe women," the brave in the middle said. He pointed to Gert. "I see you with squaws and Mangas."

"Yes," Gert told him. "I am honored to know your medicine man."

Sarah walked up behind Gert. "Is something wrong?" she asked the Indian, her voice cracking with concern.

"I Baishan," the Indian said. "Meet family leaving for fort, hear that Joe go. Apache chief know young one," he pointed at Gert. "He tell us come to watch over women. Hunt if need."

Gert nearly wept with surprise—and gratitude.

"But you don't know anything about Jackson or Slash—O'Malley men?" Gert pressed.

"No. Woman with them very strong, even no gun," he said.

Sarah gripped her arm with her own profound relief.

"Thank you," Gert said, and touched the side of the hatchet to her heart. "Thank you for my mother and myself, and for Joe."

"Joe and little woman," Baishan said. "They are brother and sister to Baishan."

Gert did not know what her grandfather would think to hear that, but it was a great honor and she earnestly hoped he would be flattered. She was.

"Baishan," Gert said. "You say that the woman, Clarity, is strong. What did she do?"

The Apaches all laughed. Baishan replied, "She call one man belly of snake before they ride through village."

That comment, that strength of hers, finally caused tears to spill from the corner of Gert's eyes—and those of her mother as well. They both thanked Baishan. He may not have understood why, but he had given them hope.

Baishan said something to the others in his tongue. Each horseman turned and rode in a different direction. Gert saw that they would be taking up positions that they had undoubtedly scouted previously. Each approach would be watched. The women would be protected.

Gert turned back into the station, her mother stepping back and exhaling loudly. Gert replaced the lantern, and Sarah set the carbine against the table.

"Thank God," Sarah said.

"Go back to sleep," Gert told her. "You have time before sun-up."

"I could never sleep now," Sarah said. "It will take that long for my heart to stop fluttering."

Gert felt the same. She went over and touched her mother's cheek. "I've seen those men at the settlement but never met them. This is more significant than you know."

"How is that?"

"The Apache do not regard White women with much respect," she said. "They think we are soft."

"I suppose, compared to their women, we are."

"For Clarity to have impressed them—that is something," Gert said. "Something very unique."

Gert went back to her room. She washed her face in the basin, dressed, then went back to the main room. The first hints of day were just beginning to light the horizon, and then the lowlands. She looked out the windows that faced north, east, and south.

She saw no sign of the three braves.

Maybe they are as much spirit as flesh after all, she thought.

She went about her morning chores, which began with milking their only cow who lived in the stable. Her mother, today, would be checking their chickens for eggs.

As the women went quietly about their work, they felt pride and gratitude that the O'Malleys—men and women both—had earned the respect and communal support of these people and so many others around them. Whatever way things worked out, the combined efforts Leonard Tatham—whoever he really was—and General Guilford could not take that from them.

* * *

Joe woke to a sound that was soft and fluttery.

He was still half-asleep and wasn't sure, at first, if a spider or a trickle of sweat had gotten into his ear, or if he was hearing something else. Maybe it was sandstone pebbles dislodged by a bird and sliding down the face of the rock wall. Maybe it *was* a bird.

He tried to go back to sleep but the sound didn't stop. Now that he was a little more alert, it didn't sound like it was on him or even nearby.

Grumpily, he raised his hat, immediately covering his eyes with the flat of his hand. Slowly, he opened his fingers and looked into the unforgiving daylight. His gaze was immediately drawn to a wavy ribbon of sunlight where it should not have been—

Joe swore and jumped to his feet. Squinting but not taking his eyes from the rippling glow, he ran barefoot across the hot stones. He was headed toward the wagon, watching, on the near side, as their water spilled through the bottom, sparkling as it drained from the open spigot in the barrel.

Joe threw himself across the sideboard and slammed the nozzle shut with his palm. The cask shook in a way it should not have. The container was more than two-thirds empty, most of it coating the rocks and wheels. Joe examined the ladle. It was dry, unused. He tossed it aside, found a blanket in the back, and pulled it out. He threw it below the cart to soak up what water he could.

"Joe?" Gonzalez said in a daze. "Is everything all right?"

"For someone it is," Joe answered bitterly.

He looked around quickly, squinting up and down the surrounding stone walls, out both ends of the valley, saw no one. Then he turned angrily toward the Mexicans, all of whom were now awake and staring. His bare feet were burning on the stones, and he walked back to pull on his boots.

"Like I thought, no one's out there," Joe said. "One of you cost us over half of our reserve water," he added accusingly.

"Intentionally?" Sanchez said. "Are you suggesting sabotage?"

"Yeah, and I'm also suggesting that we get out of here right now," he said.

"The sun's moved about two hours higher in the sky. There's no sense waiting seven, eight hours till dark. Not with a few water skins and a mostly empty barrel." He stood and regarded the men. "I just told you to get up. We have to get to one of the freshwater creeks which toddle off the Santa Ana River, and those are about a day and a half due west."

The Mexicans started to move.

"What makes you so sure it was one of us?" Gonzalez asked.

"Because this wasn't meant to kill us," Joe announced. "It was intended to stop us from going forward."

"But sabotage?" Gonzalez said. "Maybe—maybe someone forgot to close it?"

"The ladle was dry," Joe said.

"The heat, the sun—"

"Ladle was in the shade of the barrel," Joe said dubiously. "And when I first said it, why didn't one of you *say* you had a drink when you saw what happened?"

"I—I was afraid," Álvarez spoke up suddenly.

The other men stared at him. Joe walked toward the frightened, cowering driver.

"You went for water?" Joe asked.

"*Si.*"

"And forgot to close the spigot?"

"It m-must be. I—I was not so awake."

"Not awake enough to hear the water splashing onto the ground?"

"I think I was not."

Sanchez shook his head. "Joe, we have known Álvarez many years! He is committed to our cause."

"Álvarez," Joe said. "You were the one procured this cistern, right?"

"*Si.*"

"Why didn't you get a barrel with a flip-top?" he asked. "That's how they mostly come."

"It came with the wagon, from the owner of the *cantina* who sold it to me," Álvarez said. "I had no choice!"

"I believe him," Gonzalez affirmed.

Joe did not know whether to trust the man or not.

"No matter," Joe said. "We have to go back or we turn west to find water."

"We can't go back," Sanchez said. "That would put us three or four days behind schedule."

"Like I said, then, we gotta move out now," Joe told him.

The three Mexicans looked from one to the other, as if someone might come up with an alternate suggestion. No one did.

In disgust, Joe walked back to the wagon to reclaim the water that was soaking into the blanket. He folded the fabric then held the ends with both hands and a slight bend in the middle. He squeezed the ends so that what had been collected pooled in the center. Then he held it out to his horse so the animal could lick it up.

He repeated the process, squeezing until there was nothing left. There would not be enough to give to the other horse. They would have to use their ladle to give the old pinto some of what was left in his cistern. The rest they would have to save for themselves.

Joe tossed the blanket in the wagon. It landed atop a crate with a splat and he came back into the shade.

"We'll have to drink from whatever's in our canteens," Joe said. "The rest is for the horses." He looked again at Álvarez. "Let me have your supplies."

The driver didn't move. He looked like a rock, still and ivory in the shadow.

"I asked you for the canteen," Joe repeated.

"He had it in the buckboard," Sanchez said.

Joe walked over. It was not there. He came back and stood over Álvarez.

"Where is it?" Joe demanded.

Both men moved at once, the Mexican to get up and away and Joe to stop him. The frontiersman had expected the man to run for Joe's own horse. He was not mistaken and caught Álvarez around the waist from behind. Both men fell forward, Joe atop his quarry. The hard earth tore at the Mexican's flesh, spotting the ground around him with red.

Gonzalez and Sanchez ran toward the men. Though injured, Álvarez tried to claw away, dislodging smaller rocks as his fingers sought larger ones. Gonzalez grabbed the man's arms from behind and hauled him up as Sanchez came around front. Joe backed away.

This was not his struggle any longer.

While Gonzalez tightened his hold on the man's arms, Sanchez slapped him hard and yelled at him in Spanish.

Joe knew a few words of their lingo, but the Mexican's tone alone expressed his anger and concern. Sanchez wanted to know why their ally of so many years and countless engagements had done this.

The driver refused to say anything. Sanchez smacked him again, then with a backhand. Gonzalez had to grip him tightly to keep him from dropping.

"Talk!" Sanchez ordered.

"Forgive me," Álvarez finally muttered.

Sanchez hit him again, this time from rage, not coercion. "It was Maria, wasn't it?" he demanded angrily.

Álvarez said nothing. His bleeding cheek was struck again, hard. Gonzalez struggled to keep him upright.

"Talk to me!" Sanchez screamed.

Álvarez raised his lined, bloody, tired face. "Someone . . . someone heard us talking, at night . . . about the wagon."

"So? You needed a wagon!" Sanchez yelled.

"Maria . . . was afraid. She did not want me going to Vallicita . . . alone."

"So she did what?" Sanchez asked.

"She . . . made sure no harm would come to me."

"By engaging with the *Juaristas*?" Sanchez said.

Álvarez did not answer.

Sanchez threw up a hand and turned away angrily. Gonzalez did not drop his captive but lowered him to his knees and then to the ground. Álvarez fell forward, sobbing. Gonzalez walked over to his partner. Sanchez was standing with his shoulders back and his fists tightly balled.

"Joe is right," Gonzalez said. "We must leave."

"We have to find out what else he knows," Sanchez said.

"Yes, but not now," Gonzalez replied. "He is not going anywhere. We can see to that."

"There may be dangers ahead," Sanchez said.

"I don't think so," Gonzalez replied. "He clearly thought we would turn back."

There was a pause as the two Mexicans considered their next step. Joe had more immediate concerns.

"Gentlemen, every minute we stand here brings us closer to dying from thirst," Joe said. "That's a very real possibility. And every breath you take through your mouth dries your throat. I suggest we tie him in the wagon and move out. I agree with Sanchez. Y'all can settle this later."

"Joe, are you sure it would not be best to wait for sundown?" Gonzalez asked.

"The horses'll go through most of the barrel by then," Joe said. "Better to get as far as we can while we can. We may get lucky and find a pool along the way." He shook his head. "Though . . ."

"You doubt it," Sanchez said.

"Yeah," Joe agreed. "It is not livable, the place we're going. But either we go that way or we turn back." He regarded the men in turn. "Which is it? Which is more important to you two?"

"It's not just the mission," Sanchez said. "It is—a man does not turn back from duty. Not if he wishes to remain a man."

Gonzalez nodded in accord.

"Then we go," Joe said. "But I want it understood by the two of you that you gotta do what I tell him. There's a dispute, I win. I don't intend to die out here."

"It is really that bad?" Gonzalez said.

"No," Joe said. "It's worse, 'cause it's not yet winter *and* it's daytime in a desert. We agreed?"

The men nodded.

"Should we lighten the wagon?" Gonzalez asked. "For the horse?"

"Not unless you want to lose your bulletproof vests, which is the big weight," Joe told him.

The men both shook their heads.

They tore off Álvarez's shirt and used it to bind his arms behind him, after first ripping off a sleeve to tie his ankles together. Álvarez continued to whimper, though he did not ask for forgiveness. It was more like he was ashamed at having been caught, as if he had told someone, maybe his wife, that he would not be *good* at betraying his comrades.

His face was left to bleed and he was flung into the back like a canvas sack of flour. Flies came after him at once. Joe went back to the side of the wagon and wrung a few stubborn drops of water from the blanket. He shook these onto the man's face and used the fabric to wipe away the blood.

"Gracias," the man sobbed. *"Gracias."*

"You may be a spineless man, but yer still a man," Joe said as he tossed the blanket beside him. Only a few determined flies returned, most of them to the bloodstained blanket.

"I would breathe through my nose and stop crying," Joe added. "You need all yer tears and spit on the inside, not out."

While Sanchez climbed into the driver's seat and Gonzalez sat beside him, Joe took the ladle, tilted some of the barrel water in it, and fed it to the wagon horse. Then he gave a little more to his own. They would need more than that, but it would get them going.

A very short time later they were underway, perspiring away precious water and sticking to the shadow beside the valley wall. When that was ended, there was nothing but blazing plain. Each man adjusted his hat, mouthed a prayer, and prayed as much for the horses as for themselves.

Chapter 14

The busy harbor at San Diego served not just the growing maritime city but several towns to the north and as far east as the Temecula Valley. The number of small warehouses, businesses, and wagon transport concerns had exploded in the seventeen years since California became a state in 1850. The dredging of the harbor at San Diego had added considerably to the number and size of large ships that could weigh anchor there. Goods ranging from lumber going out to cotton coming in, from wine to oranges bound for the Far East and Canada. All found precious space on the ships that sailed here from around the world.

The population of the harbor consisted of as many seamen as it did local workers. Most of the sailors were from the anchored ships, though many were also looking to ship out. Among those, a portion were criminals hoping to escape the law, and a significant number of them were both Union and Confederate soldiers who were desperate for work. A third group, most in the shadows, were purveyors of drink and conjugal comforts. The sin peddlers made more money than the other two groups combined.

Only the foreman of the local stevedores made nearly as much. Most of their income did not come from the harbor companies but from bribes, which was the only way ships with perishable items got to load or unload in a timely way.

It was a tight community, abiding by its own rules and broaching no interference from state or federal authorities. They, too, made money. The agents stood out by their fine clothes and carriages as they came, collected documents and bank notes, and departed—many also with bribes as they left behind papers and passports with the proper stamps, signatures, and seals.

The wharves themselves were sturdy if well-worn, like many of the men who manned them. Outside the natural harbor, the Pacific was unkind to its shores. Cliffs and sections thereof literally fell into the sea with regularity, undermined by waves that hit with the ferocity of great, relentless fists. What the water failed to destroy, the wind or earth tremors or rains managed to pull down. Here, however, the structures and the people managed to endure.

One of those sturdiest of people was Harbormaster Rog York. He had seen a great deal in his half-century of life. Little was ever new along this coast, along any coast. Nothing that happened ashore in the port surprised him.

York was from Boston, where his father got wanderlust and dragged the family west, perishing along the way. York routinely went to the harbor in Texas to steal food for his mother and younger sister—and one day he stayed. Not quite ten years old, York had apprenticed in Galveston, where the weather was worse than in Boston or California. The territory was still Mexican then, just as California had been Spanish when he first came to the West Coast.

York thought that he had seen it all. Then he experienced

three unexpected events that began in San Diego before the day had even fully dawned.

The Dundee was not expected, that was the first surprise. She and her captain were well-liked in San Diego, and also by the harbormaster. Swift was not just York's poker buddy, their faces looked enough alike to be kin. Swift was convinced that their lines must have intersected somewhere in the old country, but York believed that his own people had originated farther south, in London.

"Besides," York had more than once observed, "we are not built alike. You have the porpoise-like body of a sailor and I have the bearish build of a lubber."

To Swift, that was simply a matter of their livelihood. But York had been born big. That was what made him employable on the docks.

Still, it was fun to talk with the jovial Swift whenever he was in port. He was the only one who was not required to pay a "duty tariff," as the stevedores called it. He was unloaded first and fast and damage-free as a courtesy to York.

Having walked to his office from his slightly inland home, the rotund York had just pulled on his tight-fitting blue jacket to begin the day. That was when he spotted the schooner from his second-floor window overlooking the bay. It was still dark due to the overcast skies and the mountains to the east that delayed the dawn. But the lanterns and streetlights illuminated the name painted in red on the vessel's white hull. The harbormaster tried to see what was amiss.

They would not have turned back if all were well, he thought with concern.

The masts and sails had looked all right. Perhaps they had been breached by the squall that blew through earlier.

No, York thought. *She's not listing at all.*

Nor would they have come back for illness. Doc Puckett was a bad poker player but a good physician. York appreciated him on both accounts.

The harbormaster grabbed his spyglass and hurried down the stairs. The thought crossed his mind that Swift's ship may have been struck by pirates, in which case he would have to send a messenger to the U.S. Navy vessel *Manhattan* at anchor off San Luis Rey. The sloop of war was charged with protecting these waters from buccaneers. They patrolled daily, and he only had to send them out once, for gun runners in a rowboat. He knew by the waterline they had been traveling heavy, and what they had been heavy with. He grabbed the weapons hidden in cotton bales while the navy grabbed the men.

Because of his size, York was not suited to the narrow corridors of these structures or the narrow, winding streets. But he was only a block from the main thoroughfare, and he made his way through it with purpose that broached no interference. The harbormaster emerged in the early morning when seamen were just hauling themselves back to their vessels from bars or cheap apartments that rented by the hour. Both his imposing girth and his uniform with its big, shiny brass buttons announced his coming and caused guilty men and women to duck into the shadows. Those who were too inebriated to move swiftly were ordered, "Move!" with a bark that drew immediate, involuntary compliance.

York cleared a shoreline row of closely spaced shacks and sheds to reach a clearing where he had a full view of the harbor. Much closer to *The Dundee* now, he saw what seemed to be wisps of smoke pluming above a hatch—but that could be morning mist on the unseen port side of the ship, he wasn't sure. That was when he received his second surprise. Though it was dark, a blob of movement at the stern seemed to indicate that the rowboat hanging from a pair of winches just below the mizzen course had been swiftly lowered. Dropped, it almost seemed from the rapid descent of what was either the boat . . . or possibly a body being thrown overboard. York couldn't be sure because the hull blocked most of his view. As the vessel continued to sail forward, he raised his spyglass and tried to make out whatever may have fallen.

It was indeed a rowboat, moving away from *The Dundee* to the north, though he could see nothing of its passenger. It was just a dark, pyramid-like shape.

The harbormaster watched for a minute as the small craft moved farther from the larger one. That was when he was jolted by a third surprise.

The side of the large schooner, directly amidships, above and below the water line, exploded.

Gabriel Martinez did not stop to watch the result of his handiwork. He was too busy rowing, hard and fast. It had taken quick, precise movement for him to do everything that needed to be done. The first was to remove a single stick of dynamite from the crate and distribute the rest of the deadly but not entirely fragile sticks among several canvas bags. Second was to slice off a thick piece of sail used to cut patches for repairs. Third, he had to throw the lantern he had lit against the far wall of the hold, where kerosene and other supplies were kept. Then he had to use the lantern matches to set a long fuse on the single stick and hurry aft. He had made sure, first, to place a spare pulley along the burning strand.

Martinez knew that no one would bother him when he lowered the rowboat. They would be too busy fighting the fire he had ignited against the forward wall of the hold. The pulley and then the smoke would obscure the lit fuse. None of the frantic crew would see, hear, or smell the lighted fuse.

He had put the sacks of dynamite into the boat before lowering it to the sea. Then he climbed down the poop ladder to board.

The fuse would burn for three minutes. He had used all of that time by the time he started rowing. He did not know which side of the hull—possibly both sides—would open up as a result of the blast. His only goal was to put distance between himself and *The Dundee*.

That he had done.

Once Captain Swift had told the first mate to change course, their fate was assured. There was no way Martinez could avoid an inquiry. Not just about the cargo but about the attack on the captain. He could not afford to be arrested, questioned, and exposed. The delay would be trouble enough, though he would find a way to get where he needed to go—and in time.

The Mexican was sitting with four bags containing eleven sticks of dynamite. They were stacked on the folded bundle of sailcloth to raise them from any water that might wash into the boat. Concentrating entirely on rowing, on looking behind him to navigate to safe haven on the shore, Martinez was actually startled by the explosion. It was also a revelation: until now, he had no first-hand knowledge of how powerful the dynamite was. All he had was the testimony of the Spaniard who had witnessed a test, who had told them about the train that would be carrying the dynamite.

"The inventor, Mr. Alfred Nobel, maintains that the power of the explosion will increase in an enclosed place, where there is no way for the force to dissipate—except by knocking things down," the spy had instructed. "The smaller the place, like a cellar or a cave, the more destructive the blast is likely to be."

The hold of *The Dundee* was not only small, it was underwater. Martinez suspected the explosion would find more resistance in the sea than in the air. It would stay inside, pushing harder against and splintering the wooden hull.

And so it did. Above the surface, a red cannon-like blast shot through the boards of the hull, pulverizing them. Simultaneously, below the surface, a yellow light pushed through the wood without ripping the material to pieces. They snapped outward, releasing the explosion— then just hovered there in the water, like stiffened seaweed caught in the momentary glow. Then they broke away, floating to the surface as driftwood. The fallen shreds of wood immediately mixed with the water to form a pulpy scum. He could see it in the light of the burning ship as it drifted after him, carried by the waves.

The sound itself was equally dynamic. A pounding roar burst from the top, but died quickly. A longer, deeper rolling thunder growled beneath the sea but stayed there. It, too, perished, supplanted by the sound of madly flooding waters. The only sounds after that were loudly creaking and groaning structural material . . . and shouting sailors, some of them having been thrown into the sea and crying for help.

But everyone who could help would either be dead, below deck, or in the water themselves.

The impact on the vessel was instantly devastating. The masts and sails shook violently, some of the spars cracking and tumbling in delayed response. A few broke when the vessel rocked from side to side immediately after the blast, as the hull unevenly took on water. It dipped toward the stern as water flooded in that direction. The aft section cracked audibly as it struck subsea rocks it would not otherwise have been near.

In the glow of flames burning below and now above the deck, Martinez finally saw a few sailors run from below. They ran around, looking for life preservers and anything else that would float—not for their fellows but for themselves. Whether Swift had ordered it or not, the ship was being abandoned.

With deep satisfaction, the Mexican turned his attention to the shore. At least now it was lit by the burning ship. A final gift from a fatally reluctant captain.

If only you had obeyed the orders you were given, Martinez thought angrily.

The coast was liberally studded with off-shore rocks large and small. The current carried him in. Most of what Martinez had to do was avoid being dashed against them. The closer he got, the more he used the two oars to intercept and push off rather than row. He had to place the oars precisely to keep from slipping off, but within just a few minutes he was in water shallow enough for him to go ashore. He cradled the four sacks, still within the canvas sheet. The thick bit of sailcloth absorbed the splashes of water. He wanted to get away from the rowboat as quickly as possible. He would not even waste time trying to sink it, since parts of the boat—even if it were just the oars—

would be carried off by the current and remain visible whatever he did.

Carrying his precious cargo ashore, Martinez discarded the sail canvas when he reached the beach. He set the sacks on dry land then went back and collected one of the oars. He attached two sacks on either side. It would be easier to carry them across his shoulder rather than in a big bundle as he had planned.

However, there was one difference between the man who had left *The Dundee* and the man who had come ashore. He had seen what one stick could do. He was impressed and humbled. And his mind was now abuzz with the possibility of what he might do with what remained of the dozen.

He began to walk inland, briskly, along the scrubby sand-and-rock coastline. The light and sounds of the ship receded as the sun rose.

It hadn't been a dignified exit, he reflected, but at least it had been a quick and efficient departure. Now, he had to work. That did not frighten him.

As with the small cabin, Martinez was not accustomed to luxury. Not since he was an orphan boy in San Pablo Guelatao in the state of Oaxaca. He knew what it was like to be very poor, to sit at the roadside and beg for coins or food scraps from the nobles who came by on horseback or in carriages. The soldiers he met back then were kinder, happy to throw the thin boy *something*. Martinez had seen enough of the wealthy to study how they carried themselves, how they spoke. He learned to impersonate them so that when he stole his first fine set of clothes he could get a meal or a drink without paying first—or at all, if he were fast enough or clever enough to slip away.

When he was older, he joined the *liberals* and worked

as a spy, infiltrating the finest parties and dinners simply because he looked like he belonged. That was how he persuaded the agent of the Scotsmen who owned the ship to give him the control he wanted. He had money. And he had a title. However discredited the wealthy might be in Mexico, they held sway among Americans who had no politics, only a hunger for profit.

Martinez stopped and made some adjustments with the sacks. This was due to the added weight on his left side because of the dynamite. The better balance required more muscle on the opposite side, but it would allow him to walk quickly. Whenever his hands or arms tired, he slowed, let the oar rest on his shoulder, shook it out, and continued inland. He knew that he dared not go to San Pedro. At this time of the day, when everyone was just waking, the return of *The Dundee* would draw a crowd. He, with his parcel and damp clothes, would stand out.

Santa Barbara was too far to walk, and would take too much time to reach. He knew the coastline from maps. Buena Ventura was nearer, and there, he would be able to purchase a horse and cart.

Martinez headed northeast, the gold jingling in its pouch with every step. As the smoke-and-cloud-grayed countryside spread out before him, the man's step grew stronger rather than weaker as his iron determination rose with the sun.

Witnessing the fires and the failing integrity of the ship, Rog York did not stand lead-footed on the street. He was already in motion before he knew exactly what he was dealing with.

"Get lines and life jackets!" he cried. "Lines and life jackets!"

He hadn't addressed anyone in particular, but those who heard him, who knew him, would also know what to do. The cork vests were kept in many establishments along the shore to rent to fishermen or swimmers who wanted to ply the choppy coastline. Some, attached to lines, would be thrown into the water to help anyone who might have jumped from the stricken ship. Others would be worn by rescuers to save anyone who might have been thrown unconscious from *The Dundee*.

He repeated the call-to-arms as he ran, his voice booming over the shouts and wails of those who had come out to see what had happened.

"Boats!" he shouted when he saw Anna Lewn on her back patio.

Anna was a gray-haired, sixty-one-year-old Civil War widow who rented rowboats and rafts to treasure hunters, gold seekers, and marine scientists who wanted to explore the coastal seas.

"That's why my flapjacks are getting cold!!" she shouted over her shoulder as she ran to the floorless shed built on coastal rocks.

Anna always had time for a backtalk last word. Nothing fazed the woman. She physically grabbed two young men by the arms as she ran, impressing them into service.

The entire harbor was mobilized, people moving quickly and efficiently. They did so even as the spectacle of the sinking, crumbling ship struck at the heart of each of them.

Upon reaching the shore, York found people boarding anything that could float. They were forming chains of boats, planks, even a broken piece of mast. Rope was slung between them so the crew of *The Dundee* could swim to shore or else be pulled from the water and carried, if they were injured.

Seven men were swiftly pulled from the cold, sloshing water with minor injuries. They had been among the first to go over the side, before the vessel was pulled more and more into a roll to port and finally onto its side due to water pouring into the hold. What remained of the masts fell pointing west, the sails slapping the sea and forming pockets where more water could collect, dragging the ship farther to its side.

Within a few minutes the fires were out and the ship was clouded with gray smoke. The only sounds were the creaking of timbers tearing free or buckling under the weight of the ship and the ocean.

York was standing on Saucer Point, a flat rock that was as far out as one could walk without getting wet. He was using his glass to search the waters for any sign of Captain Swift. He and Doc Puckett had not been among those recovered as yet.

All he saw were bodies bobbing on the waves. Just over a dozen men in all. They were facedown and would wash ashore soon enough. It was difficult to say who they were. His heart heavy, he returned to shore to see about the living.

Suddenly, amidst the respectfully silent din, the harbormaster heard a voice calling his name. He stopped, looked around.

"Good God!" he bellowed.

It was Russell Puckett. The man was lying on his back, in the water, being passed along by people who were kneeling on several of makeshift platforms. It was easier to move him that way than to raise him, especially if he had broken any bones.

York stepped thigh-deep into the water and sloshed toward him. The man's shirt was charred and he had burns on his scalp and chest. His hair and eyebrows were mostly gone. But he was conscious and trying to help the rescuers by mentioning where he had seen people trapped in the boat.

"Doc, what *happened*?" York asked when he reached the man's side. "And where's the captain?"

"Swift . . . Swift was in his cabin," the medic said, spitting out seawater that washed over his chin. "I tried . . . to get to . . . him. He was injured."

"Injured?"

"Head . . . concussion."

"I'll go out there at once," York said. "Look for him."

"No!" Puckett shook his head. "Injured . . . *before* this. *Attacked!* His cabin . . . flooded. Water pushed me . . . back. I . . . I couldn't . . . get . . . there . . ."

"Attacked by who?" the harbormaster demanded. He had a friend missing. He also had an investigation to conduct.

Puckett struggled to say more as a trio of strong men waded from shore and lifted him onto an old door being used as a table. Wincing with pain and crying out, Russell Puckett lost consciousness.

York remained in the water for a moment, trying to understand what could have happened. The ship was fully on its side, the hull blown out bilaterally. He had seen boiler explosions that could do damage of this type but *The Dundee* had no engines. Black powder detonations were damaging but not so local. Cannon fire could punch a hole in a boat—but not this size and not *through* a ship.

At best—or worst—they went in one side and then down. He could think of just one explanation.

Anna came up to him after the living and dead had been pulled from the sea.

"You see this happen?" she asked.

"Not directly," York answered.

"Folks say it was bright, like lightning."

"Under and over the water line? On two sides?" York said.

"Didn't say it *was* from the sky," Anna protested. "Just how people described it."

York reminded himself that everyone was going to be testy, himself included. He let the comment pass.

"This looks to me like it hit a floating torpedo," York said.

"A what?" Anna said.

"A large metal shell packed with explosive powder."

"Floating?" Anna said. "A *metal* ball?"

"They were used during the War," the harbormaster told her. "Some seaports were riddled with them. If you didn't have a map, you didn't get in."

"What will God's sick children think of next?"

"I am not sure I want to know," York admitted.

The woman dragged a floral bell sleeve across her brow and pushed strands of gray hair behind both ears. "If such a contraption did this, someone had to have left it," she said. "We only had this ship go north today."

"Maybe they were transporting it, dragging it, lost it, came back searching."

She shot him a look. "They would have brought that to the harbor when they was in? You knew Swift! Would he'a been that stupid?"

The harbormaster shook his head slowly. "No, but—aw

hell, Anna. The doctor said there was something he had to tell me. But he passed out."

Anna turned as one of the locals, a one-eyed banjo player named Eustace Lee, who came rushing over from the direction of her shack.

"Miss Anna, y'all got flotsam washin' up your shack," he said. "Want I should start polin' it away?"

Anna looked at the elderly Black man and smiled. "You're hired," she said, knowing that this was not a task for a man with no sense of depth. "Just don't fall in and drown."

"No, ma'am!" he enthused.

"I'll be along presently."

"Yes, ma'am!" he said, hurrying off.

Anna's gray eyes turned to where York was looking, out at the damply smoking wreckage. It was a sinister silhouette against the starry sky.

"Thanks for your help, Anna. Let me know if you lost any craft or any was damaged."

"I think we're okay, but I appreciate the gesture," she said.

Anna walked away after Eustace. York sighed heavily, took a last look at his friend's ship, and walked through a line of onlookers back to town. To everyone who asked what could have done this, he gave the same answer: "I do not yet know, but I will find out."

The harbormaster went to the street where cots and blankets had been set up for the dead, dying, and wounded. The sky was still overcast, and lanterns were suspended from every available eave. Poles, rakes, and fence pickets had been jabbed between the cobbles to hang more. York found Dr. William Cronkite, a Civil War surgeon, working on Doc Puckett, whom the medic knew.

"Hello, Billy," York said.

"My God, Rog," was his reply.

"Yeah. You'll tell me if he comes around, says anything," York said.

"His back was burned through to the bone," Cronkite told him. He did not bother saying more.

York clasped a thick hand on Cronkite's bony shoulder and continued on to his office. He encountered his wife Victoria, whose long red hair and red shawl were windswept as she ran to help with the wounded. She gave him a long, hard hug.

They didn't speak, not then. She knew he was going to write his report, was already composing it in his head. She did not want any of the details to slip from his memory. She kissed his cheek and moved on.

Climbing the stairs with water-logged boots and trousers, he placed each heel in turn in the iron bootjack at the door to pull them off. He rolled the legs of his trousers to his knees. Water dribbled out as he tightened the fabric. Removing his jacket and closing the window to shut out the sounds of salvage and rescue, York went to his shelf stocked thick with nautical books. He selected an annual volume of cannon and maritime weapons and paged through it carefully.

He was confident no cannon could have done this—if nothing else, they would have heard a shot up to four or five miles away. He was trying to find something, possibly of European ancestry, that might explain what had happened. Anna's disbelief had been well-founded. Most of the "torpedoes" he read about—which were named for a breed of fish—exploded on contact and could indeed do this kind of damage. However, they were attached to poles or spars for support. They did not float—at least, not as of the 1866 edition of *Naval Warfare: Armaments*.

No weapons in here float! he told himself as he turned the pages. *Maybe attached to a rock? Or—wood floats. In a barrel? But how would that keep from being dashed against the shore or carried out to sea? Weighted by a chain?*

Someone would have seen that, he decided. There were always eyes on the sea, from the shore and from vessels. A suspicious barrel or raft would have been pushed away by a long pole.

Deeper into the bleak morning, with the noise of the street finally beginning to subside. Mrs. York arrived with her usual, if belated, plate of biscuits—and news. She quietly informed her husband that Russell Puckett had died.

York nodded gravely.

"Poor man," he replied. "A truly *decent* man. And with him went whatever he had been trying to tell me."

"But that is not the only news," she said.

Victoria told her husband something that caused Rog York to jump from his desk and run from his office.

"Your shoes!" she yelled, running after him with a spare pair he kept in a footlocker.

Chapter 15

Throughout the morning and early afternoon, Jackson remained with his son by the banks of the Colorado River. It wasn't just comfortably distant from the fort. The shoreline was the coolest spot anywhere in the region. In addition to the tree cover, the waters cascaded against and over rocks, sending a refreshing mist toward the shore.

Not that the older O'Malley had anywhere else to go. They were waiting for Merritt—anxiously, at first, afraid that his early return would mean another setback. The longer he did not come, the more their speculation and even hope began to arise.

"If the fort padre had nothing to offer him," Jackson finally said, "they'd've sent him riding by now."

"Maybe they let him visit with Clarity," Slash suggested. "That would take some time."

They sat on a long, flat stone, sometimes turning to put their feet in the invigorating water. Now and then, Jackson turned his thoughts to the women back at Whip Station. He was not just concerned about them being alone. He knew how distracted and upset they would be worrying about Slash and Clarity.

He also wondered, then, if maybe he and Joe pushed the wrong decision on Slash. Jackson felt that his two strong women would be less upset having to defend themselves from Guilford than hearing that Clarity was actually being hauled off to Kentucky . . . or worse. And that Slash was trailing them.

For that reason alone, Jackson also knew it was dangerous to leave the boy by himself. Since Slash was three and chased a fox from the small chicken coop, he had been nothing if not impulsive. Often unwisely so.

Then, and on many occasions thereafter, Sarah had cause to say, "He got those hawkish ways from your father. None of the Brunners ever behaved like that."

"None of the Brunners had barnyard animals," Jackson had reminded her more than once. "And only cart or carriage horses to get around."

It was true, Sarah knew. Her family were well-to-do German merchants who, in 1850, established an outpost to sell raw and finished textiles on the Mississippi. They competed directly with Southern vendors, who resented the foreign intrusion but liked the idea of competing with an aristocrat instead of grease-stained laborers from the North. With so many European settlers in the western territories, the Brunners had a wide-open market.

Young Selda—her name, then—had come with her father Adelbert when he first came to hire a manager and run it for a time. She had been to school in Frankfurt and London and found the open lands of the West more magical, more like a fairy tale, than any European forest she had ever seen.

The Brunner Outpost was where she met Jackson and his parents. At the time, the O'Malleys were planning on joining a family ranch in Texas.

"A ranch. With cattle?" she had said to Jackson in her lightly accented voice.

"Well o'course!" he had replied with a smile that was mostly big teeth. "But I won't be droving. I wanna break horses."

Selda had gasped loudly at that, and Jackson immediately had to explain that he meant taming horses, not actually destroying them.

It was a short meeting between Jackson and Selda, that day and, the woman later admitted, her heart was still beating hard when the O'Malleys left. A short time later, when Jackson rode his palomino back just to see her, she said her partly broken heart instantly healed itself and beat faster still.

He smiled, now, vividly remembering how he had dismounted, showed his smile again—even bigger now—and brashly hugged her without a word. Selda's mother, noticing this through the open door of the storeroom, was aghast.

"It was like being held by this entire new land," the young woman had said—not even sure, at the time, exactly what she meant by that.

Jackson stayed another day, they found a preacher, and they married. The bride's family disowned her for a litany of sins, which included changing her name and taking a husband below her station . . . an American cowboy no less.

In the weeks that followed, Sarah understood better what she had said to her mother. Young Jackson was virile, confident, even cocky. He was a new breed of "ruffian," as her father described them—the American. That was one of the reasons Sarah had loved him from the start.

The Brunners had gone back to Germany before the Civil

War. They left behind them a business that was thriving and self-sustaining. The two families were still not speaking.

Sarah's parents heard of Jackson's accident, by post, from a chuck-line rider, a scruffy loner who carried news from ranch to ranch in exchange for food. The man used to work for the Germans and probably imagined that the job of returning Sarah to them, and then to Europe, would fall to him.

The Brunners wrote from their estate to invite their daughter home—just Sarah. Adelbert was brimming with certainty that his daughter would have realized her mistake by now and eagerly return.

Sarah had sent back carefully bound snips of the twins' hair and a note that said simply, "I love and am fully devoted to my husband and our beautiful chickadiddles."

Unfortunately for Adelbert Brunner, his ability to judge wars was as flawed as his knowledge of human nature. He advised their local manager that if it came to a choice, he should sell to the South instead of to the North. He obeyed. Debts went unpaid and raiders from both sides intercepted shipments of goods. Adelbert had anticipated strong support from the European aristocracy for their fellow landowners in the Confederacy. That never materialized and, less than six months into the conflict, the Brunner establishment—by then, two warehouses and a store—was burned by Union troops.

That was the last the O'Malleys heard from, or of, the Brunners. Jackson always felt bad about that for the sake of his wife and their children. But there were some things—weather, war, in-laws—over which even a righteous man had no control.

The chickadiddles, Jackson thought as he stole a look at his grown "chickadiddle." The river seemed to burble the word behind them, over and over. Sarah and Jackson had indeed adored the two from the day Dolley O'Malley put them in their mother's arms.

"Like the tablets of Moses himself," B.W. had described them the first time he saw Joe carrying them. "Straight from God."

Or the devil, Jackson often thought with amusement. Slash was his father's son. Gert was her mother's daughter. They were like dust devils, little windstorms that swept the plains and stirred everything up, from dirt to grass to spiders. Keeping up with the adult Slash was one of the things that helped Jackson recover from his injury. And Slash knew it, which is one reason why he never bothered to tame his rambunctious nature.

Jackson often thought that the only things missing from his life were his own dear ma and witnessing first-hand exactly the depth of horror his in-laws would have felt seeing their rough-and-tumble grandson and Indian-loving granddaughter loving their lives on the range.

"You interested in anything from the chuck tables?" Slash asked. He had been silent for a long time, seemed to have forgotten that the other man was there.

"No, thank you," Jackson said.

"Where is Merritt, d'you think?" Slash asked. "Been— hell, it's gotta be over an hour. Closer to two. How long does it take to talk to a parson? Or Clarity?"

"Maybe he is with the general," Jackson offered. "Or filling out papers. Cavalry's got more forms for more activities than the Bible's got pages. He'll be here."

Moments later, as if God were listening, the horse bearing the reverend emerged from the compound and started down the road. Slash rose, hunched like a wrestler poised for a fight.

"Don't go out there, son," Jackson cautioned. "They may be watching to see who he's got here."

"I don't care," Slash said, leaning against the tree and pulling on his boots. "I just don't care, pa."

Jackson didn't argue. He had learned you don't argue with a rabid wolf. You leave it alone or shoot it.

"Fine, but I can't sit a saddle right now," he lied. "We walk."

"Sure, pa," Slash said distractedly. As long as the waiting was ended and he could move, he didn't seem to care.

Jackson put his own boots on with effort—his feet were wet and the leather was dry—and, with both men pulling their horses along, he limped after his son.

They picked their way through the throngs of shippers, sellers, buyers, and soldiers who were moving among the boats and unladed crates, maneuvering between tables set up for carpenters, an ironworker repairing bits and oarlocks, seamstresses, and doctors to repair whatever had gotten broken, torn, or injured on the river. There was one dentist and two barbers, all of them with customers. A veterinarian was treating horses, cats, and dogs while a tented pastor treated souls.

Jackson's eyes remained on their own preacher. He was trying to read the man's big, open face, get a clue about what they would have to deal with. It looked to him as if Merritt Michaels' mouth was moving. The closer they came, he saw that it was—in prayer, he realized.

That did not seem like a good sign.

Slash first, then his limping father, reached the reverend as he came to the foot of the winding path that intersected the trail. The reverend dismounted. His normally pale face was utterly blanched of color. His eyes were dead.

"Clarity is to be sent north, with Tatham—and a military

escort," Merritt reported. "The judge is upriver in Needles. She will be tried there."

It took a long, shocked moment for that information to settle in.

"How do they know where the hell the judge is?" Slash asked.

"Yesterday, when Tatham went to talk to the general—you remember, Jackson, after we arrived?"

"Yes," Jackson said impatiently.

"Guilford dispatched a messenger to the judicial seat there. The messenger returned this morning with a written offer from Judge Alterman to hear the matter there in three days or here in two weeks. Tatham chose the former."

Jackson saw his son begin to bubble over and put a cautioning hand on his upper arm. Slash shook it off.

"Don't, pa. Don't."

"Son, we won't let that trial happen. But we *are* going to talk this out before we do anything."

Slash exhaled like a bull. "All right. Yeah. I'm sorry."

Jackson turned back to Merritt. "When do they plan to leave?"

"In the morning," Merritt said. "They expect to reach Needles by noon the following day."

"Did you ask to accompany them?"

Merritt laughed bitterly.

"Why is that funny?" Slash demanded.

"Because I was informed, after the provost gave me this information, that if I return to the fort, I will be arrested and tried as an accomplice," the pastor said. "I pressed my protest of this entire matter, but I was rebuffed. That's another of their calculations. Marshal Landau showed me the regulations about what it takes to be part of a military escort. First"—he held up fingers in turn as he recited the requirements—"there has to be a reasonable threat against your personal safety if you are traveling to the trial. Second, there has to be a reason for you to reach the place the escort is going—"

"A witness!" Slash said. "You are needed!"

"I made that point, but it is conveniently not for General Guilford or Tatham to decide," Merritt said. "The judge must rule on that, in which case I will be summoned. They cannot bar me from Needles, but I will have to get there myself."

"We'd go with you," Slash said.

"Which brings up the third reason my request was denied," Merritt went on. "Tatham has said that if I return, I will be arrested as an accessory to the flight of a killer. I was advised, by the marshal, that if I am seen around the fort or along their route, I will be taken into custody and tried along with Clarity."

"They are swine, all of them," Slash hissed.

"Worse," Jackson said ominously. "They are daring us to do something. For the general, Clarity and Merritt are just bait."

"I swear, they will get their wish!" Slash vowed.

The boy seemed to be deciding what to do next. Jackson stepped over and grabbed his reins.

"Pa—" the young man protested.

"No!" Jackson warned. "We have to act rationally and together. You hear me? *Together*. Boy, *think*! We are outnumbered, outgunned, and they got your wife! You act rashly, and Clarity will be a widow! Now calm down or we may die here, today!"

The words had a more sobering effect on Merritt than they did on Slash. The preacher turned away, coughing, afraid he might vomit. Perhaps, if he had eaten since the previous day, he might have.

"I don't want to live without Clarity!" Slash told his father, calmly but through his teeth.

"And she wouldn't want you to die," Merritt said, turning back toward them. The reverend looked at Jackson. "Tell me—what are you considering? What can we do?"

"I'm considering . . ." Jackson started, then backed his thoughts up. "Where did all this start for us?"

"For us, back in Murray," Merritt said.

"True, but we can't get there and back in time to prove this charge may not be official," Jackson replied. "No, here I mean. It started at the station with the arrival of that man Tatham."

"Who I shoulda hamstrung," Slash muttered.

"Wouldn't've solved *anything*!" his father reminded him angrily. "He was right when he said we would've had Guilford to deal with. What we have to do is get the cavalry to back off from this matter."

"How?" Merritt asked helplessly.

"None of us believe Tatham is who he says he is," Jackson said. "He's most likely a bounty hunter with a policing background. The—what's their name? The family?"

"Roche," Merritt said.

"Right. The Roches leaned on their local law to get a dead-or-alive warrant. He picked it up, knowing we'd likely resist."

"That don't make the Kentucky warrant any less enforceable, however it was obtained," Slash offered.

"Unfortunately, you're right," Merritt said forlornly. "I spoke to Marshal Landau about that. He showed me a book. It's in the Constitution, Jackson. I copied it down, figuring we might need it."

The reverend pulled a piece of paper from his vest pocket. He unfolded it with trembling fingers. The ink had smeared from folding it wet. He had more difficulty reading it due to his misting eyes.

"Article IV, Section II, Clause 2," Merritt said. "'Person charged in any State with Treason, Felony, or other Crime, who shall flee from Justice, and be found in another State, shall on demand of the executive Authority of the State from which he fled, be delivered up, to be removed to the State having Jurisdiction of the Crime.'" He carefully folded the paper away. "Officer of the state or bounty hunter, Tatham is within the law."

Jackson considered this. "Assuming such a warrant was issued, and was valid."

"Yes," Merritt said. "I wonder—do you think that's why Guilford wouldn't show it to us?"

"I don't know. Tatham wouldn't've rode all this way with nothing to back him up."

"Unless he's not even a bounty hunter," Jackson said. "He could be a hired killer. There may not be a warrant at all."

"That would be a big risk for the general to take," Merritt said.

"Not so big for a man who tried to start a new war out here," Jackson replied. "Tatham may only have stopped for supplies—or to ask directions."

"Sure," Slash said. "That brass bully is out to get us, and he's got an army behind him. Guilford could've given him that paper so Tatham wouldn't have to risk his life with a shooting. My wife could probably outgun him."

"Which is why we have to figure a way to go around them," Jackson said.

He regarded the preacher. "What did you make of Landau?"

"A good man in a bad situation," Merritt said.

"You don't have to be a bad man to be a party to bad things," Slash said.

"Just a coward."

"Cowards break both ways," his father pointed out.

Slash considered his father's words then went silent. There were times when wisdom could overcome even youthful anger.

Jackson returned his son's reins to him as he thought about the reverend's comment. The sounds of the busy riverfront were strange to ears accustomed to the silence of the plains. But they were also stimulating, in their own way. It reminded him how different the O'Malleys were from the people who lived and worked here—and at the fort.

Jackson regarded Merritt. "Did you talk to Malibu and Sisquoc?"

"They were around, keeping busy, but I did not want to draw suspicion on them," the reverend said.

"One more question," Jackson said. "What do you think about getting yourself arrested?"

"Not much," Merritt admitted. "Why?"

"I have an idea," Jackson said after a long moment. "Something they will not be expecting."

A pair of soldiers started down the road. They were probably not coming to see the three men but Jackson did not want them to overhear anything he had to say.

"Come back to the river," Jackson told the others. "I want to go where I'll be able to think out loud."

There was not a cloud or tree to afford Joe and the Mexicans shade as they crossed the arid frontier. The rock ledges, along with the rocks themselves, were fewer. The only difference between this lowland and a desert was the fact that no one passing through this region had bothered to name it. If they had, Skull Territory might have been appropriate. The deeper the men went, the more animal bones they encountered.

The rationing of water was miserly, the horses taking priority. The apples they brought also went to the animals. Joe watched them carefully and would stop whenever the animals showed signs of wavering or their heads sunk low. He would give them drink and feed them a clump of dry grass and move on. Sanchez did not so much guide the wagon horse as allow the animal to follow Joe. Even when it was past noon, the sun still seemed to be directly overhead, its rays smeared across the sky like a forge that paid no heed to its own iron boundaries.

The problem for Joe was not just water. It was knowing exactly which way to go. General direction was easy. He had the compass for that. Even before he owned one, he would line up the sun with a spot on the horizon and he would be perfectly on-course. Out here, where there were little jags and jogs in the route, the particulars mattered. A slight turn off the westerly line he had chosen, and they might miss the Butterfield Trail. Or they might aim for a spot farther from due-north, adding possibly calamitous hours to their journey. Finding the trail would not solve their problems, but it would save them from endless wandering and death.

Then he spotted something. Something that did not belong on the pale, arid landscape.

"Hold!" Joe said.

It seemed as if he were speaking to the horse since the Mexicans were sprawled where they sat or lay, unresponsive in their own steaming sweat.

The cart horse stopped when the lead horse did. Joe dismounted and walked ahead. His swollen feet hurt, and he was glad he was wearing moccasins. His step was uncertain, but he was upright and relatively alert. He stopped beside a blackened knot of tumbleweed. He placed his boot on it. The mass crumbled to powder.

"Hallelujah and thank you, Lord," he said under his breath.

Joe looked ahead, lowering his hat brim to shield his eyes. There was another small, black mass slightly to the northwest. There was no wind now, but there would be a small one at night. It would blow southeast.

It was a sign, and it was exactly right.

With a livelier step he walked to the wagon, kicked the wheel to rouse the torpid occupants.

"Get up!" he rasped in his dry throat.

Sanchez and Gonzalez roused themselves. Neither spoke. Their mouths were too parched. They squinted down at him.

"We're near," Joe said. "Two weeks ago, I set a tumbleweed fire on the trail. When it blows, wind here travels northwest to southeast."

"Wind . . . here?" Sanchez said.

"It's hot, but it's wind," Joe said. He pointed to one side.

"That line of ash—that's our pointer. We're prob'ly two, three miles from the trail and outta this hell hole."

"And then . . . what?" Sanchez asked.

"Oak Grove," Joe said. "We can be there by morning."

"Morning?" Gonzalez laughed. "We have . . . a sip of water each, left."

"I know. We gotta leave one horse, drink his share now," Joe said. "We reach the trail, Moore Creek is ahead. Summer was dry and the ponds will've dried, but the creek should be okay. We refresh and finish the trip overnight."

Sanchez's creased eyes turned to the back of the wagon. "Then we talk to Álvarez."

Joe drank his share of water from the near-empty deer-skin at the side of the wagon. He passed it to Gonzalez and then mounted.

With shaking fingers that lacked other than rudimentary coordination, the two Mexicans wasted no time measuring the last of the water in the ladle. They drank and, momentarily refreshed, they watched as Joe took the saddle and gun from his own horse. He heaved them into the wagon beside their prisoner and gave the rest of the barrel water to the cart horse.

Then he faced his own steed.

"You're welcome to follow us," he said into the eyes of his mount, stroking it along the jaw. "I reckon you got the mind to, maybe not the muscle." He kissed the animal. "I wish you Godspeed or a quick end."

The horse seemed relieved to be free of his rider and gear. Joe climbed into the buckboard, took the reins, and turned the horse slightly off west to northwest, in the direction of the blackened foliage. The other animal stood dumbly for a moment and then followed along, casually, as if it had no concerns. Now and then it paused to tug at a bent, dry piece of grass. And then, at some point, Joe no longer heard the horse's gentle clopping or strained breathing.

He did not look back, even when he heard nothing behind him at all.

Chapter 16

Harbormaster York was exhausted.

There was the physical strain of the early-morning events, of not being able to rest when even the overworked stevedores did, and of not having eaten since supper the previous night. He had taken a biscuit from the plate his wife brought him from the house, but left the eggs covered with its tin lid.

There was also the mental and emotional strain. Death was on the street and, still, in the water . . . along with limbs separated from their owners in the explosion. The currents made it difficult for men to reach them as they bobbed this way and that. They also had to pause to beat away fish who competed for these remains of men who had probably been in their hammocks, judging from the location of the holes. In a moment, the lives of survivors had been altered without any hope of being restored. Not just limbs but hearing and sight had suffered—so much gone for those who needed every part of them to be working. Seamen could work without a finger or two that got frozen to a shroud, or even a peg leg or a hook for a hand. But they would have to offer a crew something else to compensate—experience, geographical knowledge, skill with a wheel or keel or language. Most of those who were injured in the explosions would have no such options.

And God knows the maritime merchants will do little to help them, York thought. Profit-minded men would not allow able clerks or designers or secretaries to be shouldered aside for charity. The owners of *The Dundee* were a small concern. They did not have the financial resources or public image to uphold of a major shipping line like Pacific Steam or Australia Royal Mail.

There had been some consolation, however. Something intangible that kept him going. To be around the good in people, their eagerness to help, was inspiring. It did not erase the horror and suffering. Nor did it heal the deep, permanent chafing on the soul. It was something, though.

But then Victoria York brought news that struck York with the force of a massive wave smashing against a sea wall. All other considerations fell away as the tired man bolted from his chair and followed her from the building, through the street, weaving around people, dogs, horses, carts. They were heading away from the wreck, and the crowd here was mostly stragglers, watchers, who had arrived from a community north of the shore, away from the sight of the blighted ship, away from the charnel smell of the smoke and dead.

"Move, move!" he instructed the gawkers. He faced them each specifically so Victoria would not think he was addressing her.

Privately, though, he did wish that his dear wife's dress was not so starched and wide, her feet and steps not so petite, that her calm demeanor matched the urgency of his own.

New England women, he thought—but with love. When

storms or a cluster of arrivals or strikes or riots rocked him, her poise was his anchor.

As they walked, York saw his wife wincing slightly and, reaching forward, offered her his handkerchief.

"Thank you, but I'm all right," she lied.

The harbormaster's wife did not wish to appear weak. He immediately forgave Victoria her careful step.

The couple reached a second area on the main road. That's where the cots and blankets were arrayed, the first street having been turned over to the care of nurses and other volunteers. There was nothing more the doctor himself could do. They found Dr. Cronkite here now, bent over one of the patients.

"There! William is with him now!" Victoria said.

York kissed his wife on the side of her head.

"Thank you," he said as he maneuvered around her. "Why don't you go home now."

"I'll go to the office," she said. "Someone may come looking for you."

"You're an angel," he replied in earnest, smiling back at her as he hustled forward.

York moved around the untrained volunteers who were washing and giving water to the injured, or simply standing there holding the hands of men who were in pain or unconscious. York came up to the doctor unobserved. The harbormaster looked down.

There, on the table, was a face he knew well. There were deep lacerations and several burns, some missing hair. But Captain Alan Swift was breathing regularly and the white sheet that covered him did not bear any bloodstains.

"How is he, doctor?" York asked.

The physician was applying salve and bandages to the wounds on the man's face. He did not stop from his labors.

"Considering the amount of water I forced from his lungs, it's a true miracle he is still breathing," Cronkite replied. "I do not know how he got out, but he managed. These cuts—they're from glass."

York leaned closer. The cuts were deep and wide—heavy glass.

"Cabin windows," York suggested. "Doc Puckett said he was in his cabin. The stern went under, may have hit a rock."

"This concussion," Cronkite replied, indicating the man's head. "Pretty severe. And his breath smells strongly of laudanum. I doubt he'd have been able to swim."

"He may have been washed out with the flood," York said. "The water was what prevented poor Puckett from getting to him. The effort may have cost him his life."

"Dr. Puckett was a fine man," the physician said gravely.

"He was," York agreed. "Has the captain said anything?"

"Not a sound."

"Will he?" York pressed.

"I know what you want, but he needs time," the doctor told him. "The sun will help, if it comes out. The light, the warmth. His body was very cold." The doctor turned toward the harbormaster for the first time. "I'll stay within earshot, Rog, I promise. I want to know what happened as much as you do. Any ideas?"

"I was looking in the ordnance books. This is unlike anything, as far as I could find."

"Something new," Cronkite said. "If only we had medicines to keep pace with the new guns and cannon."

The harbormaster thanked the doctor. Before turning

away, he took one more look at the face of his unconscious friend. He bent close.

"We've got the lifeline rigged, my friend," he said. "Use it."

York did not leave the makeshift hospital but visited with the other helpers and their patients. It was not an entirely charitable act. He asked the locals if any of the victims had spoken, said anything about the accident. The response was always the same: none of them was awake or alert enough or saying anything coherent enough to offer any help. Those who spoke—and briefly—were asking about their condition or imparting messages for wives or mothers and fathers. But as the patients' limited energies flagged, that had stopped. Added to the frozen activity on the ships themselves—which would have to wait for the stevedores—the silence was eerie and death-like.

It was nearly noon before York went back to his office. The sun had come out, and the breeze from the sea was invigorating. Nonetheless, after taking a few bites of cold egg, York lay down, shut his eyes, and fell asleep with a prayer on his tongue.

As Jackson walked back to the river, with the other two, his mind struggled with the challenge of the move he was considering. A plan had taken form, minus much detail, but he had no idea how it would play out—not just among their enemies but among their friends.

He sent the others ahead to the river while he remained among the vendors for a while. Slash went petulantly, Merritt attending to him, but Jackson had work to do here.

It was nearly an hour before the older O'Malley made his way back through the packed humanity and joined the others. The two had settled in farther from the tree, since the collection of merchants and tents had spread. They were now entirely out of view of the fort. Trees and a rising hill blocked it. That was probably a good thing, Jackson thought. He felt a little less tense than he had when he was watching for signs of the detective or the Mission Indians or even Clarity in the company of—anyone.

"What've you got in mind, pa?" Slash asked impatiently as they stood with their horses, the river sparkling as it raced by.

"Give me some room to organize my words," he said. "I'll tell you in a minute."

"You stalling me?" Slash asked suddenly.

"And you're pushing, son," Jackson said. "I know you're hurting, but we're trying to help."

"I love and respect you more'n anyone outside o' grandpa, but time is moving on and this is my wife we are—"

"I have a wife I love dearly too, Slash," Jackson said quietly. "I want to see her again. Give me another minute or two, son. That's all."

"We'll end up doing what I said from the first we should do," Slash said. "Take her and run."

"If it's God's will," Merritt said. "He is here and will help us too."

Stifled yet again, the boy spun toward the river, no calmer but at least silent.

Jackson thanked Merritt with a nod and took the time he had requested. He considered his next words with great care. The more he thought of his plan, the more certain he was it would not be well-received.

"All right," Jackson announced. "I want you both to hear me out before you jump on my back. Yes?"

Slash turned. Merritt nodded. Slash followed his example.

"First, where we are agreed," Jackson said. "We have to get Clarity out of the fort, today. That means we have to get in, today. We are likely not to be admitted. Even at the most hopeful, if someone took pity on us, they would put us under close guard and probably admit only you, son, for a quick visit with your wife. Also agreed?"

Both men nodded.

"What it seems to me the general cannot refuse, however, is a request over which he has no jurisdiction. And that would be the *law*. Something he cannot ignore or compromise to his advantage."

"What *law*?" Slash pressed, growing impatient.

Jackson answered, "We had a guest at the station a few weeks back—angry fella name of Bill Bayard, who was heading back to Frisco, to the assayer's office. Said he had to prove that his gold-digging new bride was not on his original claim. He needed the actual paper to prove she was lying so he could annul the marriage without paying her."

"How does that help me?" Slash asked.

"Merritt, I'm gonna need your help on this." He took a breath. "We need the warrant to support your right to annul your marriage to a wanted felon."

The look of anger and disapproval that came over Slash's face was like nothing Jackson had ever seen. He didn't reach for his knife. It wasn't that kind of murderous hate. It was disappointment that left the young man fighting a battle not to scream out or jump on his father.

Jackson read that all in an instant in his son's expression. The older O'Malley did not move. It was Merritt who, after a moment, stepped forward and put a steadying hand on Slash's shoulder.

"Wait," the reverend said. "Just wait. Your father has something here." Slash did not move but he also did not relax. His mouth was a tortured scowl. "How can you even *think* such a thing, let alone speak it?" the young man demanded.

"Slash, hear your father out!" Merritt said.

"Yes, let's hear it," Slash snarled, glaring at his father. "Because, by my soul, pa, you *can't* be serious!"

The reverend stepped closer, putting a shoulder between the two. He spoke, first to Jackson. "This *is* a charade, yes?" Merritt asked.

"Of course," Jackson replied.

"Then . . . it could work," Merritt said.

"What are you talking about?" Slash demanded. His hostility was now mixed with open confusion.

Merritt turned entirely now to the young man. "The laws of God and man," he said. "When I was at St. Mary's College, we were instructed on the rules of annulment. Your father is right. It requires proof of cause. If you wish the wedding annulled on the grounds that my sister has committed a crime, you must offer evidence of that crime. That means sworn testimony or documentary proof."

"Guilford can swear, Tatham can swear, what do they care?" Slash asked.

"And when we file those written, sworn statements in Needles, they will be held accountable for perjury," the reverend said. "Lying under oath. The general will not risk that."

"He won't sign any such document," Slash said.

"He must." Merritt's voice was stronger now, reflecting his newfound encouragement. "We are free to travel to Needles today. We can be there before him and register our own complaint, that he failed to comply with the law. That matter will have to be decided before the case against Clarity can be heard."

"What if there *is* a warrant?" Slash asked. "The judge'll ask to see that."

"Depends how honest he is," Jackson said. "If we make an issue of it first, he won't risk backing Tatham."

"That is why we have to get inside," Jackson said. "Make the general hear your case and realize where his flank is exposed."

"Your plan allows for that," Merritt said. "Slash is the victim—he did not know of his bride's criminal past. He is entitled to see the proof. Then there is the annulment itself. Jackson, you were a witness—you and Sarah signed the wedding certificate. I am the one who officiated, which means I have the clerical authority to render it undone."

"So we all get inside," Slash said. "The judge is corrupt, Guilford knows it, and he blocks every move. He sees us to spit on us—again. Then what?"

Merritt turned to Jackson for the rest.

"Then you hit Tatham and get taken to the stockade," the older O'Malley said. He produced something he had purchased from the ironworker. "Cost me, but he says it will work on any prison lock."

He showed the others a skeleton key.

The Butterfield Trail was exactly where Joe O'Malley had hoped it would be.

The dirt road was as tough as the riders who wore it

into the earth. It was announced well in advance by a sudden increase in scrub and a gentle roll of the land as the seasonal influences returned, sculpting and shaping. There was even a whisper of breeze, though it was like a gale to men whose sweat had turned to dirt-infused crust upon their faces.

The water was gone, the apples they had brought were gone, and even Joe was slumped forward, his hands limp on the reins. The sight of the familiar, inviting path the width of a stagecoach brought him to a semblance of his former alertness. Though they had found the road to salvation, that still did not bring them any closer to water.

"Cactus . . ." Sanchez said weakly. "We . . . can . . ."

"No," Joe said. "Pulp'll wet your mouth . . . make you sick . . . trots'll cost whatever water's in ya."

"You should . . . get out of . . . the city . . . more . . ." Sanchez managed to taunt him.

Joe stopped.

"What is it?" Sanchez asked. "You see something?"

Joe climbed from the wagon. Ahead, waving in the heat close to the ground, were a pair of coyotes. They looked as scrawny as he felt. But that wasn't what interested him. There was dust around them.

Holding the wagon for support as he walked, Joe got one of the rifles from the back. He noticed, then, that Álvarez wasn't moving. He didn't appear to be breathing. Joe would deal with that in a minute. Crouching, the frontiersman aimed between the animals and sent them running.

"You missed," Sanchez observed.

Joe ignored him. He didn't bother explaining that he hadn't intended to kill the animals, only chase them away. Joe rose and staggered forward to where the animals had been. It was roughly a hundred yards away but it felt longer.

His feet were swollen and every step was agony. He hadn't felt anything like that since he—and his skin—were much younger.

The coyotes scurried to a spot well off in the distance. They stopped and were watching. That confirmed what Joe had suspected. The animals had left something they wanted. When Joe arrived, he saw that they had been digging which had caused the dust. And where they had pawed at the earth, the dirt was damp.

"Yer noses were right, my friends," Joe said to the ground. "Just your timing was bad."

Joe aimed the rifle straight down and put two shots in the ground. The soil dampened faster and the moisture spread to the walls of the hole.

Dropping to his knees, Joe set the gun aside and began clawing at the opening. His fingernails collected dirt and hurt and his skin bled but he didn't stop. After a few minutes his fingertips felt something cool and damp. A few moments later and he reached muddy water.

He turned to the wagon and rasped, "Here! Bring cloth—the ladle!"

The men made the horse do the work. They were too weak. The wagon lurched forward.

It wasn't much of a water hole, but after scooping it into a torn shirt and squeezing out the liquid, Joe, Sanchez, and Gonzalez were able to get a half-ladle's worth in just a few minutes. The invigorating properties of that little bit were like a shower in a waterfall.

"Álvarez is dead," Gonzalez informed the others when he once more had a voice.

"I saw," Joe said.

"Fitting, since this was his doing," Sanchez added. "But I wish we knew what he knows."

"We can ponder that later," Joe said. "Right now, we have to squeeze out water for the horse and then extra for the trip. We got till about midnight till we reach the next stop on the stage line."

Invigorated, Joe actually decided to dig a little deeper until he hit clear water. He scooped enough into the skins and sent several ladles in succession to the horse, then let the water perspire through the cloth into their water skins. The rays of the sun hurt his hands and whatever his hat didn't shade. But that was pain, this was life.

When Joe was finished, he backed away to allow the coyotes—who were still waiting—their turn at the spot. They deserved no less for discovering the place that had saved their lives.

Before leaving, the men discussed what to do with their dead companion.

"Ain't no good answer," Joe said. "We bring Álvarez along for a proper burial we invite a honeybucket o' flies and possibly worse, especially big, hungry birds after sundown. I got no desire to tangle with sharp talons and an aggressive beak trying to feed nestlings. On the other hand," he went on, "as long as we got him with us, anybody who might be following will assume he's still alive. Gives us some breathing room. Also, just as a practical matter, him being gone lightens the horse's load."

"The question is whether anyone would have bothered to follow," Gonzalez said.

"They may have expected us to turn back after Álvarez sabotaged our water," said Sanchez, who was clearly the more tactical-minded of the two. "What do you say, Joe?"

"I'm actually thinking I don't want to explain a bruised and bloodied body to the folks at Oak Grove," he said.

Joe's sober assessment did not offer any perfect options.

Gonzalez apparently had no strong opinion either way and agreed.

"I don't want him around," Sanchez finally decided. Only some sense of breeding or decorum prevented him from spitting on the corpse.

"Fair enough," Joe said. "Too much to dig a grave. We'll put him under a pile of rocks."

The three men carried the body well off the road. They brought him to a spot where stones were fairly plentiful and then buried him beneath enough of them to protect his remains—at least until they were out of sight.

"Had he been a true *compadre* of tradition, it would have been different," were the only words Sanchez said over the makeshift grave.

Gonzalez used a stone to scratch a cross on one of the headstones.

Joe got back in the buckboard beside Sanchez. Gonzalez was sitting in the back of the wagon on the chest containing clothes, ammunition, and other supplies, including the lanterns they would most likely require to finish the journey.

"You saved our lives, and I thank you for that," Sanchez said.

"You paid me to get you someplace, and I intend to do it," Joe replied. "You two keep a lookout south and east for dust."

"Dust?" Gonzalez asked.

Joe jerked a thumb behind them. "Both you men're riding shotgun now. There may be those *Juaristas* who might've been expecting us. They're probably fresher than us too, having water 'n' all."

The warning heeded, Gonzalez handed Sanchez a shotgun and selected a carbine.

The Butterfield Trail, though uneven and rutted, was an easier ride for the horse. That mattered more than their own comfort. As they rode, the men scanned the horizons, watching for anything that wasn't an animal or weather. Sanchez spotted a long, thick, dark cloud of honeybees swarming from south to north. It appeared to be a single creature as it headed toward distant fields of golden wild-flowers. As it neared, it broke into smaller shapes, each of them possessed of its own life and mind and purpose.

An hour passed, then two. The water they had drawn from the hole kept them going, and they were finally emboldened enough to chew some of the jerky they had packed. Their jawbones ached, but their bellies were grateful. So was the moderate wind, which eased their bodies and lightened their spirits.

Suddenly, with the sun beginning its descent toward the horizon, Gonzalez called out urgently.

"Behind us!"

The other two men turned around.

There was a cloud in the south, and it was moving quickly in their direction.

Chapter 17

When the Butterfield Overland Mail stagecoach began its run in 1857, Warner's Ranch was a station stop north of San Diego. The cattle ranch was famed for its meals, and riders like B.W. looked forward heartily to reaching it.

A few months after the start of the Civil War, in the fall of 1861, Union forces established Camp Wright on that site to protect both mail and travelers from Confederate expeditionary forces. At the same time, the station stop was moved twenty miles to the north, to Oak Grove. The Union moved some of its army there too, a stay lasting until the end of the war.

After the war, both Warner's Ranch and Oak Grove competed for business from the stage. The ranch still had the food, and a Butterfield contract. But Oak Grove had a more welcoming master and mistress, the just-starting-out Thomas and Erica Hampton family with their baby daughter. They welcomed all visitors from all sectors, and were among the few outposts willing to trade with Indians.

The station was a simple but well-constructed adobe structure with a sharply sloped roof. It was nestled in a bucolic setting of grasses and tall trees. A large garden announced itself, even in the dark with various fragrances from orange to peach. To the weary, it was a haven with no pressure to leave within the hour. Rates were negotiable, depending upon one's ability to pay.

It was after twilight when Gabriel Martinez arrived, drawn by a lantern hanging beside the front door. He was not just tired, he was spent. Hunger was the least of it. His shoulders were raw from the burden of the loaded oar and the care he had to take with the contents of the bags. He felt like Christ Himself on the cross as he reached Oak Grove, unable to move his extended arms from the wood between them.

He had reached the place thanks to the guidance of a leatherworker he had encountered some miles from the coast. The man was on his way to the port, and had directed him precisely.

"It's how I come down here," he had said. "The Hamptons is only three miles northeast of my shack."

The man had refused, even for several gold coins, to sell his horse.

"We been together since he was a colt," the man said. "When Janos dies, I intend to make a set of clothes from him, to keep him near."

That was that. If Martinez had had a gun, he would have taken the horse.

The Mexican moved on, aware that he possessed unfathomable power across his back—yet it wasn't useful in budging a man's idiot vision.

Tall, rangy Thomas Hampton welcomed him to the warm but otherwise unoccupied station. After introductions, the new arrival insisted on handling his belongings by himself, setting them near the door, away from the hearth. There was a baby's cradle nearby with a sleeping child. The dynamite would be safer here than by a fire.

"You got something special in there?" Thomas asked. "Glassware, from the way you're being so careful."

"Something fragile, yes," Martinez said.

He purchased a meal and drink, which he ate quickly. Then he enquired about a horse and cart.

"We only got but one," the long-faced proprietor said.

"Would you sell them?" Martinez asked. "Or perhaps—rent them?"

"It's the only way we have of getting supplies," Erica said softly, apologetically.

"Then let me ask you this," Martinez said, addressing Thomas. "Would you consider driving me to a place up north where I can purchase a horse and cart? It's very important."

"They got animals back at Warner's Ranch, to the south—"

"I must go north," Martinez insisted with a tight, insincere smile. "And . . . I cannot walk any further."

"How'd you end up on foot anyway?" Thomas asked.

"The boat I was on was lost at sea. I wandered here."

"A boat?" Thomas said. "I can take you to the harbor in the morning—they got boats."

This was tedious. Martinez was losing his patience. He looked around the fire-lit room. Then he reached into his vest pocket and carefully withdrew the purse filled with gold. The care was dictated by how sore the flesh was underneath, rubbed raw by the motion of the coins as he walked.

"I will give you all I have, fifty dollars in gold, for the loan of the horse and wagon, along with a lantern," Martinez said. "I promise to return them in less than a week's time—and you may keep the gold." He regarded Erica. "I see, around me, what seem to be ample stores until I get back. Since arriving, I believe I have heard a cow, yes?"

Erica nodded.

"There. You have milk and I came through a garden with lettuce and tomatoes in abundance, it seemed." His eyes shifted to Thomas. "This money can buy a great deal for your daughter—new clothes for your wife. Tools to fix that window."

Martinez pointed to a spot where a ball of cloth patched a rotted area of wooden frame.

"Come with me, if you like," Martinez encouraged Thomas. "Until I can get one of my own."

The couple looked at each other in silence. They looked at the purse on the small table with an uneven leg.

"I won't leave my wife and daughter," Thomas said. "Not with rain like we had before—the runoff from the mountains can get fierce, especially in the dry riverbed that runs past. You saw that too?"

"I did not," Martinez said through his teeth, his contrived amiability failing.

Thomas sighed. "All right, Mr. Martinez. You can borrow the horse and wagon."

A half-hour later, with a lantern at his side and his bags of dynamite still on the oar, suspended between the slats that made up the sides of the wagon, the Mexican was on his way.

Twilight brought a quick and thorough end to the movement of goods on the river, on the shore, and up to the fort. Most of the people who had been up with the sun had continued along the river, returned to the Butterfield

Trail, or retired for the night in tents. The loud sounds of business were replaced by the subdued sounds of occasional songs, frequent laughter, and yelling from the few heavy drinkers and poker players who had remained.

Dusk also found three men riding up the trail to Fort Yuma. Merritt Michaels was in the front, and the two O'Malleys were behind him.

It had been a long, frequently contentious afternoon for the men.

Slash had relaxed somewhat as he looked at the skeleton key his father had purchased. He asked to keep it. The key—a totem, if nothing else—seemed to calm the boy. Jackson handed it over.

Merritt had regarded Jackson. "You're saying that if the annulment fails, we fight to get her out."

"From the station till now, we followed the rules," Jackson had told him. "We were the only ones who did. Now we may have to fight."

"An army."

"An army," Jackson said. "But we have two things going for us. A cause and, hopefully, two allies inside that they know nothing about."

Merritt took a moment, then nodded. He didn't necessarily agree but he didn't see any options either.

"You were inside after I left," Jackson said to the reverend. "You have to tell us everything you saw, where everything is."

"I was distracted . . . not really paying much attention," he confessed.

Slash quickly grew impatient. "You *have* to remember, dammit!"

Merritt shot him a look. "I'm trying! You forget, brother,

this is not my world, not my way! Spying, planning escapes, conspiring. I am a man of the church!"

"You helped Clarity escape from Kentucky!" Slash reminded him.

"Yes, in a blind panic!" Merritt said, finally losing his composure. "Because like you, brother, I was concerned about my sister. But if you ask me now, that entire time is like air. I went through it, held little. Right up until the time we reached Whip Station, my only firm companions were my love for Clarity and my faith in God and His Son!"

"Of course," Jackson said. "No one is asking for a Galilee miracle from you, Merritt. But God has set you, has set us a new task. You rose to that one alone. Now you have us. Think hard. I know the general layout. What I need from you is anything you can remember seeing after I left will help."

Merritt looked at him with a pained, soulful expression. "I know. It's all been—I thought we were starting over when you took us in."

"You did," Jackson said. "This is—it's the West. It's a harder place than a more generous God would've given any man. You build your roof strong or the wind'll take it. Even then, you gotta keep your buckets handy in case of fire. Sometimes they come as a team in twister-fire that picks up all kinds of things to throw at us. Either we run or we fight. You fight, you better bring every gun, fist, knife, friend, and Bible you got. What we must do is clear. What lies ahead I can't say. So we need every scrap of help anyone can give us. And we're starting here, now, with you."

Slash had been listening not just intently but with rising spirit. Everything his father had said, he knew to be true. It had been part of his every minute, every day, for as long as he could recall. He impulsively hugged his father, wept on his shoulder, and apologized for doubting him.

Merritt did not want to intrude on the moment, and turned toward the river—not just to give them privacy but to think. He looked at the water and saw God in it, not men. He saw purity and clear purpose, not evil. He allowed his mind to flow like water. He had been trying to avoid the pain of memory, but now he embraced it, from the moment they first reached the top of the winding dirt road, with pebbles that filled the ruts from runoff . . . the clean boots and stolid expressions of the two sentries . . . the flagpole and the stone wall that surrounded it—

The reverend turned to face his two companions as he sought his memory.

"The stockade is to the west of the general's head-quarters. It has a high fence—about a head taller than the man at the gate."

Jackson and Slash both looked at him.

"Go on," Jackson said encouragingly.

"You saw, I think—Sisquoc and Malibu were to the east. The stable and a corral were northeast of where they were standing, and a row of low structures was built north and south from them. One of them had an open door on top."

"Yes, that was the quartermaster," Jackson said. "Go back to what you saw with Landau, with the padre."

Merritt closed his eyes. "There was a guard in front of the stockade. The wall was—a fence about a head higher."

"That's right. Merritt. What about the padre. Did you walk with him?"

"Yes," Merritt said. "We went to the chapel. It stood by itself. It has a small bell tower. Pews for maybe fifty or sixty soldiers. A few civilians were inside, praying."

Merritt was encouraged to tell the men every detail he

could visualize. Several comments triggered questions from Jackson. Some of those Merritt could answer. Some he could not. It felt almost like prayer, walking through memory and the unseen.

When he was done, when he had exhausted everything in his memory, Jackson and Slash squatted on the shores of the river, where there was a patch of dirt. Using sticks, they made drawings.

Merritt did not join them. He found himself asking God for His help. For without Divine Providence, there was no way any of them would survive this day.

And when darkness fell, it was time to move.

The men left their horses in the hands of a wrangler named Joe O'Reilly, whom they trusted at once. He agreed to keep them till no later than morning, when he would be busy with whatever new horses arrived for the cavalry.

Having purchased ink and paper from Sammy's General Goods Emporium, they had drafted a Certificate of Annulment, which required the signatures of the bride, groom, officiant, and at least one witness.

"In Kentucky, this paper does not require the signature of the witnesses," Merritt had told them. "I would guess the rules are the same in California."

"Whether it is or it isn't," Jackson had said, "the object is for us all to be inside while Guilford tries to find a way to stop us."

Slash did not have to say he wouldn't wait for that to happen. Fortunately, the plan they had come up with did not require it.

There were different guards at the gate, one of whom carried a message to Marshal Landau that Merritt Michaels wished to see him. The assistant provost marshal came to the gate. He was surprised to see Jackson O'Malley and had figured out, before being introduced, who Slash was.

Merritt explained why they were there. In the light of the lantern that hung at the gate, Landau seemed increasingly dubious.

"I'll inform the general," the officer said. "I cannot guarantee he will be sympathetic to this request."

"Please point out to the general that this is a civil and not a military matter, entirely independent from the charges pertaining to the Kentucky matter," Merritt added. "He does not have the authority to deny this request."

"I'm not sure he will be moved by that either," Landau said.

"He should be," Merritt replied. "Rank and force-of-arms have no legal function in civil matters."

"You a lawyer, Reverend Michaels?" Landau asked.

"No, but I am certain to find one in Needles if it comes to that."

Landau left. The reverend's calm demeanor impressed Jackson.

"Was any of what you said true?" Jackson asked.

"He has to assume so," Merritt replied. "I do not believe that Guilford or Tatham want us to go to Needles."

"He has to know we'd follow Clarity, wherever they go," Slash said.

"I do not believe he intends for you to survive that long," Jackson said bluntly.

While they waited, Jackson grew anxious—though he didn't let it show. Now that the showdown was near, he wondered about the wisdom of it. He liked Clarity but he loved his son. The thought of losing him over this was torturing him—especially when the young woman did by her own admission shoot a man to death. How could he even think to ride home to Sarah and Gert with the boy's body draped over his horse.

Because living with the knowledge he could have done something would be worse for him, Jackson told himself. There was at work here a confused and difficult mix of the boy's love for his wife and pride.

But Slash would never forgive his father for backing down now. Even if it did mean the young man's death.

Landau returned to the gate after a few minutes.

"The general will not see you, any of you," he said, looking at them in turn.

The eyes of the assistant provost marshal stopped on Slash.

The young man cried, the shout seeming to rise from his knees, right before he struck the officer.

Chapter 18

The day had never cleared and darkness came early to the port of San Diego.

The spirits of Harbormaster York were equally dreary throughout the afternoon and into the early evening. He had finished his report on *The Dundee* and then took time off to review the ships that were scheduled to arrive over the next few days. Tragedy or no, the port remained operational.

He was just finishing a list to give to the foreman of the stevedores when rapid footsteps came clomping up the stairs. York looked up just as Eustace swung through the open door.

"Doc wants you now!" he yelled breathless. "Cap'n Swift is woke!"

York shouldered past the man, apologizing as he sped down the stairs. His heavy footfalls obliterated Eustace's reply. The harbor was still crowded, only now with workers who were exhausted from the day's salvage work and sought food and drink—mostly the latter. A great many had carts loaded with goods and items that had evidently come from *The Dundee*. There was only one local salvage company, Mansfield and Fitzpatrick, and both owners had come to the harbormaster's office during the day to complain about the haphazard way the wreck was being managed. York had apologized sincerely but pointed out *The Dundee* was in the harbor, brought there by its own crew, and was technically not abandoned.

That didn't address the real problem of looting. However, York made the decision to overlook it. Everyone who took something from the ship had to search the vessel, and that might turn up remains or possibly survivors. In his mind, the benefit outweighed the illegality.

The lantern-lit medical area shone yellow-orange in the dark, and York easily picked out the doctor. He was with Captain Swift, now and then looking over to see if York was coming. Dr. Cronkite seemed relieved to see the harbormaster on the way. The physician stepped aside as York arrived, charging not brusquely but urgently to the captain's bedside.

The captain's eyes were open and staring straight up. His breathing was strained but regular. As soon as York loomed over him, Swift's gaze shifted. He smiled weakly.

"My friend," York said to him. "My dear friend."

He had intended to say more, but words collapsed and he had to fight back tears.

"Rog . . . where is . . . Martinez?" Swift asked.

"I don't know this man," he answered, stealing a look at the doctor.

Cronkite shook his head and shrugged.

"Gabriel Martinez," Swift went on. "He did this. Brought cargo . . . explosive. Bound for . . . Frisco."

"For what? Construction? Prospecting."

Swift shook his head. "I think . . . war." With difficulty,

the captain raised trembling fingers, touched them to his head. "He did this . . . when I tried to . . . check cargo."

"You didn't know what he had onboard?"

"No."

"The forms you filled out here when you stopped—"

"In . . . complete . . ." he struggled with the word, then forced it out. "Incomplete. Orders from . . . Ritchies."

"This man sailed from Mexico en route to San Francisco with explosives," York summarized. "I saw a man take the aft rowboat after the explosion. Him?"

"Likely," Swift said. "I was . . . washed from . . . cabin."

Dr. Cronkite moved in then. "Rog, I wanted you to talk to him, but we must get him out of the cold. We'll take him to my office."

"Yes, certainly." York straightened and took a step back. He looked down at Swift. "You do everything Dr. Cronkite tells you."

"Puckett?" Swift asked. "Where . . . ?"

"It's been pretty chaotic here, but I'll try and find out," York said. "You get rest first."

"First Mate Sullivan."

"I'll get the names of everyone we've got here, and I'll let you know after you've rested."

The captain nodded. He continued to stare at the surly skies, even as Dr. Cronkite waved over two men to pick up the stretcher he was on.

Ever a seaman, York thought. Gravely injured but watching the skies for weather.

York did not wait for them to carry him off before he turned and went to see Anna Lewn. She was still near the wreck, supervising the effort she had made to collect flotsam and jetsam from the ship. She was poised on a rocky promontory holding a torch, her dress blowing in the wind.

She looked to York like a magazine image he had seen of a revolutionary French woman holding the tricolor aloft.

"Anna," the harbormaster said. "We have to keep people back from the wreck."

"Why?"

"There may be more of an explosive we know nothing about," he said. "I just heard it from the captain. I also need you to do something for me. I'll pay, of course, but I need you to do it because it must be done right."

She took a moment to call everyone back to shore, her people as well as everyone else, saying there was news about dangerous conditions onboard. Once that was in motion, she turned back to York.

"What do you need, Rog?" she asked.

"Go north to San Luis Rey and deliver a message to Captain Landry of the *Manhattan*," he said. "Tell him what happened here and that it's just a sample of what's being planned for San Francisco. There is a new and obviously powerful kind of explosive. Tell him that we believe the culprit went ashore, that his target may also be the ship carrying Benito Juárez, and that this information comes from Captain Alan Swift of *The Dundee*."

Anna listened without expression. When York was finished, the woman started down the rocks to go to her shed.

"You have all of that?" York called after her.

"Yep."

"When can you leave?"

"Nos," she said. "Wind's favorable. I'll take my sailboat, be there before dawn. You see Eustace, send him to me! I'm gonna need a mate!"

"I will!" York said. "And thanks!"

Something else occurred to York, something he had seen on the shipping manifest for two days hence.

"Anna!"

"Yes?" she yelled back without stopping.

"Please remind Landry that Benito Juárez is, we think, on his way to San Francisco," York said. "It might be him that's the target!"

She waved in the torchlight to signal that she understood, while York turned and went to find Eustace. He did not have to look far. The man was standing at the foot of the rock.

"Figured you might need me," the banjo player smiled.

"You'll be sailing north with Anna," York told him. "A dollar every two miles, when you get back."

The man smiled broadly and hurried away.

York wished that all of his dealings could be settled so easily.

"Stay in the wagon!" Joe yelled to Gonzalez as the dust cloud billowed toward them. "And get the vests out now!"

"What are we going to do?" Sanchez asked.

Joe jumped from the seat and began unhitching the horse. "Mr. Sanchez, you're going to ride the hell out of here. Get to Oak Grove and stay after your quarry. We'll deal with this."

"A good plan," Sanchez said.

"A good plan for who?" Gonzalez shouted back as he opened the chest. "We don't know how many there are or even if they're—"

"Hostile? Riding like that, wearing down the horses out here?" Joe said. "They'll be shooting when long guns are in range—about a minute. You getting those vests out like I said?"

Gonzalez shut his mouth and pulled the garments out, in his haste banging each against the other and on the floorboards.

"How will *you* get away without the horse?" Sanchez asked as he helped Joe with the hitch rail.

"With their mounts," Joe said. "If they still need 'em, we'll be too dead to go anywhere."

Sanchez smirked at the dark humor. It was one of the reasons he had come to like and admire this man.

The moment the horse was free, Sanchez jumped on its back. Joe handed him a carbine and one of the water skins.

"Matches!" Sanchez shouted.

Gonzalez tossed a box to Joe who handed them up. The Mexican was gone before the shooting began. Joe hurried back to the wagon. He looked south along the trail.

"Damn," he said as the cloudy onslaught closed in.

"What?" Gonzalez asked. He was in the process of slipping one of the vests on. He handed the other to Joe.

"There's no time to turn over the wagon," Joe said as he pulled on the heavy metal vest. The unexpected weight caused his knees to quiver. His back was already straight because the vest wouldn't let him bend. He had to hunker up his thighs and lock his legs to stay upright. "Listen carefully. You take the shotgun. Go up front, right side, stay behind the wheel to protect your legs. Do *not* fire till they come around your side an' you got a clear shot at their side or back. I'll try to see that they don't get the chance."

"How?"

Joe didn't answer. He stood behind the left side wheel and watched their approach. As he had predicted, the oncoming riders opened fire as soon as they were within range. The men appeared to be wearing peasant garb—no doubt the Mexicans that Sanchez had feared might be waiting for them.

"They had to've found Álvarez!" Gonzalez said as bullets flew wide and punched the dirt.

"Seems likely," Joe said. "When we didn't turn back and make for the Butterfield Trail, where they could pick us off, they came looking."

The attacking riders began to separate, forming two groups to surround the wagon. Now that they were clear of the dust, Joe counted six. Watching the men on his side, he rolled quickly to the side of the buckboard, aimed at the horse of the first rider, and fired. The animal dropped, tripping the horseman behind him. Amidst the cries and neighs, Joe fired at both men. The first attacker fell back, his hands clutching his right side. The other man took a bullet in the chest, spun, and dropped. The third rider had to swerve wide to avoid running into the two downed horses.

With his side cleared for the moment, Joe immediately stepped farther along his side of the wagon and picked off the first rider on the right, though he missed the low-riding second and third. He heard the hoofbeats of the third rider on his side. Dropping the carbine, he drew his revolver and fired as he turned.

The onrushing Mexican also fired.

The bullet clanged off Joe's chest, knocking him back against the wagon, hard, and throwing his shot wide. Leaning against the sideboard, Joe unloaded the revolver on the man, sending horse and rider into the ground in a pillar of dirt and blood.

There was another rifle in the back and Joe reached over to grab it. The plainsman had intended to jump into the wagon for protection and a vantage point, but the vest was too heavy, too constricting. He aimed across the wagon at the same time as Gonzalez fired. The Mexican's shot missed, and he took two ringing hits in the chest as the riders blew by. There was an audible escape of air and Gonzalez slid down the side of the wagon.

As the Mexicans spun to charge again, Joe fired. One man went down. The other charged the wagon, having discarded his own carbine for a Colt. He was tucked in low, the horse's head blocking him from Joe.

The rider's shoulder exploded red and he spun backward and flew from the saddle. Gonzalez's shotgun blast rolled across the plains and died—along with the man he'd hit.

Except for the surviving horses and the moan of one of the men Joe had shot, the Butterfield Trail was once again still and silent.

Groaning, Joe holstered his gun and threw off his vest.

"Christ, God," he said, rolling his shoulders as he hurried to the first man he had shot.

The man was middle-aged, lying on his side facing Joe and panting. Joe pulled the canteen from the man's dead horse and knelt by his side. His guts were exposed where he'd been hit above the waist. Blood was running over his clutching fingers. There was no saving him and Joe poured water into his open, gasping mouth. The man coughed, choked, and Joe stopped.

Gonzalez walked over, the vest clunking on the ground as he dropped it.

"The others are dead," the Mexican said.

"Figgered."

"These are *Juaristas*," Gonzalez said. "I am only sorry they do not get to die in their homeland."

Gonzalez squatted beside the dying man. He asked him a question in his own language. The man answered. It was the last thing he said.

"Anything helpful?" Joe asked.

"Nothing I did not already know," Gonzalez replied. "He said I will spend eternity in Hell."

"I thought I recognized '*infierno*,'" Joe said. He rose, rubbing his chest where the bullet had struck. He walked out and grabbed two of the horses, brought them back to the cart.

"Thank you for covering me," Gonzalez said. "I am not so good at fighting as I am at planning to fight."

"A common affliction," Joe said. "I'm used to shooting animals, not people. But I owe you too. They woulda had us without your vests." He handed Gonzalez the reins and went around gathering up the canteens. "Maybe progress is like people—ain't all of it bad."

Gonzalez took a swallow from one of the canteens as he looked north along the trail. "We have wasted a lot of time, Joe. The wagon is going to slow us."

"I know," Joe said. "We're leaving it behind. Take the water, guns, ammunition—just what we can carry."

Gonzalez looked longingly at the vests.

"War is about losing stuff," Joe said. "You can't sit around regretting it."

The other man agreed and collected only those items from the wagon that he could carry—the guns, water, and a hatchet. He knew, from hunting, that sometimes it was necessary to kill in silence.

"The bodies?" Gonzalez asked as he went to one of the horses, a sturdy Appaloosa.

Joe cocked his head to dark lines in the southern sky.

"Buzzards are already on the way," he said. "An' we ain't got the time to gather rocks."

Gonzalez did not like the idea of leaving his countrymen as carrion, but he did not argue. Unless they made their way north, there would be a great deal more death.

Giving the horses water from the barrel before leaving it, the men mounted up and rode briskly along the Butterfield Trail to catch up with Sanchez.

Martinez wanted only two things in life right now. One was to be in San Francisco. The other was to rest. He was beginning to realize that one of those would not be possible. As for the other, at some point the horse would need it as much as he did.

The trail north was monotonous, but he could not afford to sleep. The thought of traveling some five hundred miles by land to reach the Barbary Coast was a daunting unreality, he realized. It wasn't just the time and distance. The dynamite was also a consideration. On the sea, in a relatively quick journey, he would have been able to control the climate, even the rocking to a degree. Out here, he would have no control over the heat, rain, or the surface of the trail.

As the horse clopped along, he found himself conceiving a new plan that would allow him to complete his mission and also get a few hours of sleep. Allowing the horse to continue on its unvarying path, Martinez took the map from his jacket pocket. He unfolded it and leaned toward the lantern. Oak Grave was not marked, but he knew approximately how far he had traveled from San Diego.

"You don't have to go so far," he said, looking along the coastline. "Not all the way up there."

Though his associates wanted to attack the lucrative Barbary Coast and kill their own leader Benito Juárez, the port of San Pedro in Los Angeles was on the president's itinerary. And it was much, much closer.

"It might be possible to beat him there," Martinez muttered. And a dynamite attack on Los Angeles would be a fair prize.

Los Angeles it would be, roughly one hundred miles distant. He could make the trip in fifteen or twenty hours—including a rest for himself and the horse. He still did not know if there was anyone who might be looking for him on the Butterfield Trail. It had always been his biggest concern, which was why he had gone by sea.

It was still a concern.

Since he had no weapons—at least, none that would fail to blow him to Heaven—he would wait until he found a suitable spot. Then he would conceal himself before retiring. The bumping of the wagon also made him nervous the longer he rode. He would have to do something about that.

And it occurred to him that by getting rid of the cart he could perhaps solve two problems at once, if necessary.

"It isn't the plan we crafted," he said, "but it is the plan we have. In war, that is a compromise you must make."

Chapter 19

Three men grabbed Slash O'Malley after he struck Assistant Provost Marshal Landau. The two sentries set their rifles against the wall and grabbed his arms from behind. His father grabbed him about the waist.

Landau had staggered against the gate post. He recovered immediately, pushed off, and delivered a powerful uppercut toward his assailant. Slash was able to pull his head back enough to avoid the main force of the blow. But he couldn't duck a rifle butt in the gut. It was delivered by a fourth soldier who came running through the open door and grabbed the Springfield one of the sentries had set aside.

All the air left Slash's body. He doubled over, limp save for the waggling of his head as he swore at the men who held him and the general who had jailed his wife.

Jackson backed off at once. He stepped beside Merritt, who was neither surprised nor upset by what Slash had done. He seemed numb, as if he had been expecting the boy to break. At the same time, he looked like a man whose last, best hope to save his sister had gone up in an act of futility.

Maybe all if it was, he thought sadly. The Devil had won.

"He has a knife!" Landau said, stepping back and rubbing his palm against his bloody jaw. "Get it!"

"I got it," Jackson said, backing away. He made a point of slipping the boy's beloved Bowie knife in his belt. "There's no need for the fighting to get more serious."

"Oh, this is serious, O'Malley," Tatham said.

The man walked up as the sentries disappeared with Slash. Landau followed them, leaving the detective with Jackson and Merritt.

"Heard the commotion and came over," Tatham said. He grinned. "You understand, of course, that I've been expecting something like this." He laughed. "Annulment. Do you imagine that we are as gullible as you, vaquero?"

"Is that what we were?" Jackson asked. "'Gullible'?"

Tatham stopped talking. For Jackson, that cinched the deceit . . . the lie.

In the dark, by the lantern light, the man seemed especially sinister. Or maybe, Jackson thought, it was the crooked smile—the first he had seen on the man's face.

"Well, O'Malley, this is where we part," Tatham said. "Except for you, everybody's got what they want. Your son will be reunited with his new bride."

Standing slightly behind, Merritt had been looking at Jackson, not Tatham. In particular, he had been watching the naked blade that hung at his side, in the shadow.

The reverend gently put his hand on the man's elbow.

"I'm all right," Jackson said, turning slightly aside.

When he turned, the blade caught the light of the lantern. Tatham snickered. He stepped to one side, the same light showing his bare hand resting on one of his own revolvers.

"We the people of these United States," he said almost

gaily. "Trusting each other as we would an Indian in war paint."

"Less," Jackson said.

"Have it your way." Tatham smiled, showing teeth in the light. "Feel free to follow us to Needles in the morning. You'll get two hangings for the price of one."

Merritt tightened his grip, but there was no need. Jackson had no intention of giving the man cause for a third hanging.

Trailing laughter that was part satisfaction, part cruelty, Tatham turned and went into the fort. One of the sentries had returned and, stepping back outside, shut the door.

"Go away at once," he ordered the two men.

Moving as though the life had been burned out of them, the husks of Jackson O'Malley and Merritt Michaels began a long, sluggish journey back down the road.

Merritt was praying. Jackson, as soon as he was able, was thinking.

"I'm wondering, Merritt, if the boy did that for a reason," Jackson said when they were well away from the gate.

"He was possessed by—"

"No . . . I mean a getting-in-the-fort reason," Jackson clarified. "Slash can read animals and their moods better'n anyone save Joe. It was clear we was being turned away. That was his best chance."

"To what end?" Merritt asked. "He can't even fight— you took his knife."

Jackson held it up, admired its dark contours. "He loves this blade. I didn't want him to lose it. That was one of the reasons I took it."

"Lose *it*?" Merritt said. "What about his life?"

Jackson replied, "He has made your sister his life. In these two weeks, I never saw such a change come over a man. If he hadn't attacked Landau, tonight, he would have charged that Cavalry escort in the morning—single-handed, if it came to that."

"I read *Ivanhoe* and *The Count of Monte Cristo* to Clarity when we were children," Merritt said. "But romances do not always end in a storybook way."

"This one still may," Jackson said. "At least, that's what I'll be hoping while I figure out how to get this knife over the stockade wall."

Merritt stopped and faced him in the dark.

"Brother Jackson, what in the name of Dear Jesus are you talking about?"

Jackson stopped a little ahead and looked back at Merritt. "I'm saying that there was another reason I took this knife."

Merritt frowned as he forced himself to think back. "Yes, you mentioned that there were 'reasons.' Would you kindly share the others?"

"I had only one," Jackson said. "I didn't want the soldiers to go searching their new prisoner."

"Why?"

Jackson replied, "He still had the key."

Slash allowed himself to be half-carried, half-dragged through the courtyard to the stockade. He yelled out as he did so, apparently in rage, in actuality hoping that either Sisquoc or Malibu would hear.

They had.

"I want my knife!" he shouted desperately. "My pa took it. I *want* it!"

The sentries ignored Slash's entreaties as they manhandled him forward.

The two Mission Indians retreated to the stable. They did not want to be spotted by Guilford—or, more important, Master Sergeant Graves, the man who had given them permission to go to this boy's wedding. Graves might not know who it was the sentries had arrested.

Not yet. But soon, the Indians knew, he would.

"They are destroying O'Malleys," Malibu said.

"We have to see Jackson," Sisquoc said. "Decide who are we with."

"I will go," Malibu said. "If I'm missed, you can say I went to help Jonata pack up her beads. He will believe that."

"*I* would believe that," Sisquoc smiled.

When the stable boy wasn't looking, Malibu left by the back door. Sisquoc remained, mucking the stall of his horse, hoping the grateful boy wouldn't come over and ask where the Indian's companion was.

Malibu avoided the trail and hurried down the steep hill, sure-footedly making his way to level ground and a bend in the river. It was there, as it happened, that Jackson and Merritt were just arriving with three horses in tow.

Jackson spotted the Indian coming toward them.

"Malibu!" he said quietly but with relief that spoke to the kind of day it had been.

The Chumash came over and embraced the man. Then he bowed politely at Merritt. The reverend's face also described the pitiful state of things.

"I saw them pulling Slash to the stockade," Malibu said. "He was yelling about his knife."

"To you, I think," Jackson said. He handed the Indian the blade hilt-first. "I can't ask you to do this, old friend, but the boy is going to need it."

"I know. But—he will kill to get out?"

"Not from the jail," Jackson told him. "He has a key. The challenge will be getting out of the stockade and then the fort."

"I would say not to try," Malibu said.

"That isn't a good choice for either of them," Merritt said. "Guilford wants Slash dead and Tatham will hang my sister."

"I did not say surrender," Malibu clarified. "We can keep them hidden. When the soldiers ride out to find them—that is the time to go. Yet I worry what will happen then. The general will not give up the pursuit."

"We will have to get Slash and Clarity to safety, most likely Mexico," Jackson said. "I won't like it, none of my family will. But the choice is seeing a firing squad and a hangman do their dirty work."

Malibu understood. "I can get to him by bringing water," he said. "There is a place I can take them where searchers will not think to look," he said.

"Where?" Jackson asked.

"The mortar magazine," Malibu answered. "The general had it stocked last month. There is no reason for anyone to enter."

Jackson nodded.

"And if anyone does find them there," Malibu added, "he is not without the ability to bargain."

Jackson embraced the Indian again. "I hate for you to risk so much, my friend."

"Would any O'Malley fail to do the same?"

"No," Jackson answered. He glanced back at the reverend. "Nor, I think, any Michaels."

Leaving the two, Malibu returned the way he had come, rejoined Sisquoc, and left the stable.

Sebastián Sanchez reached Oak Grove shortly after midnight, an hour before his companions arrived.

He had been lucky. The lantern showed rutted wagon marks off to the west of the Butterfield Trail. He assumed the trail went to Warner's Ranch, but the ruts took him to Oak Grove. He was right. Though Sanchez knew he should go on, he also knew that without rest he would not be able to go on. Not effectively.

His arrival woke the Hamptons. He introduced himself— apologizing for the hour—but they were only too happy to welcome him.

"It's been a long ride from Vallicita across the desert," he said. "Drink and rest are all I require."

"Your horse? Shall I stable him?"

"No, no. He is fine," Sanchez said. "He has been eating grass along the way."

Thomas put him in a small bedroom that had once been an officer's quarters, on the same cot the officer had used. The man accepted lemon-flavored water and lay down. He did not bother to undress or take off his shoes. He was too tired.

It was quiet. Sanchez allowed himself to forget the chase. His tired mind drifted to Mexico, to his sister Anita and her new baby, and her sister-in-law Patricia who was waiting for him to be done with war.

And in the quiet, Sanchez heard the woman say to her husband, "It is strange to have two Mexicans visit us on the same day."

Patricia vanished, and he repeated the words he had just heard, making sure he had heard them correctly. At the same time, he was moving his legs, his tired arms, forcing his eyes open.

He rose from the bed, opened the door, and stood there like Samson between the pillars of the Philistine temple.

"Sir?" Thomas asked. "Is something wrong?"

"The man who was here," Sanchez said. "I—I am supposed to meet him. How did he leave? And when?"

"He purchased our cart and horse to go to Los Angeles," the proprietor told him. "He was very generous, said he needed it to carry his bags."

"Did he tell you what was in these bags?" Sanchez asked. He added quickly, lest they get suspicious, "I am seeking a man who would have been carrying very delicate things."

"Then that is your man," Thomas said. "I remarked on how carefully he handled them."

The Mexican left the room at once, fishing a coin from his pocket and placing it in Thomas' hand.

"One more thing, please," he said. "When did he leave?"

"It was, I think, about two hours ago," Erica answered. "He was in a hurry to get on the road."

"North, yes?" Sanchez asked.

"That's right," Thomas answered. "To Los Angeles."

Sanchez asked one more favor: a description of the horse and wagon. Receiving it, Sanchez thanked him, left another coin, and ran out to his horse. He was gone at a gallop before the Hamptons knew what to make of the exchange.

Thomas did not think on it for very long. Gathering up

the two coins, he said, "We should wish for more Mexicans," he said. "It has been a very enriching day!"

Anna loved the sea. She loved it more than Eustace who, up at the prow, using a lantern to watch for rocks, kept wishing he were somewhere else.

"On a farm," he said at one point. "Like I grew up on, only not owned by someone. My own."

Anna let him talk. She was focused on the sail and the coastline. She didn't need a spyglass, like the others. She grew up here, the daughter of a fisherman, and she knew the California shore better than she knew her own lined face. Both, in fact, got their character from the sea.

Eustace's lantern illuminated enough of the coast so that she could stay near to the shore without being afraid of running into it. She knew the currents well, and compensated with artful shifts of the sail and tiller. Whenever the sail blocked her view, Eustace called out to warn her to alter course west or east.

They spotted the high, proud masts of the *Manhattan*. The vessel was at anchor in its deep cove some two hundred feet from shore. Lights burned on deck, and they had no trouble navigating alongside. They had been spotted by the night watch and, after Anna identified herself and who she had come to see, a ladder was lowered. While Eustace dropped the sail and secured the boat, Anna was taken to see the captain. Morgan Landry was in his late forties, of medium height and build. Though he had obviously been abed when she arrived, he did not meet her in a robe but in a shirt and trousers. The lamps on the wall had all been lit.

Captain Landry met her with a courtly bow. "I've met you, I believe," he said.

"Yessir, in San Diego on Independence Day," she said.

"Of course. The boat rentals. Would you care for anything?" he asked.

"No, sir. Thank you."

The captain gestured to a seat, but Anna remained standing. The woman's gray hair was wildly free of its ribbon, her clothes soaked with sea spray, and her expression grim. Landry did not return to his desk, as he had intended.

"You have a message from the harbormaster?" he asked.

"Important one," she said. "I have to say it because there was no time to write things down. Early today *The Dundee,* a schooner, left port. Came back about two hours later with holes in both sides, and sinking. It went down before making it all the way back."

"Captain Swift's boat?"

"That's her. I never seen a wreck like this . . . many dead."

"Is Captain Swift—?"

"He survived, badly hurt. But he was able to tell Rog York—the harbormaster—that there was a man transporting a new kind of explosive and he intentionally sunk the boat before going ashore."

"I will immediately organize a party to go after him," Landry said, moving toward the door.

"Sir, that isn't the only concern," she said. "I don't fully understand, but Rog seems to think that Benito Juárez is in danger. He's—"

"Coming north on a diplomatic trip," Landry said. "We

were told to expect him later today and meet him with a sixteen-gun volley."

As Landry spoke, he went to the door, opened it, and then called for First Lieutenant Jack Wyndham. The man arrived promptly and was told to rouse the Barbary Seven, a contingent of Marines who had trained at the Washington Navy Yard and distinguished themselves on blockade duty during the war.

"I will be on deck to give them their mission ashore immediately," he said. "Send a man ahead to the stable master, they will be mounted and riding hard. Also, we will be setting sail with the sun on an interception mission to the south."

The young officer acknowledged, saluted, and hurried to the crew quarters.

Landry turned back to the woman.

"You have my gratitude and respect, dear woman," he said. "Is there anything we can do for you?"

"My friend Eustace is below. We could use some rest and, now, I'll thank you, food and drink before we can take the winds back. Probably, if you got 'em, dry clothes for Eustace."

Landry smiled. "You'll have what you ask for as soon as Mr. Wyndham returns, though you won't need to sail back. We will take you in tow and leave you off when and where we intercept the Mexican president."

"Thank you." Anna smiled. "I know Eustace will be most grateful."

While Landry went to his coastal charts, to calculate the likely point of rendezvous, Anna and her mate were taken to the galley where the tired, wet, hungry, and arm-

weary Eustace Lee accepted the hospitality of the ship—
and enjoyed the bustle of activity surround him. Once the
Marines had departed and the big ship put to sea, the great
white sails were not half as wide and proud as the chest of
the former slave.

Chapter 20

Sanchez assumed that the man he was following would take the Butterfield Trail. At night, it was the only way to travel safely, especially with volatile explosives.

Plus, he is traveling in a wagon, the Mexican thought. His only chance at speed was taking a well-laid path.

Though tired, Sanchez was alert. Because of the sound of the horse's hooves on the trail, he wasn't able to hear any cart ahead of him—or behind. He did not see how Joe and Gonzalez could have survived an attack by a superior force, but he prayed they had. Not just for the men but for the mission.

The darkness of the night prevented him from seeing anything other than vague, dark shapes in the landscape. But he was confident the *Juarista* would have gone this way.

From Los Angeles, then perhaps by sea to San Francisco, he thought as he entered a pass between the hills. *That is the only way he can hope to reach the Barbary Coast in time.*

He reflected for a moment, wondering if that was still the plan. It seemed rather random and sudden for a lone rider, with explosives, to buy a wagon from people he had just met.

Sanchez slowed as he entered the pass. It was black here, not just dark, and the only sounds were insects on the ground and the occasional owl. He could not see any trees above, except where foliage blocked out stars.

He rode with one hand on the reins, the other holding the carbine. He did not know what he could possibly shoot at in this darkness, but it made him feel safe just holding the rifle.

Suddenly, Sanchez thought he *heard* something just to the left. For just a few paces, as he walked by, there was a slight change in the sound of the horse's hooves—as if they were echoing against something hollow. It was off the trail, but it didn't have the shape of a boulder or tree. It could have been a shed, a small cave—

Or a wagon.

Maybe his quarry decided to rest until sun-up. Sanchez thought of striking a match but decided against it. That would be painting a bull's-eye with light.

He stopped the horse and listened. He heard his heart louder than the crickets now. He was tempted to move on, more concerned about it being a bear rather than a man. But if it were the man he was chasing—

If he knew the others were coming, he would wait. But he did not know.

You have to find out, he told himself.

Dismounting slowly and very, very carefully, Sanchez reached into his saddlebag. He felt for the box of matches and struck one.

The object ahead was a wagon, tucked close to a steep rock wall. The horse was gone, possibly taken to where it could graze. Or maybe the owner was afraid of bears or other predators. Sanchez had to see what was inside. If the Hamptons were correct, and if this was their wagon—it matched the description the proprietor had provided—it might contain bags of explosives. Sanchez marked the location and shook out the match. If the owner of the wagon were watching, he did not want to give the man a target. He would feel his way.

The Mexican started slowly, cautiously across the western side of the trail to where the wagon sat athwart the path. He would step, listen, then step again. He held the carbine in both hands, ready to swing it in the direction of any sound.

The horse heard the hiss before Sanchez did. The Mexican stopped, very still. He thought it was a rattlesnake somewhere just above, or perhaps in the wagon—a trap, or perhaps a signal. The horse backed away and Sanchez did as well.

Light and movement from above caught his eye. Sanchez looked up and saw what had caused the sound. It was a small, flickering light and it was falling toward him. He did not know how high it was, how large the light was, anything about it other than that it was getting bigger. His last thought was whether it might be a shooting star falling to earth.

Martinez had moved the horse and emptied the wagon not long before he heard the man's approach. He would have let the unfortunate fellow pass but for two things.

First, he had been riding a horse with a saddle belonging to his *Juarista* militia. Martinez knew all those men. The match revealed the markings and the fact that he was not one of them. Even absent all of that, the man's rings, gleaming in the match light, announced him as a nobleman. One who, no doubt, had learned of Martinez's plan and had been pursuing him.

Now he was dead. Evaporated, with the wagon and the *Juarista* horse, in a loud, brilliant flash.

The fact that the man had that saddle suggested that some misfortune had befallen the men who were supposed to be protecting Martinez's flank. It also meant that the plan—at least some of it, perhaps all of it—was known. There was no time to rest, no time to waste. Hopefully, this was the only man pursuing him by land. Perhaps the rest were at sea, watching and waiting for a ship that would never come.

Upon entering the canyon, he had lit the lantern and looked for a place to hide the horse. He found it in a tor that had been left by the ancient collapse of the hill around it. There was a stone run around it, rubble from what used to be solid rock. Retrieving the dynamite from the wagon, Martinez had climbed the field of rocks and carefully packed the dynamite into as few bags as possible.

He had been told to check the sticks periodically to make sure that they were dry. It was not exterior moisture that he should be concerned about but the oily nitroglycerin sweating from the inside, leaving the sawdust and clay compound to bead and crystalize on the exterior of the tube. This was a result of age and motion. After a few months, the separation was inevitable. Shaking and jostling made it happen even faster.

Two of the remaining eleven sticks had a slightly sweet odor. That, as he had been warned, meant the explosive content was near the surface. Those sticks could explode with the slightest bump.

One of them just had. He did not even have to light the fuse, ignite the blasting cap to make that happen. He had done so just to be sure.

Finishing his work, Martinez went back to his horse and carefully secured the bags to both sides of the saddle. Hopefully, they would survive the rest of the trip. If not, he would not know the difference.

Before leaving, he walked the lantern back to where he had thrown the single stick. The wall of the canyon seemed to have liquefied, sliding down across the Butterfield Trail in a sheet of rock and pebble. Everything else on the road was gone. At least, anything that could be identified as a wagon, a horse, or a man were no longer there.

Again, as on the ship, the power of this explosive impressed him beyond all expectation. The stagecoach line would not be happy, but before leaving he would ignite the other sweet-smelling stick and destroy the opposite side. That would bring down more rock and effectively seal off the path. In the event that this man was an advance scout, the others would find it difficult to pick their way through this hilly region to the north.

The Mexican rode the horse down the road a way, then walked back with the stick, lit the fuse, and ran. Thirty seconds later, exposed to a naked blast for the first time, he was slammed by a roar louder than any he had ever heard and knocked forward, off his feet, by the force of the detonation.

Despite this, despite the choking dust that surrounded him, despite the fact that he could barely hear his own voice over the ringing in his ears, Martinez was laughing when he got back on his feet.

"This is what God must feel like!" he cheered into the swirling, choking mist.

On wobbly legs, Martinez moved ahead quickly to where he had left the horse. Though he had just nine sticks remaining, that would still be enough to fill the hearts of the people of Los Angeles with terror . . . and hatred for the nobles of Mexico who would be blamed.

Joe O'Malley and Rafael Gonzalez had not quite reached Oak Grove when they heard the first, and then the second explosion from farther along the Butterfield Trail. Both times, they saw light bulb up into the sky.

The first blast had caused them to stop.

Joe had looked across the sky. There were no thunder-clouds. It could not be lightning.

"Your explosives?" he asked Gonzalez.

"It could be, but why out here?"

They moved on, even faster when they heard the second explosion. Joe thought back to what had happened at Civil Gulch two weeks earlier.

"They're closing the trail," he said.

The Hamptons were both standing outside their station, alert and peering along the trail when Joe and Gonzalez arrived. There was a wailing baby in the woman's arms, a lantern in the man's hand. They turned to greet the new arrivals.

Joe tipped his hat to apologize for not dismounting. "Sorry for the intrusion, folks, but did a gentleman name of Sanchez happen to come through here tonight?" he asked.

"About an hour ago," Thomas answered. He pointed the

lantern to indicate the road north. "Say, you got any notion what's going on here?"

"Nothing that'll come this way," he assured them. "Sanchez was chasing an outlaw. Did any other riders stop here before him?"

"An outlaw?" Erica said. She did not mention the gold. If it was stolen, she had no intention of returning it.

"Just one," Thomas replied. "He didn't give a name. Mr. Sanchez said he was hurrying off to meet him."

"Your friend seemed especially interested in whatever the other man was carrying," Erica added.

"Handled it with a lot of care, I can tell you," Thomas added.

Joe thanked them, and the two men rode on.

Thomas ran forward, the lantern waggling. "Do you need any food or drink?" he called after them.

Joe waved his hand briskly back and forth without turning. The proprietor walked back to his wife. The couple deflated a little, and the baby fell silent.

"Mustn't be greedy," Erica said, as much to herself as to her husband.

"That is God's own truth," Thomas replied, shaking his head. "This has been a mite strange night."

The stockade at Fort Yuma consisted of three brick cells on opposite sides of a narrow courtyard.

The loud opening of the main stockade gate and the commotion of the two sentries and their captive brought Clarity to her feet. She watched as her husband was drawn by, followed by Landau.

"Slash!" Clarity cried, her hands gripping the bars,

her face pressed hard between them. "My love, *what* did you do?"

"He struck me," Landau called back as the prisoner was taken to a cell. He was holding a fistful of arrest forms he had just filled out. "You know, I sorta felt bad for him, for you both until that. I'm thinking now maybe he is just the hothead they've all been saying."

Slash was placed in the northernmost cell on one side. Clarity was in the southernmost cell on that same side. Except for when the party walked past, he and his wife were unable to see each other.

Landau and the sentries left, and the stockade guard closed the door, bolting it, leaving Clarity and her husband alone in the quiet compound. There was only a dog to keep them company, a mongrel whose job was to bark if anything was amiss.

"Slash?" Clarity called out. "Please answer me!"

"Are you all right?" he asked.

"Well enough. Why did you do that?"

"No talking," he said. "Make friends with the dog."

Clarity drew her face back from the bars. Her expression was puzzled as she looked down at the scruffy animal. "You mean that?"

"In earnest," he said. "Quickly."

Confused but kneeling, Clarity stuck her hand through the bars. She didn't know the animal's name, but she had called him Dirt because there was more of that than fur on him.

While his wife let the dog lick her hand, Slash dipped his hand into his shirt. He was glad his father was as sharp as he was. He hadn't taken the knife because he was afraid Slash would use it. He knew the soldiers would do that, and then they would search him. Without the knife, they might not bother.

They did not. Which was why they did not find the skeleton key he had fixed onto the necklace he wore, the one Clarity had given him before they parted.

He wasted no time. He was willing to bet bullets to bowties that Tatham or Guilford or both would be along presently to gloat. Of course, getting out would not be enough. He needed something else to happen—which was another reason he hoped, he prayed, his father had acted.

The lock opened with some effort.

"How's the dog?" he asked before he opened the door.

"Fine, I think." She didn't ask what he was doing. The guard might overhear.

She heard an unoiled creaking as the door opened. Clarity did not ask how her husband came to possess the key. It did not matter. A moment later the dog scurried to where they had placed Slash. Pressing her face against the bar she could see him squatting and playing with the animal. He picked it up, stroking it, then came forward and passed his wife the key.

She wanted to kiss him more than she wanted to get out, but that passed as they heard the dead bolt at the front of the gate being pulled back. Clarity dropped the key down her blouse. Slash placed the dog on the ground and ran back to his cell. He shut the door.

The guard admitted a man carrying a canteen and a tin cup.

It was Malibu. Dirt ran over, his tail swinging wildly. He dropped a piece of biscuit on the ground. The Indian nodded at Clarity and went to Slash's cell with the water.

"We already had the boy trained," Slash said as the Indian stepped to the cell.

"I should have expected as much," Malibu said. He did not give the young man the canteen but pulled the Bowie knife from inside his uniform. "Be wise with this," he cautioned.

The Indian offered Slash a drink, but the young man declined.

"Go, so we can get out," Slash said. He pushed the door a little in explanation. "And thank you, my dear friend."

Malibu nodded and looked at the youngest O'Malley. "May your ancestors watch over you both," he said.

"Thank you," Slash said as he sheathed the knife. "And thanks for your friendship even more."

Malibu left and Slash waited until the outer door was bolted before leaving his cell. Clarity had already turned the key and opened her own door. Despite the urgency of the moment, she threw her arms around Slash and held him in a way that made him forget their plight—but only for a pair of elated heartbeats.

He kissed her lips as he was pulling away.

"Where do we go?" she asked in a whisper. "I haven't seen anything of the fort, but I suspect the rear is safest?"

"Maybe," Slash said. He pointed straight ahead. "But we're going out that door."

She looked at him with a mix of curiosity and alarm. "What are you talking about? They'll shoot you—*us*—for trying to escape!"

"No, they won't," Slash assured her. "The guard—he has a rifle."

It took her a moment to get his meaning. "You expect me to shoot someone?"

"No," he replied. "I've got it figured out. We are not leaving."

"I don't understand," Clarity told him.

"I've decided not to run," her husband said firmly. "I was checking the layout while they brought me here. I have a plan to get to the general's headquarters."

"And do what?" she asked with alarm.

He replied, "Bet my life on Tatham being a liar."

Chapter 21

The two men barely stopped their horses before running into the wall of rock. Only the sudden deadening of the sound of their hooves alerted Joe to an impediment.

"He is not that far ahead of us," Gonzalez lamented as Joe walked his horse along the blocked roadway. "But it might as well be a continent!"

"We gotta go around," Joe said, "but we'd best rest till sun-up. We'll move faster if the horses are rested and we can see where we're going."

"It isn't that far from Los Angeles, Joe," Gonzalez said. "He may *be* there by morning."

Joe considered this. There was no waterway they could use or follow and just hills on either side of the Butterfield Trail. The rocks were piled too high to even think about moving them.

"The only other option is to go on foot," Joe said. "We climb these and set out. What the hell day is it?"

"I don't even know," Gonzalez admitted.

"Butterfield stages come every three days—Virgil Pierce'll be coming north, Sten Wilson going south. They'll both

stop here and have to go back to the last station for help
cutting a path."

"Then we leave the horses and go," Gonzalez said, already dismounting.

Joe took his weapons and water, wondering how a man
who had intended to run a stagecoach station continually
ended up back in the plains, his life in constant peril.

A prairie dog don't change his fur, he thought as he went
to unsaddle the horses. His hand fell on something in a
leather loop on the saddle.

"Hold it," Joe said.

"What is wrong?"

"Maybe nothing," Joe replied. Leaving the horse, he
went to the rocks piled in front of them. He felt his way in
the dark, moving along the wall lengthwise.

"Did you think of something?"

"High but not so steep in spots," Joe said.

"Meaning what?"

Joe said, "We're going to rest. Soon's the sun is up.
We'll walk the horses over the wall."

"How?"

Joe answered, "There's trees over us. I can see the
leaves. We got a hatchet. Come first light, we cut branches
and lay in a ramp up one and then down the other. If there's
a spot on top to stand, we can use the same wood."

Gonzalez was suddenly heartened—mostly. He did not
like the idea of sitting here, waiting. But he knew that
having the horses rested was far more desirable than pro-
ceeding on foot with no plan. He reluctantly agreed. Joe
rode back a way and positioned himself facing the eastern
horizon so he would be up with the sun. He told Gonzalez
to stay where he was.

"If something happens to one of us, the other can continue," he explained.

The men unsaddled their horses and used them as rough but acceptable pillows. Despite their concerns about the enemy who was moving closer to Los Angeles, sleep—and dawn—came quickly.

Joe examined the wall and found the lowest spot, which also had the shallowest incline. It was about ten feet over their heads.

"It'll be like going up a snow-covered slope," Joe said. "You walk the horse with hard tugs so it doesn't decide to stop—and you're over."

Gonzalez looked skeptical but had no choice but to trust the experienced frontiersman.

Joe was pleased to see that there would be less chopping than he had expected. The trees on the wall of the valley were old, and erosion had dropped several of them over time. Their limbs were scattered among the saplings. Joe easily scaled the sloping wall and, with the help of his companion, and with additional chopping, they collected a stack of suitable logs in less than two hours. There were enough for a three- or four-foot-wide walkway on both sides.

Half of the logs were laid upright, side by side, at the spot Joe had selected.

When the men were finished, they were still about two feet short of the top.

"I'll go up and push the rocks down the other side," Joe said.

"No," the Mexican said. "I will. If you get hurt, I'm stuck here."

Joe grinned. "I appreciate the concern."

"In matters such as these, I have learned to be professional, not personal," he explained.

Gonzalez went up on his palms and toes, as he had seen monkeys do in Chapultepec Park. Joe was impressed. He would have crawled up.

The rocks did not fall easily but they finally gave way, Gonzalez leveling the spot on top. He told Joe to wait while he ran along the wall to grab some rotted logs as filler. Kneeling, he patted the mulch into the spaces between the rocks large and small so the horses would not catch their hooves or fall. When he was ready, he came down, walking himself down on his back.

"Nicely done," Joe said as the man got to his feet.

"I really want that man, Joe," Gonzalez said. "Let's do the other side and get over."

The men carried the rest of the logs up. Joe had decided it would be easier to make the up-and-down trip in one piece rather than try to get the horses to settle on top while he and Gonzalez hauled these logs from one side to the other.

When they were finished, Joe went first, walking and pulling the reins of his horse. He stomped with every step, making sure the logs would not slide or crack beneath him. The animal went reluctantly at first, then faster as it became eager to get back on firm ground. When they reached the top, Joe turned the animal so it stood lengthwise along the top of the wall. He steadied the animal with strokes on the neck and soft words. He wished he had a hood to cover the horse's eyes so it couldn't see the road so far below.

"But I don't," he said quietly, "so we're gonna turn now, and I'll try to help you get your footing."

Tugging the rein sharply, the animal turned and had no choice but to put its forelegs on the downward slope. It resisted the descent, trying to back away. Joe had to put his shoulder into a tug, pulling ahead and down hard. The horse came, but it came so fast it nearly ran him over. Joe half-ran, half-stumbled down, staying ahead of the horse—but just barely. He finally jumped from the ramp when he was about five feet up. He landed hard but he didn't break anything.

More important, neither did the horse.

"Joe?" Gonzalez cried.

"We're down!" he yelled back. "You come over—let me do the other one."

"No!" Gonzalez called back. "I, too, have ridden for many, many years."

"In corrals or on rickety slopes?"

Gonzalez didn't answer. Joe heard the hollow clop of the hooves on the logs. He admired the Mexican's gumption. He never liked being out with a partner who needed hand-carrying.

The sounds were uneven, uncertain, and Gonzalez yelled frequently. Joe listened as they rose and was relieved when he saw the head of the Mexican appear over the top.

"Well damn you for a fool!" Joe said. It was less of an oath than an expression of admiration.

The man was riding the horse.

The two did not pause the way Joe had but came over the wall and down the other side. Gonzalez was leaning well back, helping the horse to maintain its balance. They cleared the rocks faster than Joe had.

"In a corral," Gonzalez said, reining up beside the unmounted plainsman, "where I jumped stone walls."

Patting the panting horse on its flank, Joe mounted his own steed and the well-rested, invigorated quartet galloped off.

"Guard!" Clarity yelled. "*Guard!*"

Private Victor Tufts had been half-dozing, upright, at his post in front of the stockade. It had been a long, typically uneventful night until now. All he wanted was sun-up and his cot.

And his discharge. He had been too young to serve in the War, and when his older brothers got out, his pa insisted that he go in. The Cavalry was not for the eighteen-year-old. He wanted to study medicine, and he was lied to, told by the recruiting officer that he could. Until he was sick, he never even met the fort medic.

Tufts certainly did not want to deal with that woman. She had been quiet until the other man arrived. There was a rumor that she would be leaving come morning. He hoped so. He liked it when the cells had soldier and civilian drunks who just slept.

Collecting his energies, he unbolted the door, took the lantern from its hook outside, extended an arm, and looked in. The woman was up against the bars, looking out.

"What d'you need?" he asked.

She pointed ahead, on the ground. Somehow, she had lost a shoe and the dog was chewing it.

Tufts made a face. "How the heck did that happen?"

"I was teasing Dirt with the string," she said. "He pulled it."

Tufts walked in. "I'd let him keep it, 'cept he might choke."

No sooner had the soldier entered than there was a very long, very sharp knife laid across his throat from behind.

"Wha—?"

"Move even a finger and you die," Slash told him.

Clarity had already come from the cell. She grabbed the man's rifle and lantern before he could drop either. Behind her, Dirt continued to chew her shoe. She retrieved it while Slash walked his frightened young captive to Clarity's cell. The door was still open. Slash moved faster, entering the cell and driving the man's head, hard, into the brick wall in back.

There wasn't time to bind him and gag him. This was the fastest way to keep him quiet. He dropped the dazed boy to the ground.

"You ready?" he asked Clarity.

She had already examined the rifle and sighted it. She held it across her chest, looking like herself again. That, and a resolute expression, was her answer.

"I'm gonna set you in a spot to cover me," he said. "When I get inside the general's place, follow if you can."

"I'll be there," she promised.

Slash left the door open. Anyone who looked over and saw the guard absent from his post would assume he was inside. They didn't need to delay any arrivals for long— only until they were in position.

Moving along the shadowy outside wall of the stockade, they made their way to the row of adjoining structures immediately to the east. The office of the assistant provost marshal was first. It was dark. There was a yew wood chair outside, Windsor style with slats on the high back. Slash moved it out slightly, still keeping it in shadow, and motioned for Clarity to get behind it.

She had not needed to be told. Slash could not see the confident set of her jaw, the hawk-like purpose in her eyes, as the woman got on one knee and slid the barrel between two slats in the middle. From there, she could cover the entire compound right to the front gate.

"I love you," she whispered as her husband continued to the next door down.

Slash was too close to the general's headquarters to risk responding. The light was on, the window was open, and there were voices inside.

"Who's out there?"

The voice broke from near the flagpole, where Landau was just returning from a card game.

"Go!" Clarity urged her husband.

Slash bolted ahead, threw open the door, and entered the office. He stepped toward the desk when he heard a flurry of gunshots getting nearer outside. That would be Clarity, shooting high as she made her way to the door. She entered and kicked the door shut. The general and Tatham were both seated behind the desk, studying a map. The rifle was pointed at both men before they had even responded to the presence of Slash and his drawn knife.

"Thought I'd find you both here," Slash said. "Blood brothers."

"You will hang," Guilford said thickly through the smoke of his cigar. "Tonight."

"Put your hands flat on the desk, both of you," Slash said.

Tatham obeyed slowly. Guilford did not. Clarity put a bullet so close to the edge of the desk that splinters hit the officer in the face.

"I've got nothing to lose," she said. "Next one goes through the brass button third from the top."

Guilford reluctantly obliged her.

Slash approached. There was an uproar outside the door but no one entered. Without lowering the rifle, Clarity went to a spot where she could not be seen from any of the windows.

"First man who looks in loses his face!" she yelled through the open window.

"Everyone stay back!" Guilford yelled. "I will handle this!"

"Yes, you will," Slash said. "I want just one thing from you, general. The warrant that this man said was put out for my wife."

"I don't take orders at gunpoint," Guilford answered.

"How about knifepoint?" Slash said. "We asked kindly, several times, and you didn't help us then either."

When Slash was nearly at the desk, Tatham looked as if he were weighing a leap across it. Clarity put a bullet in the wall, just under his ear. He felt it go by. He went very, very still.

Guilford rolled the cigar from one side of his mouth to the other.

"There is no warrant," the general admitted. "Fortunately, I don't need one now. I don't even have to transport you to Needles. In front of the entire company, you have commandeered a Cavalry facility, held its top-ranking officer hostage, and will die, here, for that."

A voice came from outside.

"We are coming in," the speaker said calmly.

"Who's there?" Slash demanded—recognizing the voice but unable to place it.

"The man you struck, Assistant Provost Marshal Landau," he replied. "I'm with the two Mission Indians."

"You there, Malibu?" Slash asked.

"I am," he said. "Marshal speaks the truth."

"General," Landau said, "we heard what you just said. Several of us did. Under Cavalry Regulations, Section—"

"Don't you *dare* quote the regulations to me!" Guilford ordered.

"Very well, sir, but I am placing you under arrest. Colonel Burke—who is with me—will be assuming command."

The general just glared at Slash. The younger man showed no emotion, other than unrepentant resolve to see justice done.

Tatham rose. He looked at Clarity. "Put the gun down. I have something to settle with your husband."

Slash let his gaze shift to the man. "You're no detective," Slash said. "Not even a bounty hunter."

"That's correct," Tatham said.

"Hired gun," Slash said.

Tatham did not have to reply. "I don't care about this man," he said, indicating the general, "or his fight with you. But I will finish the contract I came to execute or I will die in the effort."

"You will die in the effort," Slash informed him.

Tatham grinned. "You once said you could take me, boy. Can you? Can you do that without the help of a woman?"

There were faces in the windows now, and light spilling in from lanterns. For the first time, Clarity seemed anxious. But she said nothing. The challenge back at the station had been Slash's. This was not her fight.

"Outside?" Tatham said. "Knives?"

Slash looked from Tatham to his wife to the door. Without a word, he went outside.

Clarity suppressed a sob. She understood. She would do no different herself, if challenged by anyone. But she also knew that pride was the wrong reason to continue a war that was over.

Tatham's guns, which she knew well, were hanging on a hook by the door. Clarity lowered the barrel as Tatham walked by, still grinning. She wanted to shoot him even more than she had wanted to shoot Bill Roche. But then it *would* be murder, not self-defense.

Tatham stepped onto the walk then down to the dirt. A circle of soldiers had formed, lanterns high. Slash was in the middle. They parted to admit the man. Behind him, Clarity emerged from the headquarters. Passing the rifle to Landau, she joined the circle. She had to be there for Slash, either in joy or sorrow. Her expression was stoic.

Both combatants ignored her. They were regarding each other, nothing else.

"I'm not wearing," Tatham said to no one in particular. "Anyone have a blade for me?"

"I got one!" a voice shouted from outside. It was the cook with a butcher knife. The men made room so he could toss it at Tatham's feet.

The killer picked it up and made a few diagonal slashes in the air. He was still smiling. He crouched, the blade held forward, belly high to Slash.

The younger man had fought for fun with his father and grandfather, to train, not to kill. He took a moment to think of Gert, of the Apache, of the way they pushed their human spirit aside to become a cold, hungry wolf or eagle or snake.

He stood straight, his right arm across his chest, the blade pointed outward, flat side up. His other arm was low, below his waist, clawed—like talons. That was how he once stood off a puma, when they happened on one another. The cat was on a ledge. If it jumped, Slash had been ready.

Tatham was on the outside and began to circle. Slash remained in the middle and turned along with him. In his mind he was hovering, looking down, ready to strike when his prey moved.

Slash was scared, just as he'd been with the mountain lion. But that made him sharply alert.

The killer made a few test lunges, shouting each time. Slash did not react to either the movement or the sound.

"He's trying to make you afraid!" someone shouted.

It was the only sound from the circle. The men were respectfully silent as word spread of what had happened in the general's headquarters.

Tatham began to tighten the circles, spiraling closer. Slash extended his arm slightly to create more of a buffer. His feet did not move from his spot, except to turn.

And then the bigger man lunged, as if he were stabbing with a sword. It came toward Slash's left side and he deflected it with his arm, the blade slicing through buckskin and the flesh of his forearm. The sleeve quickly stained with blood.

For that moment, though, Tatham's own left side was exposed. Slash did not want the man's arm, he wanted his heart. He cut outward from his chest but Tatham met him with his own free arm. In a moment, the two adversaries were locked, Tatham laughing.

The killer was the stronger and more experienced of the two and easily threw Slash to his back. Tatham dropped on top of him, pinning his knife arm with his knee. The killer put his fingers around Slash's throat, Slash grabbed his knife-wrist, and the two struggled.

Slash's blade was pointed away from Tatham. He was

struggling for air. He bucked at the hips and could not dislodge the man. His resistance to the downward-pressing knife was weakening. With great effort, Slash released the knife arm. As it came down, the man's weight shifted to that side. Slash used the support of the ground to shift to his right. Tatham's knife buried itself in the dirt. Momentarily free of his choking fingers and knee, Slash was able to pull his right arm free.

His knife went into Tatham's exposed left thigh.

The bigger man yelled, snarled, and raised his knife, intending to put it into Slash's chest. But Slash had not withdrawn his own blade. He twisted, hard, the blade tearing a wide circle of flesh and muscle. Tatham fell to his right side, reaching for the knife. Slash withdrew it, squirreled from beneath him, scrambled to his knees, and cocked his arm back. There was a clear, clean line to the man's gut.

There was a gunshot. Landau stepped forward, entering the ring, his pistol still raised.

"I will take things from here," he said. "Slash, take your lady and go. I promise this man will be dealt with."

Slash rose unsteadily, blood running down his left wrist. It was the medic, not Clarity, who reached him first.

"Let me have him first," he said to the woman.

Slash sheathed the knife. "I think that cur needs you more," he said, indicating Tatham as he took his wife in his good arm.

While the doctor sent two men for a stretcher, an old soldier came over to the victor, admiration splashed across his face.

"Ma'am, you got a spunky man there," he said to Clarity—though he was looking at Slash.

"Thank you," she replied graciously.

"I—I did something like you, once," the man went on. "It was agin' a *moose*. Had me pinned *just* like that!"

"I learned it fighting with my collie," Slash said, adding, "and also, from my sister."

Leaving the puzzled man behind, Slash walked with Clarity toward the infirmary.

Chapter 22

The arid plain gave way to lush countryside as Joe followed his compass north.

The two men remained on the Butterfield Trail, keeping up a brisk pace. As Joe had expected, they met Whip Sten Wilson riding south. Joe hailed him from the middle of the trail with an upraised hand.

"Joe O'Malley, what're you doing hereabout?" the former Pony Express rider asked.

"Looking for someone. Loner, likely large sacks for saddlebags? See him?"

"About three miles back," Wilson replied. "Riding real easy, if I may say. What's the story?"

"Tell you another time," Joe said. "Way down, way is blocked by a big landslide. Can't go around. Better to head back to Chino Hills Station and bring men."

"Aw, hell," Wilson said. "Don't suppose you can ask for me? On yer way."

"We really need to catch this fella," Joe said. "You'd have to sit there an' wait for help anyway."

"Yeah, that's true," Wilson said. "Okay, Joe, thanks for the warning. See you at Whip Station. And good luck."

"Thanks," Joe said, kicking the horse to a gallop as he rounded the stage.

Gonzalez followed, leaning forward in the saddle with a sense of urgency—and reckoning.

Martinez hated the slow pace he was forced to take, but he was heartened as the first signs of civilization budded on the horizon. There was a wooden bridge over a dry riverbed and, beyond it, a barn and what looked like a residence.

"The outskirts of an expanding city," he said.

He continued at his steady walk, eyeing the bridge and thinking it might be a way to announce his arrival. Bring people out to see what had happened, leaving their homes and businesses beyond open . . . and unprotected.

The air was clear, the wind low and quiet, and the sound of the hoofbeats behind him clearly heard. He looked back.

Two men were coming hard in his direction. He did not have to imagine who they might be. He had no idea how they got around the roadblock, but it didn't matter. He looked ahead. He had to cover the quarter mile to the wooden bridge and destroy it before they reached him. The explosion would not only delay them, it would provide smoky cover so they couldn't get a good shot at him.

The problem was, they were gaining on him. He dared not speed up. Reluctantly, as he rode, he unlashed the top of one of the sacks. He reached in and carefully, with his fingertips, withdrew one of the sticks of dynamite.

He did not light it—yet. He could not afford to let them get as close as the other man had, since they would be armed. But he wanted to do damage.

"And they won't shoot me," he uttered confidently.

"They don't know what might make these explode, how much damage they will do."

He risked a little more speed. When the men were nearing rifle range, he stopped and lit the stick in his hand. The fuse would burn for about thirty seconds. He released it behind him in an arcing overhand throw and then continued his ride. The dynamite landed, sizzling, on the trail.

Martinez heard the horses neigh as the men wrenched them around, east and west. He had been counting, turned back just before the dynamite tore a large crater in the ground and sent rocks flying and falling like hail. It pelted the two men, even though they had put considerable distance between themselves and the blast.

The Mexican continued, faster now, as the bridge loomed. He crossed it even as the two riders were still swinging their way back to the road.

This would put an end to their pursuit. The riverbed was wide with soft walls that would collapse under a horse.

He dismounted, almost casually, and wedged a stick between the last board and the ground. He watched, waited, then struck a match and lit the fuse.

Remounting, Martinez rode away confidently. He ignored the two men who emerged from the barn to see what had made the previous disturbance. They were about to get a more dramatic lesson.

The bridge went up as if it had been struck from below by a cannon firing at the sky. The sound rolled down the riverbed, the wood—some of it afire—flew up and then tumbled down, everything from boards the size of an arm to splinters the size of a fingernail. The horse flinched but Martinez steadied it, even as the heat and force of the yellow-red fireball reached them.

The horse stayed the straight course past the barn, past

the house, as Martinez looked back. There was nothing left for the men to cross. He turned back to the road and looked ahead at a row of structures on a main street.

They would not be there for very much longer.

When Joe reached the riverbed, he threw himself from his horse, grabbed his rifle, and skidded down the side of the riverbed, first on his heels, then on his backside. He reached the rocky bottom, bruising his feet with the impact. It hurt to run across but that was what he did. Every part of him ached from the logging and wall-climbing, but he wasn't going to stop now.

Gonzalez was behind him, mimicking what the frontiersman had done. Reaching the other side, Joe tossed his rifle up and grabbed the largest piece of board he could find—the signpost that had stood at the eastern side of the bridge. It was charred and still burning around the edges. He slapped it against the steep bank, grabbed the top, and held on there as he tried to dig his boots into the loose earth.

Neither the boots nor the dirt would cooperate. He slid back down.

"Boost me!" he said as Gonzalez arrived.

The Mexican bent by the bank, cupped his hands, and Joe stepped his right foot in. Gonzalez strained to raise him, Joe stretched his fingers out—

And then the men from the barn came over and pulled him up.

"Tarnation was *that*?" one of the men asked.

"Later," Joe said, finding his rifle and kneeling.

He aimed at Martinez and fired. The man was just out of range.

"We gotta stop him before he reaches the town," Joe said. "He's got more explosives."

"Can you ride bareback?" the other man asked.

"Like an Injun," Joe answered as they ran toward the barn.

Before they got there, their quarry stopped suddenly. A dead halt, facing straight ahead. He was still two hundred feet or so outside the town, too early for an explosion.

Joe didn't waste time thinking about it. He bolted ahead, his arms churning, wanting only to get within range before the man moved. He was nearly where he wanted to be when the Mexican flew backward from his horse.

"Now what?" Joe asked as Gonzalez came up behind him.

Joe resumed running forward, the Mexican at his side. They stopped when they saw what had knocked Martinez from the saddle.

A contingent of United States Marines. Six of them dressed in blue, all mounted and in a row.

"Now if that don't beat all," Joe said. He came forward, holding up his rifle with both hands so no one took a shot at him.

The man at the far right of the group came forward.

"Who would you two be?" asked the man, a lieutenant by his markings and about thirty by his sun-darkened but unlined features.

"I'm Joe O'Malley of the Whip Station down San Diego way," he said. "This is Rafael Gonzalez representing lawful interests further south. We been following this man, the one you shot. He's been blowing stuff up with a stolen explosive called 'dynamite.' Intended to blow up more. And you, sir?"

"Lieutenant Jim Grand, seconded to the naval vessel *Manhattan* at San Luis Rey," he answered.

"What brought you here?" Joe asked, "and at a right good time, I might add."

"Someone blew up *The Dundee,* a schooner outside of

San Diego harbor," Grand replied. "We knew his general direction on land. When we heard the explosion—"

"Gave himself away, the blasted idiot," Joe said.

He regarded the men ministering to Martinez. Beyond them, having heard the explosions, the townspeople had begun to come out. At a sign from Grand, two of the Marines left to urge them back.

"Why didn't you kill him?" Gonzalez asked.

"Not our orders," Grand said. "Do you gentlemen have any idea why he did what he did?"

"He's a *Juarista*," Gonzalez said. "He wanted to attack an American city and blame others."

"Blame you?" Grand asked.

"Not directly," the Mexican answered. "But, you know, what you cannot achieve with diplomacy, you seek to win with deceit and blackmail."

"I'm glad my job is easier than that," Grand said.

"Excuse me," Gonzalez said, stepping around him. "There is something I must know."

"Hold up," Grand said, swinging his horse around. "He took a bullet in the neck—he's in no condition for interrogation."

"No interrogation, lieutenant," Gonzalez answered. "Just one question."

The men reached the fallen Martinez at the same time. He was awake, his throat having been deeply grazed but not punctured. The wound was being closed with catgut.

Gonzalez stood over him, a Marine stepping between them.

"What happened to my partner?" Gonzalez said in Spanish, speaking around the American.

Martinez laughed painfully, causing the two Marines

holding his shoulders down to lean into him even harder. Looking up, the Mexican just expanded his hands mimicking an explosion.

Gonzalez scowled and then spit at him.

The Marine pushed him back. Gonzalez stalked off. Joe let him be. He walked over to the lieutenant. A corporal had confiscated the bags and the horse. He was carefully examining one of the sticks. Grand motioned for him to hand it up.

"These are the explosives?" Grand asked Joe.

"I believe they are," Joe said. "First time I've seen one close. They sparkle, so I guess it's the fuse makes them blow. Though given how careful he was riding, I wouldn't go juggling them or anything."

Lieutenant Grand nodded.

Joe took a step closer. "Would you mind if I take one of those?" he asked.

The officer frowned. "It's evidence."

"Partly mine, I'd say," Joe answered. "Reason I ask is, there's a Butterfield coach on the way south. Won't be able to get through 'cause this fella brought a rockslide onto the road. I figured the least we could do is clear it."

The officer considered the request. With reluctance, he handed Joe the stick. The older man looked at it the way he handled it: respectfully.

"A cigar that can take down a mountain," he said, shaking his head. He regarded the lieutenant, then pointed to the corporal. "I'd treat those like sacks of butterflies. You only seen the smoke. I saw what they can do if they get angry."

A stretcher arrived from the office of the local doctor. Civil War surplus, Joe knew. The best thing to come of that conflict was all the horses, lanterns, and other goods sold inexpensively to the public.

In another few minutes Martinez was being carried into town by locals, and the Marines were mounted and ready to go.

"Thanks for your help, Joe O'Malley," Lieutenant Grand said.

"Appreciated but not necessary," Joe said. "This is my home . . . my country too."

The lieutenant smiled down, threw him a sharp salute, and joined his men.

Joe turned back to Gonzalez, who stood looking back at the riverbed.

"I'm sorry Sebastián was not present to see this," he said. His voice was low and choked.

"I know some who'd say he *is* here," Joe said.

Gonzalez snickered. "I am not a very religious man. I would prefer to be shaking his hand or patting his back to"—he gestured vaguely in front of him—"to talking to the air."

"I know what you mean," Joe said. "I feel that way about my dear wife, except for one thing."

"What is that, Joe?" Gonzalez asked.

"She's with me always," he said. "Here, home, wherever I go. If that weren't so, what kind of sense would life make?"

Gonzalez found a smile. "I am sorry you miss her, Joe. And perhaps you are right."

"Sure, I am," Joe said. "You happen to catch the name of that riverbed?"

Gonzalez shook his head.

"Angel Creek, City of Los Angeles," Joe replied.

Chapter 23

Captain Swift would recover.

That was the word Rog York received from the doctor.

Benito Juárez was intercepted in the harbor of San Diego and remained there until Captain Landry received word that the passage north was safe. Anna Lewin personally received the thanks of the grateful Mexican leader.

York was grateful that a personal loss and an international disaster had been averted. He was proud of the way his people had performed. But as the exhausted harbormaster prepared to go home to his caring wife, he knew that this was not the last salvo but the first of a new kind of warfare. One waged with a terrible new device, with a knack for indiscriminate killing.

It was a frightening new world he faced on an otherwise satisfying new day. And already, his mariner's mind was working on ways they would have to secure the harbor against other, as yet undreamt-of dangers . . .

Joe and Gonzalez dragged themselves south on the Butterfield Trail.

They used the dynamite to open the blocked canyon passage of the Butterfield Trail. Driver Wilson and the men he had gathered to undertake the effort were almost devout in their awe for what they'd seen.

There wasn't much left to bury when they reached the spot where they had fought the *Juaristas,* but they put them under rocks just the same.

Throughout the slow, three-day journey with long stops for rest, food, and a wash in the river, Joe's mind was not on what they had accomplished or where he was, only where he was going.

And to what.

To *who.*

He wondered if, to some degree, he was going slowly for a reason. As long as he was away, Slash and Clarity were still happy—at least in his imagining. He did not want anything reality might offer to change that.

But the day arrived when Joe and Gonzalez also arrived. It was late afternoon. From a half-mile up the trail, Joe kept his sharp eyes on the homestead looking for any sign of activity . . . and of hope.

The first thing he saw was smoke rising from the chimney. He also saw, finally, someone coming from the stable. It was Jackson, from his walk. He was bringing a horse out. A horse he did not recognize.

It couldn't be Wilson's team, he knew. They would have beaten Joe here by fully a day.

When he got closer, Joe saw that the horses being assembled in the yard had no saddles. Indian horses. It couldn't be Malibu and Sisquoc. They would have come on Cavalry horses.

Sharp-eyed Gert was the first to see the two men approaching. Joe could see, but not hear, her yelling to others.

They came out the back door—Jackson, Sarah, Merritt, and several Red Men Joe did not at first recognize, then did. They were the Apache brave Baishan and his two companions.

And then, drawing a lump to his throat that was more welcome than dawn itself, he saw his grandson and his wife.

"Gyaa!" he cried, startling Gonzalez who did not know what Joe had seen but quietly prayed it was what he had been waiting for.

The horse thundered across the plain, sending a storm of dust ahead of it as Joe reined back at the station as if he were trying to short-stop on a cliff. He jumped off, arms out, and grabbed everyone who would fit.

He cried for the first time since Dolley had gone. He wept openly and with more joy than he had known since his son was born.

"Thank the dear, dear Lord," Joe said. "Bless Him, bless you all."

"I'm going to tell B.W. you said all that," Gert said, also through tears.

"I don't care a whit," Joe said. "Not at all!"

He saw Baishan, heard from Gert that he had come to look after them, and had to restrain himself from hugging the Indian. They accepted a handshake, clasping the inside forearm, each man in turn.

Sarah wanted her father to come inside—along with Gonzalez, who came along slower and had not wanted to intrude. But Joe insisted on hearing everything, and Slash insisted on hearing everything back, while they stood right where they were.

They were tales told by grandson to grandfather, and grandfather to grandson, with everyone filling in what details had been overlooked. It was the living narrative of a short time. But in the union of White man, White woman, Indian, Mexican, clergy and those labeled heathens, it was a narrative much larger than that.

As the sun began to set, the six O'Malleys and their five companions went inside to eat the supper Sarah had prepared. For come the morning, it would be time to continue the story of the West they loved, of the recently bloodied nation they cherished, and of the pride and price, heroism and sacrifice it took to build and nourish them all.